A
HOUSE
DIVIDED

Also by Donna Hill

If I Could

Say Yes

Heat Wave (with Niobia Bryant and Zuri Day)

The One That I Want (with Zuri Day and Cheris Hodges)

Published by Kensington Publishing Corp.

A

HOUSE

DIVIDED

DONNA HILL

KENSINGTON PUBLISHING CORP.
www.kensingtonbooks.com

DAFINA BOOKS are published by

Kensington Publishing Corp.
119 West 40th Street
New York, NY 10018

All Kensington titles, imprints, and distributed lines are available at special quantity discounts for bulk purchases for sales promotion, premiums, fund-raising, and educational or institutional use.

Special book excerpts or customized printings can also be created to fit specific needs. For details, write or phone the office of the Kensington Sales Manager: Kensington Publishing Corp., 119 West 40th Street, New York, NY 10018. Attn. Sales Department. Phone: 1-800-221-2647.

Dafina and the Dafina logo Reg. U.S. Pat. & TM Off.

ISBN-13: 978-1-4967-0791-8
ISBN-10: 1-4967-0791-5
First Kensington Trade Paperback Printing: July 2017

eISBN-13: 978-1-4967-0792-5
eISBN-10: 1-4967-0792-3
First Kensington Electronic Edition: July 2017

10 9 8 7 6 5 4 3 2

Printed in the United States of America

To all the mothers and daughters that have found their way through.

ACKNOWLEDGMENTS

Where would I be without you? My deepest thanks go to you, my reader. You took a chance on me long ago or perhaps now for the first time. Thank you.

I want to thank my amazing children who keep me grounded and my wonderful grands who remind me of the awesome continuity of family.

Most of all I thank God for blessing me with this gift of storytelling and allowing me to share my world with you.

PROLOGUE

Zoie closed her grandmother's cedar trunk and ran her hand lovingly across the smooth finish. What a wise woman her grandmother had been.

She rose from her knees and crossed the creaking wood floorboards to gaze out of the attic window and onto the future that was now truly hers. The sound of laughter from below floated upward to meet her. She smiled in acceptance. Her grandmother knew the firestorm that her will would evoke, what it would do to her three daughters, and to Zoie.

Loss may have forced Zoie to return here, but love and commitment allowed her to stay. She understood that now. Understood that everything she'd been searching for had been right in front of her.

CHAPTER 1

Come home. Come home.

The words tumbled over themselves in Zoie Crawford's head. Her mother, Rose, had mastered the singular ability to weave her words into a mantle of guilt that she ceremoniously draped over Zoie's shoulders. The weight of it, heaped on her over the years, eventually forced Zoie to flee her home in New Orleans to build a new independent, guiltless life in New York. A life free of the overbearing, the clinging, the neediness, and the possessiveness that threatened to swallow her whole.

Not now. Not an option. Not even for Nana Claudia. Too much was at stake, and she knew her grandmother would understand, even if her mother didn't. Yes, her grandmother was in declining health. Yes, she was pushing ninety. Yes, she had been the mother to her that Rose had never been. But the world was still reeling from the horror of the Twin Towers crumbling and the devastating loss of thousands of lives. Her immediate responsibility was to dig through the debris of misinformation and present her findings. Her readers, the world, deserved nothing less than her best. It was her Nana who always told her, "You is a little black girl in a white man's world. You gon' haveta work ten times harder to get halfway to the finish line." Zoie lived by those words. Those words got her out of bed every morning. As a result, she was a rising star in journalism, and her focus remained on getting the story and the coveted prize. Her coverage of 9/11 had Pulitzer written all over it, and she couldn't do her job from the family home in New Orleans. She dropped her cell phone into her purse.

She'd call her grandmother later and listen for herself whether there was any truth to her mother's clarion call or whether it was simply another ploy to manipulate her emotions.

———

Zoie strode into the hub of the newsroom and instantly felt the familiar orgasmic rush that fueled her. She'd long since given up trying to explain why she was so hellbent on pulling back the curtain to reveal the Wizard of Oz. Her zeal and single-mindedness had estranged her from her family and contributed to the demise of her relationship with Brian Forde. Then there was Jackson Fuller—but that . . . was different. Yet her tenacity jettisoned her career, taking her from being a beat reporter to a senior correspondent. She took great solace in that fact and forged a new family in her co-workers. They understood her passion and commitment. That was the balm that soothed the raw places in her soul, the places she shared with no one other than her one friend, Miranda Howard—even though they often bumped heads over the importance of having more than work to keep one warm at night.

"Zoie! I need to see you," Mark Livingston bellowed over the cacophony of chirping phones, slamming doors, and a chorus of voices. He stood in the frame of his office door with his usual harried expression. For Mark, everything was code orange.

"Be right there," Zoie called out over the bent heads of her colleagues. She dropped her purse, coat, and laptop on her desk and wound her way around the bullpen to Mark's office.

"Close the door and have a seat," he said without preamble.

Zoie stepped into the claustrophobic space of her publisher, quietly shut the door, and was quickly sucked into the abyss of paper and the towers of files that occupied the four corners of the room. She lifted a box from the one chair, placed it on the floor, and sat down.

The organized chaos of Mark Livingston belied his brilliance. He had a nose for news and the ability to recognize that fever in others. His reputation for integrity and excellence was renowned in the field. He'd spent ten years with the *Washington Post* and the *New York Times* before pooling all of his resources and launching the *National Recorder*. In the fifteen years since its launch, it had stood toe to toe with the *Post*, the *Times*, and the *Wall Street Journal*.

When Zoie graduated from Columbia University's School of Journalism, she bounced around for two years before landing, five years earlier, a freelance spot with the *Recorder*, which soon became more of a staff post than freelance. But Zoie was firm in keeping her "freelance" title. It allowed her to maintain a sense of independence. Mark took her under his wing. He mentored her, groomed her, tested her skills, fed her the passion they both shared, and treated her like the child he never had. She was his protégé, and would be his heir apparent when he retired. She'd come a long way under his tutelage, but she would never be satisfied. She could always be better.

Mark lowered his long body onto his mud-brown leather chair, which had long ago seen better days. He linked his pink and white fingers together. The overhead light reflected off the bald patch on his head, projecting an illusion of a halo.

"What's up, Mark?" She crossed her legs at the ankle.

Mark leaned back. His disarming green eyes zoomed in on her. "I know you've been knee-deep in the Twin Tower series," he said, quickly adding, "and you're doing one helluva job," nodding his head while he spoke as if to reaffirm his own affirmation. He cleared his throat, and Zoie instinctively held her breath. "I have another angle that I want you to follow. I want you to turn your notes and your contacts over to Brian."

It took a moment for what he'd said to register. Zoie's eyes narrowed in shock an instant before fury exploded. She leapt up from her seat.

"Are you freaking kidding me, Brian? Oh, hell no. I worked this series." She jabbed her chest with her finger for emphasis and began to pace the tiny space. "No." She vigorously shook her head and folded her arms in defiance, then swung toward Mark. "No!"

Zoie planted her palms on the quarter inch of available desk space. "This is my story," she said again, in a singularly deliberate tone. "I've worked inhuman hours, turned in stories that no other paper has done." Her voice rose with emotion. "This is what you groomed me for, and you want me to turn it over to Brian Forde. Why in God's name would I ever agree to that?"

"Have I ever steered you wrong?" he calmly asked.

Zoie tried to focus on her breathing and not the numbness that began to rise from the soles of her feet. Her heart raced, and she had to rapidly blink to stave off the hot tears that threatened to expose that part of her she kept hidden.

"You'll continue to receive a co-writer byline."

Her nostrils flared.

Mark flipped open a folder and turned it to face her. "Kimberly Maitland-Graham."

Zoie couldn't focus. What the fuck was he talking about? She shoved it back. "What about her?"

"She's running for New York State Senate against the Democratic incumbent and she has a groundswell of support. Especially now. She comes from money and is being propped up as a star in her party. If she wins, it will be a major coup and shakeup up in Albany."

Now he had her attention.

"I want you on this from the beginning. I want her life, her policies, her stump speeches, everything she's ever written, and every job she's ever held. I want interviews with her staff and friends, the works."

"Are we positioning the paper as her supporter? Since when have we backed a Republican?"

"We aren't." He leaned forward. His green eyes darkened.

"That's why I want you to cover her. No one else on the team has the tenacity to turn over every stone to get to the truth."

"What truth?"

"Who she really is, not this picture-perfect brand that her people are creating. I know there's something there. I feel it in my gut, and you're going to find it." He pushed his face forward. "If she wins, she'll tip the balance in the State Senate."

Zoie's thoughts swirled. Excitement bubbled in her veins. Her reporting could very well help set the narrative of the state's politics.

"But it must be balanced."

"Of course." Zoie reached for the file and slid it toward her.

"I don't want this to come off as some kind of witch hunt. Facts, facts, facts," he reiterated with a slap of his palm on the desk. "I've already gotten you assigned to her press pool." He opened his desk drawer and took out her credentials. "You'll have full access."

Zoie glanced at the laminated tags. "How'd you know I'd agree?"

Mark grinned, deepening the lines around his eyes. "When have you ever turned down anything this big?"

Zoie bit back a smile. "You know me too well."

"This is it, Zoie. This is the story that will get you that Pulitzer."

"And Brian is on board with this whole co-byline thing?"

Mark nodded. "Listen, I want you on this like yesterday."

Zoie pushed out a breath and stood. "Okay." She snatched up the folder and press tags. *Come home.* A flash of guilt knotted her stomach. "I'll get started." She turned to leave.

"You won't regret this."

Zoie opened the door.

"Send Brian in, will you?"

Her step halted for a moment. "Sure."

———⇒•⇐———

Brian Forde was smart, driven, an excellent journalist, and an expert lover. One would think they'd be a perfect match. That's what Zoie thought, too. But it was those very qualities that imploded their very tempestuous relationship. They were too much alike, and the fire that flamed between them burned them both. Their fights were epic, their voracious work ethic combustible, and after six months, their monumental lovemaking couldn't overcome the very qualities that made them so damned good at what they did.

Zoie stopped beside Brian's desk. His total focus was on his computer screen. His earbuds blocked out the office noise. If she pegged it right, he was listening to John Coltrane, his go-to guy whenever he was deep into a story. The hand of melancholy tried to grab hold of her, but she shoved it aside.

She tapped him lightly on the shoulder. His head snapped up as he simultaneously snatched the buds out of his ears. His initial expression was pure annoyance at being disturbed until his focus settled on Zoie.

"Oh, hey." He swung his chair around to face her and took her in with a single eye sweep.

Brian had the uncanny ability to look at her as if she were naked.

Zoie cleared her throat. "Mark wants to see you."

He folded his arms. "You cool with the co-byline?"

Her lips thinned. She found a smile. "I'm good. I've done the bulk of the work."

He slowly stood, forcing her gaze to follow the rise of his hard-packed body until she found herself looking into his eyes. Her pulse quickened. She swallowed and took a half step back.

"I'll keep you in the loop," he said.

The deep timbre of his voice swung like a metronome in her stomach. "Great." She turned away, headed to her cubicle, and realized that her heart was pounding.

———— ⋆•⋆ ————

"This could be big. It *is* big," Zoie said while she sipped on her margarita.

Miranda crunched on a nacho loaded with guacamole and cheddar cheese. "Hmm," she mumbled and chewed. "So you don't have a problem handing your work over to Brian?"

"Of course I do. But this assignment is bigger and has teeth."

Miranda turned her focus from their shared plate of nachos and directed her full attention on Zoie.

"Since when have you been about destroying someone, especially another woman?"

"You're being dramatic."

"Am I?" She stared until Zoie shifted in her seat.

"This is not about destroying. It's about uncovering. There's a difference. This woman's win could very well shift the balance of political power in Albany. Should she be there? What are her beliefs, her policies, her allies, and her vision? Those are the things I want to find out and things the voting public needs to know."

Miranda reached for another nacho. "Okay. As long as you're clear. I know how you can get when you sink your teeth into something. This poor woman has no idea what she's in for."

Zoie chuckled, then sipped her drink. "Got a call from Rose."

"Is everything okay?"

Zoie waved her hand in dismissal. "You know my mother—always the alarmist. She left a message saying that Nana wasn't well and that I need to come home."

"When are you leaving?"

"I can't. Not now."

"Why the hell not? It's your grandmother."

"I know that. But—"

"Don't tell me it's that fucking job, Z."

Zoie glanced away and focused on the dissolving foam in her glass. Bit by bit, the white froth became consumed by liquid until the foam was gone.

"There's more to life than work."

"We've had this conversation, Randi."

"Apparently, I was talking to myself." She tsked in disgust. "I don't believe you."

Zoie jerked forward. The tips of her fingers clenched the table. "And why not, Randi?" she challenged. "What has home ever done for me? A mother who tried to suck the life out of me, and two aunts who can't decide whom they dislike most—me, my mother, or each other. And Nana . . ." Her taut expression eased. She pushed out a breath. "There's only so much one person can do in a den of vipers."

"Zoie! That's your family," Miranda said, her voice rising.

Zoie slowly shook her head. "You come from this big ole happy family that actually enjoys being around each other. My family portrait is next to the diagnosis of dysfunctional." She finished off her drink, then craned her neck in search of the waitress.

"It's been almost ten years, Z." She reached across the table. "People change, mellow with age," she added with a soft smile. She squeezed Zoie's fingers.

Zoie's throat clenched. "But the hurts, the slights, the suf-fo-cation—I had some time to let all that scab over. Ya know." She looked into the eyes of her friend. "Going back is like picking the scab. I don't think I'm healed underneath." A tear slid down her cheek. She sniffed hard.

"Listen to me." Miranda leaned across the table so that their heads almost touched. "You've lived in the biggest, baddest city in the world. You pushed yourself through grad school, landed a job in your field, and made a name for yourself in the industry. No one can take that from you—not your overbearing mother or the wicked aunties. Go see your Nana," she said softly.

Zoie dabbed the corner of her eye with the knuckle of her finger.

The waitress stopped at their table as if cued from the wings of the stage, ready to take their orders, giving Zoie a momentary reprieve.

As usual, Miranda had the waitress explain each item and how it was prepared. The infuriating habit had lost its punch with Zoie ages ago. Zoie would generally bury her head in her menu until

Miranda was finished and then smile apologetically to the wait staff on her dear friend's behalf.

She and Miranda met in college. Zoie majored in journalism, and Miranda went after a business degree, which she parlayed into a plum position with the Port Authority, and now she oversaw operations at Kennedy and LaGuardia airports.

Miranda was right, Zoie thought, as Miranda prattled on. She'd put plenty of time and distance between herself and her family. She was stronger now.

"And for you, ma'am?" the cool-as-a-cucumber waitress asked.

"Oh, yes, sorry," she stuttered, jerked from her musing. "Umm, I'll have the roasted chicken and grilled vegetables . . . and another margarita."

"Right away." She scooped up the menus and moved away as stealthily as she'd appeared.

Zoie nursed the ice from her glass.

"How *are* things between you and Brian?"

Zoie blinked several times. How did they segue to Brian? That was one of Miranda's other talents—changing subjects without warning. "There's nothing 'between us,'" she said, making air quotes. "Our working relationship is fine, if that's what you mean."

"I still think you could have worked things out." She snapped a white linen napkin open and spread it ceremoniously on her lap.

"Why does it have to be me who has to work things out?" she asked two octaves above her normal range. "What about him?"

Miranda's hazel eyes darted around the room. "Because you're the pain-in-the-ass stubborn one, that's why."

"With friends like you, Randi . . . I swear."

"Would you rather I be the kind of friend who kisses your ass even when you're wrong?"

"Yes, damnit!"

They burst out in laughter.

"You're crazy," Miranda said over her chuckles.

The waitress returned with their drinks. "Enjoy," she said and hurried off.

Zoie lifted her glass. "To truth."

Miranda tapped her glass against Zoie's. "That's all there is."

⸺◆⸺

Twelve hours had passed since she'd listened to her mother's message. With work, the shock of her new assignment, and her standing after-work meet-up with Miranda, she'd been able to relegate the words to the back of her mind and tamp down the guilt that niggled at her conscience. She simply had not had the time. That's what she told herself.

Now, however, in the aloneness of her one-bedroom condo, there was no escape. Rose's words echoed, that sinking feeling resurfaced, and the fear that she'd successfully ignored demanded her attention.

A glass of wine first. A shower next. Yes, wine and a shower. Then she would call. Nothing was going to change.

⸺◆⸺

She almost felt like herself by the time she'd finished off her wine and let the waters beat against her skin. Down the drain her worries went, along with her anxieties. She was fortified now.

Inhaling a breath of resolve, she sat on the side of her bed and picked up her cell phone from the nightstand. She swiped the screen and tapped in her password. Her heart thundered. *Three messages from her mother*. She didn't want to listen to the chastising, the questioning, the guilt trip that Rose would surely send her on.

Zoie tapped in the number to the family home in New Orleans, held her breath, and waited.

"Hello . . ."

The sound of her mother's voice drew her all the way back to the days that she longed to forget, but never could.

"Mom, you left me several messages. I'm sorry I was—"

"She's gone."

The jigsaw puzzle of words made no sense. They didn't fit together.

"What are you saying? What do you mean? Gone where?"

"About an hour ago," her mother said, her voice flat and empty as if siphoned of whatever emotion she had left. "I suppose if you're not too busy you can come home for the services."

"Mom . . . Nana . . ."

"I have to go. The reverend is here."

Click.

She couldn't breathe; her heart raced and her thoughts spun. A rush of raw anguish rose up from the depths of her soul and escaped. The keen of a wounded animal vibrated in the room, bounced off walls, and slammed back into her, knocking her to her knees.

Pain became a swirling vortex that stole her breath, shredded her heart, and whipped her around until she was weak and spent.

Come home.

"Oh God, oh God, what have I done? Nana! . . ."

She curled into a ball on the floor and wept.

CHAPTER 2

"I can take some time off and go with you," Miranda said.

"No, I'll be okay," Zoie lied. "But thanks."

"Can I get you anything?" Miranda pushed up from the spot on the couch where she'd been since she arrived after Zoie's hysterical phone call.

"No thanks." She continued to stare off into the distance.

Miranda walked into the kitchen. Zoie could hear the water run, the fridge open and close, and the tinkle of silverware against plates. Those things she could grasp. The loss of her Nana she could not. What was most difficult to reconcile was the guilt. The questions ran relay in her head, one after the other. What if she'd taken her mother's call? What if she'd spoken to Nana one last time? But she'd done neither. She would have to find a way to live with that—the fact that her Nana had needed her, and she . . .

"I think you could use this." Miranda extended a glass of wine.

Zoie blinked Miranda into focus. A half smile curved her mouth. "Thanks."

"I know what's on your mind." Miranda curled up on the couch and took a sip of wine.

"I'm sure you do. You know me better than I know myself."

"You couldn't have known, Z."

Zoie's lids fanned rapidly to keep the tears at bay. She sniffed and took a swallow from her glass. "But I did know that she wasn't well. I heard it in her voice when I talked to her a few weeks ago. But you know Nana." She waved her hand. "Said she was fine, just old, like I would be one day." She smiled at the memory.

Miranda sighed. "I'll take care of your flight, and I'll call your office in the morning."

"You don't have to—"

"I don't want you to worry about anything. I got this." She pushed up from her seat and went to get her wallet from her purse. "I'm going to book your flight, then I'll help you pack. Where's your laptop?"

Zoie mindlessly pointed to the laptop tucked on the bookcase. Miranda retrieved the laptop and got to work.

Come home. It had been a bit more than a decade since she'd been back, save for her visit for Nana's eighty-fifth birthday five years earlier. She was there for the day and returned to New York the same night.

Her mother's clinging and probing; her aunts Sage and Hyacinth, with their stories and admonishments about her lack of a husband and children and her "loose life"; the bickering and accusations between the sisters—the combination was enough to send her running into the street. The only bright spot was her grandmother, who glided through the maelstrom of her daughters' ongoing tug of war like a feather on air.

"Oh, they mean well," Nana said. "They just don't know it," she added with laughter lacing her thin voice. She'd grabbed Zoie's arm then, with surprising strength, and said, "Come with me. Got sumthin' to show ya out back."

Zoie's breath caught. The garden, which five years prior had been not much more than some green grass and rosebushes, was now lush with rows and rows of vegetables—squash, collards, spinach, red and green peppers, and plump tomatoes.

"Nana . . ." Zoie said in awe, "this is . . ." She took cautious steps. "Incredible. It's all so . . . This is what you always talked about."

"Doing a nice business. Sell to the local grocers. Good, steady income."

"That's wonderful, Nana." She put her arm across her grand-mother's shoulders. "My Nana the entrepreneur."

"Keeps me young. Your mother and your aunts don't have a green thumb between 'em."

They laughed.

"Not like you," Nana said. "You're a natural." She clasped Zoie's hand. "I'll be sure to pack you up a box to take with you."

Zoie leaned down and kissed her grandmother's head. "I'd like that a lot."

It was the last time she'd seen her grandmother.

"You're all booked. Eight tomorrow morning. Direct. Delta."

Zoie glanced across the space to where Miranda sat. "Thanks," she whispered.

"I can still go with you. There's availability."

She could use the shield of Miranda against the onslaught of verbiage that would without a doubt be hurled at and heaped upon her. The trio of sisters tended to "act right" around com-pany. But this time she would handle it alone.

"I wouldn't do that to you. I'll be fine. When is the return flight? I'm leaving right after the funeral on Friday."

"About that . . . I booked one-way. I didn't want you to feel pressured. So whenever you're ready, I can take care of the re-turn."

Tossed to the wolves without an escape plan. Under other cir-cumstances, she'd be pissed. But Miranda was doing her a favor. And Nana always said that thing about gift horses or something.

"Hey, it's fine, girl. Don't worry about it. I'll handle it."

Miranda hit a few keys on the computer. "Just emailed your confirmation and boarding pass."

"Thanks. I'll print them out in the morning."

Miranda stood and stretched. "I'm going to take a shower and turn in."

Zoie frowned. "Huh? You're staying?"

"Yeah, a sleepover. You don't think I'd let you drive yourself to the airport or pay some cab. I'm taking you."

"Randi . . ." Her throat tightened.

"I got you, girl." She squeezed Zoie's shoulder, then pranced off to the bathroom.

Zoie leaned back against the toffee-colored cushion of the couch and closed her eyes.

A rush of images and emotions hurtled toward her: Nana taking a purple plum from the pocket of her floral shift and holding it in the palm of her hand, teasing Zoie with it; those winter nights when she'd sit between Nana's knees while she scratched and greased her scalp and plaited her hair; and when Nana would sit on the side of her bed to wipe Zoie's tears away and reassure her that her mother did love her—she just had a funny way of showing it. Or Nana whooping and hollering when Zoie graduated high school and crying, but only on the inside, when Zoie moved to New York for college.

Zoie wiped away the tears that dripped from her eyes. All she had now were the memories. She pushed out a breath and slowly rose to her feet. There was nothing to be done now but face the music and get away from the musicians as quickly as she could so that she could mourn her Nana in peace.

———◆———

Even at the ungodly hour of six-thirty in the morning, Kennedy Airport was rife with activity.

"Call me if you need me," Miranda counseled as Zoie exited the car. Miranda got out and came around to the curb.

"I'll be fine. I promise." Zoie wrapped her friend in a tight hug. "I'll be back before you can miss me."

"Zoe . . ." Miranda looked steadily into her eyes. "Give them a chance. They're hurting, too."

Zoie lowered her gaze. "I know," she conceded.

"No walls. Okay?"

Zoie opened her mouth to protest and caught Miranda's censored expression.

"Fine. I'll try."

"Good." She kissed Zoie's cheek. "Safe travels."

Zoie grabbed the handle of her small rolling carry-on, gave a final wave, and was quickly swept along with the flow of travelers who ran, strolled, or were wheeled through the terminal.

———⟫•⟪———

She would be pleasant. She would not cringe at her aunties' disparaging remarks. She would not rise to the bait of her mother's barbs. Instead she would smile, and clean and cook and smile some more, and pray for the miracle that could change seventy-two hours into twenty-four.

Zoie dodged bodies and luggage as she wound her way through baggage claim and out to the exit. For a silly moment, as she watched the disembarked passengers tumble into outstretched arms of welcome, she imagined someone waiting for her. Someone who was actually glad to see her.

She hiked the worn leather strap of her purse higher on her shoulder and strode out into the Louisiana sunshine.

———⟫•⟪———

The cab that she took from the airport eased to a stop in front of 9822 Jessup. Zoie's pulse quickened. She was hot, uncomfortably hot. Beads of perspiration formed along her hairline. Her stomach felt funny, as though she might throw up.

"That will be thirty-two sixty, miss," the cabbie said as if he'd said it more than once.

"Sorry." She dug into her purse for her wallet and took out two twenties and handed them over. "Keep the change," she said, deciding that if she was going to have to play nice, she should get some practice.

"Thanks, miss!" Suddenly energized, he rushed out of the cab and came around to personally take Zoie's suitcase out of the trunk.

Catch more flies with honey than vinegar, as Nana would have said.

Zoie smiled her thanks, gripped the handle of her bag, and walked the gangplank to the family front door. Before she was halfway down the concrete lane, the door to the house was flung open as if it had been pushed in with hurricane-force winds.

Rose Bennett Crawford stood in the doorway, all five foot six inches of her; the one attribute that she'd passed on to her daughter. Even at this distance, Zoie saw the censor in her gray-green eyes, which were underlined with dark circles, and she got the irrational impression that everything that had made her mother who she was had been scooped out, leaving a shell in a dress.

Rose folded her hands primly in front of her.

Zoie forced one foot ahead of the next until she stood in front of her mother, who because of her height looked Zoie right in the eye.

"Ma . . ." she whispered. She wrapped her arms around her mother's stiff body and nearly broke in two when she felt her mother's slender frame shudder with sobs. "Ma . . . it's going to be okay," she said into Rose's neck. She couldn't remember the last time she'd hugged her mother or had her mother hug her. Tears were not new. Rose used tears to manipulate. Not this time. They were real and anguish-filled, and for the moment that she held her sobbing mother in her arms, she allowed herself to believe that they could be mother and daughter. But just as quickly as the moment came, it went.

Rose stepped back out of Zoie's arms, swiped at her eyes, and wiped her hands on her apron. "How long are you staying? I hope you took a few weeks off. There's so much to do around here. Your aunts aren't much help these days."

"Weeks . . . Ma—"

"Your job will keep. You should be important by now." She turned to go inside. "I fixed up your room. Wasn't sure when you were going to show up, but I knew whenever you came home, it would be for your Nana. Only one that ever mattered to you," she mumbled, but loud enough for Zoie to hear.

Zoie squeezed her eyes shut. Take all those words apart, and they meant nothing—just words. But mix them together, add a dash of martyrdom, a sprinkle of self-righteous indignation, and an "I'm so disappointed in you" look in the eye, and the result was the reason why she stayed away.

The instant Zoie crossed the threshold, she was no longer a thirty-one year old accomplished journalist. She was a budding young woman of nineteen in a verbal battle of wills with her mother and her aunts about her decision to move to New York. They ranted and raved and assured her that nothing good could come to a young woman in a city like New York. They insisted that she'd be raped or mugged or both. She'd never find a job. A journalist! The aunts cackled at the absurdity. College in New York! Who was going to pay for it? *Don't come runnin' back 'ere with yo tail between yo legs.*

And all the while that her aunts volleyed her back and forth between them, her mother sat at the kitchen table, shedding silent tears with eyes full of recrimination.

It was Nana who put a halt to Zoie's lambasting.

"Enough! Leave the chile be. How y'all gonna not be happy that she is grown enough to step out into the world? 'Cause y'all lived your whole lives right 'ere er'body else s'pose to?" She then turned on Rose. "You gon' drown us all in them damned tears. You had your chance. Why can't she?"

Zoie opened her eyes. She would get through this.

"You go on and get cleaned up. Your aunties are anxious to see you, so don't take forever."

"Yes, ma'am." She continued up the stairs while her mother went off to the kitchen.

Zoie crested the landing of the five-bedroom house and walked down the hall to her room at the end. The plank wood floors creaked beneath her feet. As a teen, she'd sworn that either her aunts or her mother had loosened the floorboards so that they could listen for her comings and goings. She remembered, on too many nights after getting in from a date, the creak of the floors, followed by the swinging open of doors. *Who's that? What time is it? Lawd, tore me out of a good sleep. Chile, only loose girls come in this time of the night.* Teeth sucking, eyes rolling, doors slamming, and, of course, her mother's look of shame.

"Damnit," Zoie muttered. She walked in and shut the door behind her.

One would think that, after all this time that she'd been gone, the sisters would have turned her teenage bedroom into an adult guest room. But no. Everything was pretty much like she left it, right down to the outdated VCR and the twelve-inch television set.

She rolled her suitcase over to the corner, then looked out of the window. Her view was right above her grandmother's lush garden, which appeared even more spectacular than when she last saw it.

Zoie opened the window and pushed up the screen. She stuck her head out and inhaled the intoxicating scents of recently turned earth, fresh grass, and rainbow rows of vegetables.

She rested her arms on the sill. "You did good, Nana." Her cell chirped in her pocket. She pulled it out, and Miranda's name lit the screen.

"Hey, girl."

"Hey, yourself. How was the flight?"

"Fine. I got to the house about twenty minutes ago—feels like days already."

"Z . . . Talk to your mom?"

"Briefly."

"Your aunts?"

"Not yet. I've been instructed to hurry and 'get cleaned up' because they're anxious to see me," she added drolly.

"Okay. Go. Call me later."

"I will. Bye." She disconnected the call in concert with her name being called. She pulled down the screen but left the window open. Determined not to get sucked into the discourse of discontent, Zoie closed her bedroom door and returned downstairs.

She reached the bottom landing and was guided to the gathering by the murmur of voices coming from the veranda. She crossed the foyer, passed the kitchen, the dining room, and the living room, which her aunt still called the parlor, and stepped out onto the back veranda. Two of the three women she'd known all her life were not the women she remembered.

Aunt Hyacinth, the oldest of the sisters, was draped in a shawl that appeared large enough to swallow her whole. The chestnut-brown face, still unlined, seemed small, doll-like. Her entire body was small, more frail, but what struck Zoie the hardest was the vacant look in Aunt Hyacinth's eyes. For some years, she had suffered from "forgetful spells," as her mother called them. Those spells had clearly morphed into entire episodes.

Zoe felt her heart twist in her chest. Her eyes stung. When was the last time she had called and spoken to her auntie? Her gaze drifted to her aunt Sage. Sage Bennett, the middle child, had determined, once she realized that she'd never be the youngest or the eldest, that she would find a way to stand out. She did. Sage was the caregiver, the mentor, and a master of the rapier tongue. She knew a little bit about a lot of things, and whenever anyone in the family had a dilemma, it was Sage who solved the problem. Now the once-robust, often domineering sister appeared to have succumbed to the ravages of time, and the hellfire that always beamed around her barely glowed.

Zoe pasted on a smile and stepped fully onto the veranda, quietly shutting the enclosed screen door behind her. Two pairs of almost identical gray-green eyes settled on her. The third pair remained focused—on what, no one knew.

Rose pushed up from her seat. "We were waiting for you before we had some tea. You hungry?"

"Tea is fine."

"Don't just stand there. Go and say hello to your aunts."

"Let me get a good look at your gal," Aunt Sage commanded, and then took up her glasses from the white wrought-iron table and perched them on her plump nose. She looked Zoie up and down as if inspecting a piece of furniture. "Humph. Your grandmother asked for you," she said, turning the benign words into an accusation with the skill that she had mastered.

Zoie bit down on her bottom lip to keep it from trembling. "I came as soon as I could," she offered.

Aunt Sage waved a hand in dismissal. "Too late."

Zoie turned her head to blink away the tears before facing the trio. She tugged in a breath, walked over to her aunt Sage, and kissed her cheek. "Hello, Auntie." She squeezed Sage's shoulder, then inched over to her aunt Hyacinth. She knelt down in front of her and took her aunt's smooth, warm hands into her own. "Auntie Hyacinth, it's me, Zoie."

Hyacinth blinked and settled hazy eyes on Zoie. Her eyes, once identical to her sisters', had lost their sharpness, the ability to penetrate. Instead, facing her was like looking into a window that needed cleaning. She frowned in concentration, and then a slow smile lifted the corners of her lips. "Zoie! Child, you done come home."

"Yes, Auntie, I'm here."

"And a good thing, too," she said in a lowered voice. She leaned closer to her niece. "Them two is trying to kill me." She nodded to reaffirm her words.

"Auntie! That's not true. They love you."

"Mama's gone," she said, shifting the topic. Her glassy eyes filled. "Don't know what I'm gon' do without my mama."

Zoie reach for a napkin on the table and wiped her aunt's tears. "It will be alright, Auntie," she soothed.

"Never gon be alright again." Her gaze shifted toward her sisters. She whispered, "Watch dem two."

Zoie patted her aunt's smooth knuckles, then sat down in the one available seat between her mother and Aunt Sage. A wave of indescribable sadness crept inside her, then sucked her down in its undertow. A pall hung over the sisters and the house. That was expected, of course, because of the loss of Nana Claudia. But Zoie felt it was more than that, something deeper. It was as if Claudia had left this world and taken all the lifeblood that flowed through the house and her children with her.

Nana was the thread that had held them all together. With her passing, the patchwork quilt of the Bennett family would slowly unravel.

Zoie turned to her mother. "What are the plans for Nana's service?"

Rose flattened her palms on her lap. "Reverend Carl will officiate. The wake is scheduled for tomorrow at the Holloway Funeral Parlor. You remember Gena Holloway, don't you?"

Zoie tried to place her. "Um, I think so." *What did it matter?*

"Well, Gena took over the family business about two years ago, after her daddy passed." She nodded her head while she spoke. "Doing a fine job, too. Her shiftless brother Rufus didn't want anything to do with it 'cept for the profits. So Gena stepped in. Folks were kind of skeptical at first, her being a woman and so young." She smiled. "But she put everybody's doubts to rest. She renovated, purchased brand-new hearses, and hired a staff."

"Humph," Aunt Sage chimed in. "Like Mama always said, there are two jobs that's nevah gon' lack customers: bringing folks into the world and taking them out."

Rose umm-hummed her agreement. "It's just a nice thing when family business, family legacy gets passed down."

"It's the right thing," Sage added and slapped her hand on her thigh. "Too many young folk don't care two tits about family. Just pack up and leave like all the people and all the things that made them up to be who dey is don't matter worth a damn!"

The flint of her temper scratched against Zoie's chest and burst into flames. She clenched her hands into fists until her nails dug into her palms. Now she realized where her mother's storyline lead—straight to lining her up, then shooting her down.

"Maybe we could get back to the plans," Zoie said, her chest tight with anger.

"Yes, yes, we totally got off track," her mother said in that passive-aggressive way that drove Zoie crazy. "Wake is from noon to six. Mama had a lot of friends in this town. We want to make sure that they all have a chance to pay their respects. Then the repast will be here at the house. That's where we're going to need your help." She covered Zoie's hand with her own.

"The funeral service is Saturday morning . . ." Sage's voice cracked. "Then the burial at Evergreen."

A shroud of silence wrapped around them.

Sage's lips tightened into an unmovable line. Rose's gray-green eyes clouded with tears. Even Hyacinth was alert enough to understand that her sisters were hurting, too.

Zoie wanted to comfort them in some way, say the right words, but it had been a long time since a modicum of authentic warmth had been shared among the Bennett women. In that moment, the full force of her grandmother's passing truly settled inside her. She looked from one saddened face to the other. Nana had held them together by sheer force of will. She provided the nurturing, the love, the balance. What would they do now? How would they live under the same roof without Nana's protective hand?

"The reading of the will is Monday," Sage said out of the blue.

"You need to be here for that," Rose said. "Pretty sure your Nana looked out for you. The least you can do is hear what she had to say," she added, knowing from instinct that Zoie was contemplating her escape.

"Monday? Mama, I need to get back to work." She really didn't, but she didn't think she'd survive until Monday.

"What's more important than family?" Sage demanded. "Bad enough you couldn't pick up a phone and git your New York tail down here 'fore Mama passed. And you ready to run off before she in the ground good." She sniffed loudly, then dabbed her nose with a napkin.

Zoie saw her mother's expression freeze in a mask of shame. Her sister's words, although hurled at Zoie, were meant to hit Rose, as they always did.

"I didn't say I wouldn't stay, Aunt Sage. I'm only mentioning that I do have a job, and I've been assigned to a big story."

"More on the terrorists that bombed New York?" Sage asked.

Rose leaned forward. "I told you when you ran off to New York it was a dangerous place. You wouldn't listen. Do you have any idea how scared we all were for you when we heard the news?" She pressed a hand to her chest.

Zoie wanted to believe they cared, actually cared. The truth, on the other hand, spoke for itself. She would never forget that horrific day for many reasons, her family being one of them.

———⟶•⟵———

She'd just gotten off the number 2 train at Chambers Street. As usual, the narrow streets of Lower Manhattan teemed with people rushing to their offices or the nearest Starbucks for a last shot of energy before tackling their day.

The skies were bright, the air surprisingly clear. A typical September morning. She remembered checking the time on her Blackberry and picked up her pace. It was 8:40. The staff meeting convened in five minutes. The walk would take her ten.

She turned onto Vesey Street and was stopped short by a bottleneck of people. Her gaze rose, as did those of the crush of suited and high-heeled pedestrians who stood, confused and transfixed, by the scene that unfolded above them.

Pointing. Shouting. Screaming.

Like a scene from a sci-fi movie, a modern-day war of the worlds, a plane had crashed into the North Tower of the World Trade Center.

A collective gasp of disbelief was met with plumes of black dust above, which then scattered and tumbled in concert with the debris that rained down upon them.

Panic. Terror. Running. Horns blaring. Sirens wailing. Then an explosion that rocked the earth beneath them. Flames burst from the windows of the North Tower, and the unbelievable magnified when the second plane rammed into the South Tower eighteen minutes later.

Chaos.

So she ran, blindly, covered in a film of white ash, propelled by the stampede of the terror-stricken, down the narrow streets, around the overturned trash cans and stalled cars.

She remembered thinking the world had ended—the Apocalypse, the Four Horsemen, the shit that nightmares were made of. And the sky continued to fall.

Nearly a week passed after that day before she got a call from her family. Even then it was more of a reprimand, more an "I told you so" than the concern they claimed to have. Only her Nana offered any words of love and comfort.

Zoie blinked the past away. "I'll stay," she finally conceded. "What do you need me to do?"

Self-satisfied harrumphs bounced from one to the other.

———⊷◆⊶———

Claudia Bennett's home-going service sent her off in style. It was standing room only in the Holloway Funeral Parlor, and the line of cars to the cemetery was celebrity long.

The act of preparing for Nana Claudia's final hurrah occupied so much time and thought that it left little opportunity to dwell on the loss itself. There was cooking and cleaning, and calls to be made and responded to. And, of course, there was the constant flow of mourners, who seemed to multiply by the hour.

By noon, the two-story house was stretched to the seams with go-to-meeting hats, Jean Naté perfume, wide hips, and white handkerchiefs to dab at watering eyes.

Zoie stopped counting how many times she heard "How much you've grown," "Your nana was something special," and "Did you see those buildings fall up there in New York? Just terrible."

Every countertop in the kitchen, the tabletops in the living room, and the six-foot-long dining table overflowed with trays of collard greens, deep-dish macaroni and cheese, black-eyed peas, white rice, chicken in all its incarnations, ribs, yams, whole hams, étouffée, and crab cakes, and tubs of sweet tea and lemonade that stood like sentinels in the remaining space.

Zoie found refuge in her Nana's garden, the one section of the property that remained off-limits to the guests. With a glass of sweet tea in hand, she sat on the bench that Nana had placed there for such an occasion. *Whenever I have a lot on my mind I come right here, sit in my garden and turn it over to God.*

"I'm so sorry, Nana. Wherever you are now, please forgive me. I know I shouldn't have let all the bad feelings between me and Mama and my aunties get in the way. I shouldn't have let my pride rule over my mind. I should have been here for you. What am I going to do without you?" A choked sob lodged in her throat. The enormity of her loss overwhelmed her with a grief that wracked her body. She had a mother and two aunts, but without her grandmother, she may as well be an orphan. Even though they lived hundreds of miles apart and only spoke by phone, there was a comfort in knowing that her grandmother was always there.

Alone. She was completely alone. Sure, she had her job and her one friend. That meant something, didn't it?

"I tried to say hello earlier, but you were surrounded."

Her body stiffened in response to the honey-sweet voice that she'd pushed into her past, where it belonged, where she needed it to be. She wiped her eyes and turned.

"Jackson." She drew in a slow, deep breath to steady herself. Seeing him again, even after all this time, raced her pulse and flooded her psyche with memories.

Jackson Fuller. If there existed any other reason beyond her family as to why she'd fled New Orleans, it was Jackson.

He slid his hands into the pockets of his navy-blue slacks. He lowered his head for an instant, then settled those soul-stealing eyes on her. "I'm very sorry about your Nana, Z."

Her heart lurched at the pet name. She folded her lips inward.

"I know how much she meant to you and you to her." He took his hand from his pocket and cupped his chin. "Look, I know things weren't good between us when you left—"

"Good between us?" she asked, incredulity elevating the pitch of her voice.

The glass of sweet tea shook in her hand.

"Z . . ."

She took a step forward. "Don't you dare call me that. You lost that right when you walked out on me." Her eyes burned.

The tip of his tongue moistened his bottom lip.

"I'm sorry, Zoie, for all of it. I was young and stupid and full of myself, but that doesn't mean that what I felt for you wasn't real."

She turned her back to him. "You said what you needed to say, Jackson. Now please leave. I want to be alone."

"Your go-to, get-out-of-whatever one-liner." He blew out a breath of frustration. "Cool. I'll go." He went to the door, then stopped. "It's great to see you again. New York looks good on you." He opened the door. "Maybe you should think about what part you played in our breakup. Take care of yourself, Zoie."

She didn't breathe until she heard the screen door pop close.

CHAPTER 3

"How did everything go today?" Miranda asked.

Zoie stretched out on her childhood bed, crossed her legs at the ankles, and shut her eyes. She blew out a long breath. "It went. Hard at times. Exhausting. But the service was beautiful. I had no idea that so many people knew Nana."

"I'm sure she racked up a lot of acquaintances over the years. She's lived in New Orleans all her adult life."

"I know, but it was still pretty amazing."

"And . . . how are things with you and the family?"

"All the preparation for Nana's service kept us too busy to get on anyone's nerves. Two more days and I can head home. Monday is the reading of the will."

"Okay. I'll take care of your return flight. Monday evening cool?"

"No, I think I need to wait until after everything is settled on Monday."

"Oh. Really?"

"Whaaat?"

"It sounds like a one-eighty shift in attitude. Two days ago, you couldn't get out of there fast enough. What changed?"

"Nothing. I need to stay a little longer, that's all." She paused. "It's what my grandmother would want."

"Sis, I'm not judging. Personally, I think this is what you need."

"Of course you do." She sighed.

"This is a chance for you to try to connect with your mom, Z. I would hate for you to look back when it's too late and wish that you had tried."

Zoie squeezed her eyes shut. *Like what happened with her Nana.* "How's everything on your end?" she asked to switch topics.

"Great. Andre and I are talking about a short getaway, maybe the Bahamas for a long weekend."

"Getaway. Nice. You two are getting pretty serious."

"I like him a lot. Dre is a great guy. He makes me happy and treats me like the queen that I am," she said, ending on laughter.

"He betta!" Zoie teased.

"Hey, I didn't want to ask, but I wouldn't be your best friend, ride-or-die chick if I didn't—"

Zoie cut her off. "Yes, I saw him."

"And . . ."

An image of Jackson jumped in front of her and blocked out the waning light streaming in from the window. "It was hard." She swallowed. "I didn't think it would be after all this time, but . . ."

"You never really got over him, which is why you and Brian didn't work out, even though I think Brian is perfect for you."

"If you'd ever met Jackson, you'd say he was perfect, too."

"Is that a wistful tone that I hear?"

"No. Just stating the obvious."

"Well, I don't need to meet him. You told me enough that I feel like I know him, and because I know him, I hate him for what he did to you."

"Tell me how you really feel." Unfortunately, Miranda only had part of the story—the part that Zoie had wanted to reveal.

"It's true," Miranda singsonged. "And what's also true is that you will never be happy if you don't get beyond Jackson Fuller."

She paused a beat. "Seems like you have a lot to do down there besides your Nana's will, sis."

"May-be," she said in a distant voice. "Maybe."

⋙•⋘

Zoie awoke the following morning to the smell of frying bacon and sausages. Her stomach howled in response and forced her out of bed. Living in New York, she'd adopted all the latest health-food crazes—green teas, salads, Greek yogurts, and fish as opposed to meat. She did yoga twice a week and soul-cycling on Saturdays.

However, the water in her mouth and the rumble in her belly said to hell with that healthy crap; give me some hot, greasy, salty pork! And if she knew her mother and Aunt Sage, there was a steaming pot of grits with cheese, homemade biscuits, and eggs light enough to float off the skillet.

Zoie padded off to the bathroom, did a quick wash and brush—enough to pass inspection at the breakfast table—then trotted downstairs and into the kitchen. Her mother was at the stove.

Rose glanced over her shoulder, looked Zoie up and down. "You're not dressed for church."

"Church?"

"Yes. It's Sunday. It's what we do here, or have you forgotten? I know they have plenty of churches in New York. Apparently, you don't attend."

Whatever desire she had, whatever she may have imagined sitting down to breakfast with her mother and aunts could be, dissolved.

Her heart actually hurt.

"You can fix yourself a plate, but you need to hurry. Takes us a little longer to get Hyacinth out of the house, and you know Sage hates to be late and have to sit in the back." Rose wiped her hands on her apron. She lifted the pan with the eggs and spooned them onto the platter at the center of the table.

Rose glanced up from ladling the eggs. "Are you gonna just stand there or do something useful?"

Zoie swallowed over the lump in her throat. "What do you need, Mama?"

"You can get the pitcher of orange juice out of the refrigerator."

Zoie did as she was instructed, biting down on her lip to keep from screaming.

"Thank you, baby." Rose smiled at her daughter the way she used to when she was a small child, and Zoie nearly wept. "Go on and fix yourself some right quick. If you want, you can sneak it up to your room so you can eat and get dressed. Just don't let Sage see you." She rolled her eyes. "Go 'head." She fanned her hands as if shooing a fly. "It's our secret."

Zoie took one of the plates that was stacked on the table and piled her plate high. "Thanks, Mama."

Rose grinned, then went to the sink and began to wash the pots.

Zoie hurried up the stairs and prayed she wouldn't run into her aunt. She managed to make it to her room unseen. She eased the door shut behind her but couldn't shake the childhood dread that at any moment she would be found out and chastised. The very idea that her mother had orchestrated this major breach of household protocol was still settling in her head. They'd actually had a "moment"—she and her mother. The occasion was so rare that it left her hard-pressed to process how she actually felt. A part of her, the girl that needed her mom, bubbled with joy. But the cynical woman who was a victim of the unpredictability of her mother remained wary.

She rested her plate on the nightstand, then dug in while she mentally catalogued her meager wardrobe lineup. The only thing that came close to appropriate church attire was the black dress she'd worn to the funeral.

It was the best she could do because she knew her aunties and her mother would have one fit short of institutionalization if she wore slacks to church.

She crossed the room and took the dress out of the closet and gave it a good shake. She sniffed under the arms of the short sleeves. *Good to go.*

———⬥———

When Zoie returned to the kitchen, Sage threw a brief look in her direction as she continued to fasten Hyacinth's pearls. "'Morning. Hope you ate something. Service takes a while."

Hyacinth chuckled. "Bring lunch." She laughed again. "Reverend loves to hear his own voice," she said, sounding like her old self.

Zoie grinned. Oh, how she remembered the endless Sunday service, which was exhausting if you weren't prepared. Between the incalculably long sermon, guest speakers, countless musical renditions by the choir, the required "catching of the spirit," the praise dancers, the announcements, the calling to the altar, the collections for the building fund, the pastor's fund, the roof fund (which should be included in the building fund), the sick and shut-in fund, the water fund, and the school fund—well, church could go on for the entire day. She grew dizzy thinking about it. Not to mention that around two hours into the service the aroma of fried chicken, collards, string beans, and triple mac and cheese would begin to waft into the sanctuary as the preacher preached on.

"I'm ready when you are," Zoie said.

———⬥———

Back under the eaves of the First Baptist Church of Our Lord and Savior, she saw familiar faces that were the same, yet different, and smelled the scent of lemon wood polish on the pews, mixed with the sachet and talcum powder of the parishioners, as the hum of organ music played in the background while the membership filed into the sanctuary and took their assigned seats. She remembered well the hierarchy of seating in the church and the ushers who were charged with ensuring that no one breached protocol. Inwardly, she smiled. The sense of community and genuine caring enveloped her, and she realized with a jolt of nostalgia that she actually missed all this. At least a little bit.

As promised and expected, the morning service lasted a full three hours, and between the singing, praise dancers, testimonies, catching the spirit, and, of course, the sermon, there wasn't a dull moment. Zoie was mildly surprised that three hours had passed so quickly.

Now she only had to get through one more night and the reading of the will in the morning, and she could return home—back to New York, where she belonged.

CHAPTER 4

"Mr. Phillips, Mama's attorney, said he'd be here by eleven," Rose said while she poured hot water into her mug. She daintily dipped her herbal teabag in and out until the water turned a rich reddish brown.

Zoie plucked an apple from the floral-patterned bowl on the counter. She recalled how her grandmother would fuss if the fruit bowl was ever empty and would send her daughters or Zoie running to round up fruit from the market and the backyard peach tree.

"It should be pretty quick, I would think," Zoie said.

Rose's brows arched. "Why would you say that? The quicker it is, the quicker you can leave?"

Zoie squeezed her eyes shut and slowly shook her head. "Why does everything I say have some other meaning? Why does every conversation between us have to be a war of words?"

Rose pushed out a slow breath and leveled Zoie with a steady gaze. "Maybe because you made it clear to me and your family that what you do is more important than who you are. That family doesn't come first and you are willing to sacrifice family for your own ambitions."

Zoie blinked with incredulity at her mother's reasoning. Her mouth opened, then closed. She pushed up from her seat. "I'm going upstairs. You can call me when Mr. Phillips arrives."

It took all of her home training to stop from slamming her bedroom door. Fury seared through her veins. This was why she stayed away. The constant feeling of anger bordered on debilitating. It drained her, clouded her mind, and stole precious moments of her life.

Zoie flopped down on her bed and stared, unseeing, at the ceiling. What made her believe, even for a moment, that any sort of reconciliation between her and her family was possible? The hardest part was that she never understood why she always felt like an outcast, unloved, by the very people who should have held her tight to their breasts.

Had it always been this way? She tried to remember a time when things were good and happy.

A slow smile moved across her mouth.

It was spring. Early May. A Sunday, she knew, because she could see herself in a sunshine-yellow dress with white frills on the hem, black patent-leather shoes on her feet, and white anklet socks. Raucous laughter came from the parlor. Zoie saw herself skipping down the foyer and through the archway of the parlor.

Nana Claudia seemed to be in the middle of a story that had Zoie's mom, aunts, and dad in stitches.

All eyes turned toward her, and she felt swaddled in a Technicolor blanket of love. Her mother and father held their arms out to her, and her aunts cooed and ahhed at her, while Nana looked upon her family with the self-satisfied smile of the matriarch she was.

Dad.

Zoie jerked back to the present. Her eyes were wet. She blinked against the memories. Hank Crawford had the gift of delight. He wore it like a tailor-made suit and never took it off.

Within his aura, her mother was a young, starry-eyed girl, full of laughter and with plenty of hugs and kisses to spare.

Her aunts bloomed like their names in his presence, and her grandmother glowed.

But to Zoie he was simply Daddy, the man who made her world go around, who carried her on his broad shoulders, read to her at night, and listened to her secrets.

Then he was gone, and with him the laughter and sunshine. No one ever told her why. All she knew was that the world had changed. Her family had changed.

The knock on her door jerked her upright. She wiped her eyes. "Yes?"

"Mr. Phillips is here," her mother said from the other side of the door.

Zoie cleared her throat. "Coming." She swung her feet to the floor and by degrees pushed up from the bed and stood. Crossing the room, she stopped in front of the mirror that topped her dresser. She forced a smile, smoothed her hair, turned, and walked out.

⟶•⟵

The family was gathered around the dining room table. Mr. Phillips sat at the head, where her grandmother always sat. The image slowed, then stopped Zoie's forward motion.

"Oh, Zoie, there you are." Mr. Phillips stood until Zoie fully entered and took a seat next to her mother. "Well," he said on a breath, then spread his fingers on the table, "let's get started."

He took a folder filled with documents from his briefcase, and placed them on the table. He cleared his throat and adjusted his glasses. "Claudia has willed her jewelry and her savings, totaling ten thousand dollars, to be divided equally between her daughters, Rose, Sage, and Hyacinth. Her home, her garden, and her business is bequeathed to her only granddaughter, Zoie Crawford, with the caveat that she must live in and maintain the property and business for one full year to claim her inheritance. Should you break the terms of the will, the house, the garden, and the business will be sold and the proceeds distributed to the First Baptist Church of Our Lord and Savior."

The eyes of the Bennett women turned on Zoie, who sat in wide-eyed shock. She opened her mouth to speak, but nothing came out.

"That's it," Mr. Phillips said, looking around at the astonished expressions. "Zoie, I have some papers for you to sign that temporarily turn things over to you." He closed the folder with a definitive thunk.

Sage huffed, pushed back from her chair, glared at Zoie, then stormed out. Rose assisted Hyacinth from her seat, and without a word or a backward glance, they followed in Sage's wake.

Zoie sat frozen, confused and hurt by her family's reaction. But more, she was overwhelmed by what her grandmother had done. The implication of it all was still out of reach.

Mr. Phillips came around to where Zoie sat and placed the documents in front of her. He sat down.

"I know this may be difficult for your aunts and your mother, but your grandmother was very specific in her wishes. She wanted to be certain that you would be financially secure, always have a home, and she believed that you were the only one she could entrust with carrying on the business that she built. And more important," he said, covering her fisted hand, "she wanted you to be the one to look after your aunts and your mother."

"But . . . how can I? I . . . live in New York. I have a job, a life." Her eyes filled.

Mr. Phillips pulled a handkerchief from the breast pocket of his suit jacket and handed it to her. "Your grandmother placed a heavy load on you, but she also did it with a lot of faith."

"What if I don't sign? What if I turn everything over to my family?" she asked, suddenly frantic.

"If you decline, there is the caveat," he intoned.

"That would mean my family would have to leave?"

Mr. Phillips nodded slowly. "Yes. I'm afraid so."

"Oh, God," she moaned and covered her face with her hands.

Mr. Phillips patted her shoulders and placed the pen in front of her.

Zoie looked at the pen as if it might bite. Tentatively, she picked it up. Mr. Phillips pointed to the place on the documents where she needed to sign.

"That's it, then. The house, the garden, and the business are yours in the interim and will revert fully to you at the end of one year." He gathered the documents and stood. "I'll have copies made of everything and get you the originals tomorrow."

Zoie looked up at him, her gaze imploring him for some words of wisdom. All he offered was a tight smile before walking out.

Zoie sat immobile and tried to process the unfolded events. How could she handle this? Worse yet, whatever fragment of a relationship that she had with her family was surely ripped to shreds. How could she face them? Why would her grandmother do this? Surely, she had to know how everyone would react. The questions, devoid of answers, swirled through her head.

"Well, I shouldn't be surprised."

Zoie turned to see her mother standing in the archway.

"Mama . . . I—"

Rose held up her hand. "Your grandmother loved you. That's clear." She stepped further into the room. "The truth is, your grandmother knew what she wanted. She believed that the best hands to lay her legacy in were yours."

Zoie's heart thumped. She swallowed over the tight knot in her throat.

Rose blew out a breath. "It doesn't take the sting away, the slap in the face. We've been here day after day. Now you'll have to stay and endure us, whether you want to or not. Ironic, huh?" She lifted her chin. "Up to you now, I suppose. We'll have to see how all that turns out." With that, she turned and walked out.

Zoie lowered her head and finally let the tears fall.

—➤•◀—

Zoie returned to her room, hurt, shaken, and overwhelmed by the events of the morning.

She couldn't turn her life upside down and relocate to New Orleans. It wasn't possible. With a major assignment to cover Kimberly Maitland-Graham, this was the worst time. She had a career, one that was leading her straight toward stardom in her field. She needed it, craved it, dreamed of it. Recognition. Acceptance. Accolades. They were all within her reach. Now this.

Air. She needed air, away from this house, these women who held no love in their hearts for her. She swiped at her eyes, quickly went into her room, and changed into her one pair of jeans and a T-shirt and sneakers. Jogging usually helped to clear her head. She took her ID and a credit card out of her purse, stuck them in her back pocket, and left with no idea where she was going.

The Louisiana sun was high in the sky, the glare near-blinding in spots, but its rays were not strong enough to warm the deep cold in her bones.

She started down the street at a slow jog, barely taking in the stately homes, manicured lawns, porch sitters comfortable in their rockers and bench swings, dog walkers, and casual strollers. It was all a blur as she rounded the corner and headed instinctively toward the park.

Zoie approached the entrance when a car horn blared alongside her. She slowed, turned.

The dark-blue BWM pulled to a stop. The lightly tinted window descended.

"Zoie . . ."

She stopped. Her blood, already pumping hard from her jog, kicked up a notch.

Jackson got out. "You run when you have a lot on your mind."

She hated that he still knew her so well. "If you know that much, then you should know I don't like distractions. Defeats the purpose."

He rounded the car and came to stand in front of her.

Her breathing escalated. She wanted to take a step back but could not seem to move.

Jackson, with the tip of his thumb, wiped a tear of perspiration that ran down from her hairline along her right ear.

The place where he touched her sizzled. The dampness of her skin suddenly heated.

"Want to talk?" he asked as soft as a prayer.

The gentleness of his voice, the sincerity in the brown pools of his eyes, and his tender touch combined to break open the floodgates.

Jackson immediately gathered her in his arms and held her tight against his chest.

The hurt, the loss, the guilt, the weight of her future poured out and onto his starched white shirt. She wasn't even sure how, but she found herself cocooned inside the sanctuary of his car, weeping on his shoulder.

Jackson didn't say a word. He simply held her, stroked her hair, and caressed her back until she was drained dry.

"I'm sorry," she finally muttered. She kept her head lowered, unwilling to look him in the eyes.

Jackson lifted her chin. "This is me, baby. There's nothing for you to be sorry about."

She sniffed hard. "Everything is just so fucked up," she said, her voice raspy and raw.

"How bad are things with you and the family?" he tentatively probed.

In bits and pieces and between short bouts of tears, Zoie unloaded everything that pressed down on her soul.

———◦•◦———

Throughout her confession, Jackson listened in silence. He wanted to tell her that it wasn't her fault, that she could not be responsible for the behavior of others, but he knew now was not the time. Zoie didn't need absolution. She needed an ear and a vessel into which she could pour her pain.

"Why don't I drive us into town. We can grab an early dinner and talk—or not."

When she dared to look in his eyes and allowed herself to be lulled by the easy cadence of his voice, she had nothing left in her to resist. She nodded her agreement.

CHAPTER 5

Jackson pressed a few buttons on the console and the car's interior was filled with the soft jazz that he knew Zoie enjoyed. He took a quick glance at her. She'd leaned back against the headrest, and her eyes were closed. Faint tear stains streaked her cheeks. Her lids were slightly puffy, and she'd all but chewed off her plum-colored lipstick. He'd never seen her more beautiful.

Wow, he'd missed her. He didn't realize how much until he saw her at the house, and now having her this close, holding her again . . . A part of him always regretted what had happened between them, but they were both too stubborn to have it any other way.

Zoie Crawford, his first real love. Fool that he was, he didn't realize it until too late. Young and dumb, he'd believed that he had all the time in the world to get it together. Zoie needed a strong, focused man who could shore her up against the onslaught of her overbearing mother and often caustic aunts. Intellectually, he understood what Zoie needed. But all he wanted was a career, great sex, and to hang out and live his life with as little drama as possible.

Zoie was high maintenance, on every level. He simply had not been ready for the fully formed woman who was Zoie Crawford.

They'd met in the Quarter on a Saturday afternoon in May at

Le Grille. She was sitting alone at a table across from him with her wild head of curls buried in a Toni Morrison book. Beyond reading, she looked to be taking notes. He figured she must be a student and decided to dismiss her when, as if sensing his stare, she glanced up.

That bullshit he'd always heard about getting hit by lightning was true. His body actually throbbed, and as he admitted to her after the first time they'd made love, he got hard with just that look from her.

She'd given him a cursory smile and returned to her reading and note taking.

He couldn't move and seemed unable to unscramble his thoughts after that jolt from her.

The waiter appeared and obstructed his view. When the waiter walked away, Zoie was preparing to leave. Opportunity got up and started toward the street.

Jackson slapped a twenty on the table and hurried out behind her. He caught up with her at the corner, seconds before she stepped onto the crosswalk.

"I'm going that way," he said, sidling next to her and matching her step.

Her head snapped toward him, and recognition widened her eyes. Jackson wasn't sure if the look was tempered with surprise or alarm.

"Excuse me?"

"I was saying I'm going that way."

She frowned for an instant, then picked up her pace. Jackson kept up.

"Really, which way is that?"

"Whichever way you're going."

She stopped when she got to the opposite side of the street and faced him. She folded her arms. "You were at Le Grille." It was almost an accusation.

"Yeah, I was." He grinned.

"And you're a stalker."

"I wouldn't go that far. Actually, I work over at The Shade, tend bar on Thursday, Friday, and Saturday nights. You should stop by."

She made a face and gave him a quick once-over. "Not interested." She stepped to the curb, and a cab screeched to a stop as if secretly summoned.

"Wait!"

She ducked into the cab and pulled the door shut behind her.

Jackson watched her lean forward to give the driver instructions, then recline and open her book; the cab pulled away to leave him standing on the corner. She hadn't given him a backward glance or her name.

Jackson shoved his hands into the pockets of his jeans, then headed back to Le Grille to get his car.

⸻

Jackson tried to push her to the recesses of his mind and chalked it up to a missed opportunity—hers. In his mind, he tried to convince himself that it was her loss. It was the only way he could reconcile who the real loser was. That train of thought was the only thing that helped to quell his sense of defeat.

Most women whom he met and dated became a blur in short order. Not her—whoever she was—and he didn't know what to do about it.

⸻

Almost three weeks had passed since he'd seen her. In between, he'd returned to Le Grille in the hope of running into her again. He'd even gone so far as to hang out around the university on the off chance that if she was a student, he might catch a glimpse of her walking across the quad.

If he did run into her, what would he possibly say to nix the whole "stalker" MO? He had no idea.

After a few weeks, he'd all but given up on ever seeing her again, and then there she was, sitting at an outdoor café on Chantilly Street in the Quarter.

It took a moment for him to process the image. It was her, once again with her head in a book and looking more desirable than she did before.

He darted around the meanderers and the photo-taking tourists and got to the other side of the street. He drew in a long breath of resolve and headed toward her, but he stopped short when she glanced up and smiled at the man who approached her. He leaned down, placed a possessive hand on her bare shoulder, and kissed her. They shared some words that made her laugh, and the luckiest man in the world sat down opposite her.

Jackson wanted to kick something or someone; instead, he walked away, determined to put her out of his head once and for all.

No such luck.

———⋙•⋘———

Several weeks later, his best buddy, Lennox, texted him, wanting to meet up after work for drink. They agreed to connect downtown in front of TNC Bank, then decide where to go.

He stood in front of the bank and passed the time by checking his email on his cell phone.

"Hi," Zoie greeted him, as if she hadn't given him the brush-off the last time they were together.

Jackson glanced up and did a double take. "Hey." He smiled. "How are you?"

"Good. Waiting on someone?"

He slid his phone into his pocket. "Yeah. I am. Buddy of mine. You?"

She gave a slight shrug. "Nope. Just came to grab something to eat." Her gaze darted away. "Didn't want to stay in the house tonight."

Something in her voice unmoored him. "Join us," he blurted.

Zoie grinned. "Do you always invite strangers to join you and your friends for dinner?"

"Not usually."

"Hey, bro," Lennox said, walking up to the couple. He gave Zoie a quick once-over. "Lennox Banks."

"Zoie Crawford."

Lennox nodded, looked at Jackson.

"Yeah, I was telling Zoie . . ."—he liked how that sounded on his tongue—"that we wouldn't mind if she joined us."

"Cool with me. Le Grille is on the corner. Good music, food, drinks."

Zoie and Jackson looked at each other, and the irony was not lost on him.

"Let's hit it," Jackson said.

The trio fell in step, with Zoie in the middle.

Jackson held the door for Zoie, caught the barest hint of some soft, sexy fragrance, and pretty much shut the door in Lennox's face.

Le Grille hummed with activity. The fully occupied bar left them no option but to wait for a table or find another venue. The hostess promised fifteen minutes.

"So how do you two know each other?" Lennox asked, cutting straight to the point.

Jackson shifted his weight. Zoie laughed.

"We actually don't," Zoie announced with ease. "As a matter of fact," she turned, facing Jackson and looking up into his gaze, "I don't even know your name."

For a moment, his thoughts became encrypted and he couldn't decode them. She tilted her head to the right, snapping him out of his haze. "Jackson Fuller."

Zoie extended her hand. He wrapped his fingers around hers.

"Good to finally meet you, Zoie Crawford." He knew he'd held her hand too long when Lennox's throat clearing reached the annoying level.

Much of the night was a montage of simply feeling good. Conversation flowed, along with the drinks. The music added to the jovial atmosphere, and Zoie . . . he couldn't put words to it. A light seemed to radiate around her. Her infectious laughter, laser-focused questions, and razor-sharp knowledge about so many things mesmerized him, and at times during the evening, he found himself helplessly staring.

If only things could have stayed that way. Perfect can't last forever.

⟶•◦•⟵

Jackson eased down River Road and found a parking space. He angled his body toward her. Her lids fluttered open, and when she looked at him, whatever myths he'd been telling himself about keeping Zoie Crawford in his rearview mirror dissolved like sugar in hot water.

"You okay?"

She ran her tongue along her bottom lip. "I'm good." She sat up straight.

Jackson knew the tone, knew the sound all too well. Zoie was on the verge of autopilot shutdown. The drawbridge was being cranked up, and soon the only way to reach the castle would be to chance the alligator-filled moat.

His jaw clenched. "Come on. Let's find a spot." He quickly got out and came around to open her door. He dared to place his hand at the small of her back, and when she didn't pull away, he guided her down the street and smoothly ushered her into a dimly lit café without a word of protest.

They were shown to a small banquette in the back of the café, and Jackson was relieved that they were relatively secluded from prying ears.

Zoie linked her fingers together and kept her gaze fixed on them.

Jackson draped his arm across the leather back of his seat. "Talk to me," he softly encouraged. He watched her body tighten. He reached across the table and covered her hands.

The waitress appeared, and Jackson took the liberty of ordering chicken and waffles, and two bottles of Coors. One thing he remembered about Zoie was that when she was stressed she would run and then settle in with some comfort food. And it didn't get more comfortable than chicken and waffles. Once the waitress was gone, Jackson turned his full attention on Zoie. He gently squeezed her hand.

Her gaze jerked up, then skittered away. "Nothing's changed . . . everything's changed. I don't know what the right thing is to do. Nana, the will, my mother, my aunts . . ." Her eyes filled. "It's just all fucked up, Jax. I can't stay here! How could Nana do this to me?"

"Wait. Slow down. You're losing me. What happened with the will?"

Zoie drew in a breath and exhaled the details of the will and her family response.

"Damn, Z. I don't know what to say. Are there any loopholes?"

"Not that I know of."

"So you have to stay or your family is out on the street."

"Basically."

"Hey," he leaned forward, "You're freelance. I'm sure your grandmother understood what that meant when she came up with her 'master plan.' That gives you the liberty to go where the story is. Do your writing from here. We do have the Internet here in Nawlins, you know," he said, with an exaggeration of his drawl.

The remark elicited the first smile he'd seen on her face in far too long.

"Very funny. Ordinarily, it wouldn't be a problem, but my latest assignment is in New York." She told him about Kimberly Maitland-Graham.

He frowned for a moment. "*The* Kimberly Maitland of the Maitland fortune?"

"Yes. Her."

"Hmm." He leaned back a bit. "You do know that her family is still here in NOLA. Pretty sure they will wind up being a big part of your story, and there's nothing in the will to keep you from going to New York whenever you need to." He saw a glimmer of possibility light her eyes.

"Maybe," she said, with a hitch of caution in her voice.

The waitress returned with their order.

Jackson lifted his bottle of beer. Zoie did the same.

"To possibilities," Jackson said and touched his bottle to hers.

Zoie stared at him, and for an instant Jackson swore he saw something in her eyes, and then it was gone.

"Possibilities," she replied.

CHAPTER 6

"Thanks for rescuing me," Zoie said, half-joking.

"I always wanted to do the whole knight in shining armor thing." Jackson turned off the ignition and leaned back. "You think you're going to be jogging anytime soon?"

Zoie smiled. "Probably." She glanced at the house. "I envied you. Did you know that?"

He sat up. "Me? Why?"

"The way you were with your family. How they were with you." She sighed. "You all actually seemed to care about each other." She looked at him for a moment, then turned away.

"Every family has its problems. We were far from perfect."

"At least they made you feel like you belonged."

Jackson wasn't sure how to respond. He was a witness on many occasions when Zoie's mother would make her stinging remarks, and he had seen how Zoie would visibly shrink and turn inward. He would then become her outlet for her hurt and anger, and as much as he sympathized, in the end he ultimately was unwilling to remain the recipient of her misplaced animosity.

"Look, no matter what the deal is with your people, you've risen above it. You made a life, built a career in spite of them. That counts for something." He reached out and lifted a stray curl from her face.

Zoie looked at him. "I'm . . . sorry, Jax."

"For what?"

"About everything. How I treated you—ran you away. Blamed you for not miraculously turning my life into a fairy tale."

"Takes two to make or break a relationship. I wasn't ready to be who you needed."

Her tense expression softened. "Who is this man, and where is the real Jackson Fuller?"

He chuckled. "He's a work in progress."

Zoie blew out a breath. "Thanks for . . . today." She turned to get out of the car.

Jackson clasped her arm. She glanced over her shoulder with her hand still on the door.

"I know we parted ways, but if you ever need to talk or need a drink," he grinned, "I'm a phone call away."

And then she did something she hadn't done in years; she stroked his chin with the tip of her finger. It was their special signal that everything was alright.

She opened the car door and got out.

Jackson sat and watched her walk into the house, but her touch on his face lasted for hours.

———※———

"Man, you're not tryin' to get back with Zoie, are you?" Lennox asked as they sat on the back deck of Jackson's house, sipping beer.

Jackson stretched out his legs and put his feet up on the railing. He tipped his beer bottle up to his mouth and took a deep swallow. "Naw," he finally said. "Just being a friend. We have a history—not all bad."

"Yeah, okay." He chuckled. "That woman did a real number on you."

"We did a number on each other."

"Hmm, that's true. Just think with the head on top of your neck, if you get my meaning"

Jackson cut his dark eyes at Lennox. "I'll keep that in mind."

"What about Lena?"

"What about her?"

"She know you were with Zoie?"

"Nothing to tell."

"So you say. Women have that special radar, bro. She'll find out eventually. Then what? Hell hath no fury and all that shit."

"Lena's not like that."

"She's a woman, ain't she?"

"Nothing's going on between me and Z. I saw her, we talked, had a beer, end of story."

Lennox finished his beer, set the bottle down, and rested his forearms on his thighs. "Look, I know you still care about Zoie. All I'm saying is, don't let your past screw up your present."

"That's not going to be a problem."

———※———

"Mark, I know I said I'd be back by Wednesday, but some developments have happened down here." Zoie paced across the grass while she tried to explain her dilemma to her boss.

"I totally understand. Family is important. But I need someone like you on this story, Zoie. If you can't handle it right now, I'll reassign it."

She pressed her hand to her forehead. "Listen, you know me. I can do this. The Maitland family still lives here. I can start with them and come up to New York whenever I need to and work on the interview with Kimberly Graham."

"I need you on the campaign trail, not conducting hit-and-miss interviews."

"I know, I know. I'll make it work, Mark."

She listened to his heavy breathing while her heart pounded.

"Let me think about it. This can't be half-ass. I need you fully committed."

"I am."

"I'll get back to you tomorrow with an answer."

"Okay," she conceded.

"We'll talk tomorrow."

"Fine." She stared at the disconnected call. "Damnit."

Losing this assignment was not an option. Brian was already taking over her Trade Center assignment. Somehow, she had to find a way to keep turning the pages in this new chapter of her life. The biggest problem was not the travel; it was being unavailable to manage her grandmother's vegetable business. If she was going to find a way through, she needed to get a handle on the ins and outs of the business and figure out how to keep her grandmother's legacy viable without losing everything she'd worked for in the process.

Zoie turned toward the house and hurried inside in search of her mother. By the time she spoke to Mark again, she needed to have a plan.

She found her mother watering the garden. Her back was turned, and for a moment Zoie felt a rush of sadness. She was humming a tune that Zoie didn't recognize, but in that setting her mother seemed happy, content even, as she walked along the rows of vegetables humming and murmuring and gently touching them with the kind of love that Zoie wished her mother would give to her.

"Mama . . ."

Rose glanced over her shoulder and turned off the hose. She wiped a hand across her forehead. "Just giving the garden a bit of attention."

Zoe took a step forward. "How often do we need to water?"

"Hmm, once a week, more if it gets really hot." She dropped the hose and brushed her hands along the sides of her dress. "What brings you out here? Looking over your new business?"

Zoe refused to rise to the bait. "Actually, I was looking for you."

"Oh."

"I was wondering where Nana kept her records about the business—the clients and whatnot."

Rose pursed her lips. "Far as I know, whatever records she kept are in her room up in the attic."

"The attic?"

Rose nodded. "Said the business was business, and she didn't want it overflowing into the house." She propped her hand on her hip. "Guess you can figure it all out yourself." She turned away, picked up the hose, and continued watering the garden; it was her way of ending the conversation.

"Thank you."

"Hmm."

Zoie walked away, determined to stand down any guilty feelings. If she was going to have to spend any length of time here, she would have to put on her big-girl pants while remaining respectful of her elders. It wouldn't be easy, but she had very little choice.

When she returned inside, she went up to the second floor and down the hall to the stairs that lead to the attic. She opened the door and was hit with a hot blast of pent-up air.

Once up the stairs, she was shocked at what she found. In her mind, she had expected the attic to look like those she'd always seen on television—dusty, broken floorboards, old clothes, and mannequins draped in sheets. Instead she found a wide-open space with a beautiful rolltop desk that sat in front of the small attic window, file cabinets, two comfy chairs, and even a radio. There were pictures on the wall of the family in various stages of their growing up. On the built-in shelves were the little teapots that Nana loved to collect.

Standing there, taking in the space, she turned, faced an exquisite mirror, and slowly began to recall the last time she had ventured up there. She must have been about eight, and in that version of her memory, the space was a treasure trove of adventure, a catchall for the discarded things in the house. All of the old fancy dresses with padded shoulders, high-heeled shoes, handmade quilts, and boxes of pictures and old furniture fascinated her. There were a Victrola and crates of albums. She'd emptied boxes and tried on outfits, posed in front of the tall mirror edged in heavy wood that leaned against the wall, and totally lost track of time.

When her mother finally found her, she was sitting in a corner, trying on a pair of shoes. Rose was livid, as much from anger as fear.

"Do you know you scared us all half to death? We've been looking all over for you." Her mother snatched her up by the arm, then held her tight to her breasts. "Don't you ever do that again, you hear me. Lord Jesus, if I ever lost you I don't know what I'd do. Come on. You need a bath." She took Zoie by the hand and led her downstairs. She was then scolded harshly by her aunt Sage and aunt Hyacinth for being up there, and warned to stay out before something fell on her and she would never be found again. She remembered that night, when her Nana had come into her room and sat on the side of her bed.

"They just worry about you, that's all, chile," she'd said, stroking the side of Zoie's cheek.

"What did I do that was so wrong, Nana?"

"Well, you run off, and ain't nobody know where you get to. That attic ain't a safe place for a little girl. Too many ways you can get hurt, and none of us want that." She kissed Zoie's forehead. "Understand?"

"Yes, Nana."

"That's my girl. Now, one day when you gets big enough, you can go up. Nothin' up there but junk no ways. You get you some sleep." She pushed up from the bed. "You remember what I said, hear?"

"Yes, Nana."

"Nite now."

"Nite."

The one thing she never wanted to do was to disappoint her Nana. After that day, as curious as she was, she never ventured up to the attic again. After a while, she forgot all about it.

Then she moved away.

Zoie walked further into the room, running her hand along the desk, then turned her attention to the filing cabinets. She pulled the handle on the top drawer. It would not open. She tugged harder. *Locked.* She looked around. Maybe the key was in the desk.

She went to the desk and pulled open the drawer. Pens, folders, a notepad, but no key. She frowned, turned in a circle, and went back to the file cabinet. She ran her hand across the top. Nothing. Where would Nana keep the key? She walked over to the built-ins and began to check the teapots. *Bingo.*

She unlocked the cabinet and pulled open the top drawer. Inside were neat rows of multicolored file folders, all alphabetized. She plucked out a random folder. *Fordham Foods.* Nana sold vegetables to them monthly. *Dubois Goods*, another monthly account. There were at least ten businesses that expected delivery of fruits and vegetables on a monthly basis, and that didn't include the individual households.

After nearly two hours of going over the files and taking notes, Zoie was completely overwhelmed with the enormity of what her grandmother had single-handedly built. She could barely wrap her mind around it. How could she not have known? *Because you never bothered to really find out.*

She pushed aside the files that had piled up on the desk and rested her head on her palms. She didn't have the skills for this. She worked with words, not vegetables. What did she know about running a business? At best, she had an adversarial relationship with numbers and had barely made it out of her college math classes. How could her Nana have done all of this alone? Her mother and her aunts must have helped. And if so, then why drop all of this in her lap?

Her temples pounded. She pushed back from the desk and

stood. What was she going to do? She still had no plan. All she knew at the moment were the number of clients and delivery dates. How did it all work together? She was pretty sure that her grandmother didn't drive all over town on delivery runs. But then again, knowing her feisty, independent grandmother, she very well may have.

Her gaze settled on a mahogany trunk that was tucked in the back corner of the room. Curiosity teased her, but her brain was on overload. Probably old baby clothes or something. She'd tackle that another day. She took her notes and went back downstairs.

CHAPTER 7

"Mrs. Graham, there's a reporter on the phone," her assistant said into the telephone intercom. "Zoie Crawford."

"What outlet?"

"The *Recorder*."

Kimberly frowned slightly. Small press. Small headlines. "That's the paper that wanted to send someone to shadow me?"

"Yes."

Kimberly squeezed her eyes shut and rubbed her temples. "Please take her number and find out what she wants. Tell her we'll get back to her."

"Of course."

"Thank you, Gail."

Kimberly released the intercom and ran her fingers through her strawberry-blond hair. She rotated her neck in the hope of relieving the kinks that had built up throughout the hectic day of meetings and more meetings.

Her gaze settled on the open folder on her desk. Her campaign schedule stared back at her. Contemplating the grueling weeks ahead and the toll that they would take on her and her family made her question if she was doing the right thing by running for the State Senate. Was it worth it?

Lately she'd been questioning herself and her decision more

and more. Was she running because she believed that she could make a difference, or because it was a legacy that she felt obligated to fulfill?

Since she was a little girl trailing behind her big brother, Kyle, she'd been indoctrinated into the world of politics. Kyle ran for every office in his path—from Boy Scout troop leader to class president to city council. A few years out of college, Kyle ran for and won a seat in the State Assembly. When he was in his late twenties, he was being groomed for a senatorial run when he was killed in a head-on collision on his way to a campaign rally. The drunk driver walked away with a broken arm. Kyle Maitland was pronounced dead at the scene.

Her parent's golden boy was gone. And as much as Kimberly knew that her parents loved her, she also knew that what they felt for Kyle was something completely different. With him gone, it was as if the lights had all gone out in the Maitland home. Her mother was ghostlike, and her father barely spoke.

She wasn't quite sure of the moment when she realized that in order to survive in that house, she was going to have to become the female version of her brother.

Her cell phone chirped with a text from one of her daughters, asking if they could have pizza for dinner. She smiled and quickly typed back that she would be home early and they could have whatever kind of pizza they wanted. A smiley face was their response.

She stared at her phone and then speed-dialed her husband. She desperately needed to hear his voice of reason.

"Jenny, hi, it's Kim. Is my husband around?"

"Hello, Mrs. Graham. He just came out of a meeting. Let me put you on a brief hold and get him for you."

"Thanks."

While she waited, she lifted the framed family photo that she kept on her desk. It was a picture of the four of them on their boat when the twins, Alexis and Alexandra, were about four. God, that had been a glorious day, and she was madly in love with her husband. When he came into her life, he gave it meaning beyond living the reincarnated life of Kyle Maitland. Her husband made her feel, for the first time since she'd lost her brother, that she had value for who she was, not what she could become. Yet he stood by her and cheered her on, even as she continued to attempt to fill her brother's shoes and gain an elusive seal of approval from her parents. And when the opportunity arose for him to resign as CEO of InnerVision Technologies and launch his own company, Graham Industries, she loved him enough to leave the only home she'd ever known and move with him to New York. She hadn't regretted her decision for one single moment.

"Hey, sugah," he crooned into the phone, snapping her from her reverie and sending a rush through her veins.

"Hey, sugah yourself. You should be the politician with that charming southern drawl."

"Oh, go on. You say that to all the boys."

She laughed. "I needed to hear your voice, that's all."

"Everything okay?"

"Yes. Fine. Busy day. Just a little tired, I think."

"I'll take care of that tonight. How's that?"

She giggled like a schoolgirl. "Looking forward. Oh, the girls want pizza."

"Great. Easy, early night. Listen, babe, I gotta run. See you about seven."

"Rowan . . ."

"Yes?"

"I love you."

"Love you right back."

Kimberly set the phone down on the desk, then went out to the front office. When they'd first arrived in New York, nearly ten years earlier, it was easy for Kimberly to land a job with DeVereau and Craine, one of the leading law firms in New York. Her JD from Tulane, along with master's degrees in political science and economics, coupled with her family name and money, made her road a smooth one. But it wasn't long before the partners began to see that Kimberly Maitland-Graham was a star in her own right—a fierce litigator, relentless at the negotiation table, and a devoted member of the team. All of which made her loss to the firm that much harder when she decided it was time to branch out on her own.

Starting her own boutique law firm, K. Graham Esq., which focused solely on underdog clients—those who had been hurt by the system—was difficult at first, but as with everything that she set her mind to, she excelled. It wasn't long before she began to gain a reputation as the one to go to for those hard-to-win cases, and that reputation had laid the groundwork for her political run.

"Gail, can you pull up the information about the *Recorder* and also whatever articles this Zoie Crawford has written. I know you started a file, but I want to take another look. I don't know what I was thinking when I agreed to this."

"Sounded like a good idea at the time," Gail said.

"Hmm. I guess it did."

Gail opened a program on her computer, located the virtual folder, and emailed it to Kimberly. "All sent." She glanced up and smiled.

"Thanks. We're pretty much finished here for today. Why don't you go on home? I'll print this stuff out and take it with me. The girls want pizza tonight, and I want my feet rubbed."

Gail laughed. "Sounds like a plan. I guess I'll see you in the morning then. Oh, don't forget you have an eight-thirty breakfast meeting with the Planning Committee. The school lunch budget is on the agenda."

"Right. Thanks. I better take those notes home tonight as well."

"I'll do that for you before I leave."

"Thanks . . . again. Gail, if I don't tell you enough . . . I really appreciate all that you do. You are an amazing assistant."

Gail blushed. "That means a lot. Thank you."

Kimberly went into her office and opened the file that Gail had sent, printed out the documents, along with PDFs of several of Zoie Crawford's articles, tucked them in a folder, and shoved the whole stack of papers into her favorite oversized Gucci tote.

———

Kimberly eased her Mercedes coupe to a stop in front of her Sutton Place address. Herb, the valet, hurried around to the driver's-side door.

"Good evening, Mrs. Graham."

"How are you, Herb?" She took his proffered hand to step out of the vehicle.

"Pretty good."

"Did you apply to the colleges that we talked about?"

He lowered his gaze. "Not exactly."

She rested her tote on the hood of the car. "Look at me," she said softly.

Reluctantly, he did.

"What does 'not exactly' mean?"

"I . . . we couldn't pay for all the application fees," he mumbled, and Kimberly heard the shame in his voice and felt his disappointment in those few words.

She cleared her throat and slightly lifted her chin. "Print out the applications, fill them out, and get them to me. I'll take them to my office and make some calls."

Herb's eyes widened, then he frowned. "Why? Why are you doing this? Why do you care?"

"Because I know that there's a great big world of opportunity out there for you, and it's hard as hell to take advantage of it without an education. Or how about the simple fact that you deserve it?" She handed him her car keys. "The thing is, Herb, you have to believe in yourself before anyone else can." She rounded the car and walked toward the entrance.

"Evening, Mrs. Graham," the concierge greeted.

"Good evening, Lester. How is everything?"

"Can't complain."

Kimberly smiled. "Tell your wife hello for me."

"I certainly will."

She crossed the lobby to the elevators. The doors soundlessly opened, and she slid her access card to the penthouse in the slot.

Riding up, she replayed her conversation with Herb. She knew why he reacted the way he did. In his mind, no matter how nice she was or how fat her tip was at Christmas, she was still a white woman—the enemy. Or, at best, a liberal do-gooder come to save the downtrodden. But she didn't want to be painted as some "great white hope." She honestly loved what she did and believed in her causes and the equal rights of everyone, not just the chosen few.

Would she be any more authentic if she lived in a tenement somewhere and was poor and uneducated? What she had been born into and acquired should not be held against her. What she wanted to do with her so-called "white privilege" was make a real difference.

The doors opened, and she was immediately greeted with squeals of delight.

Alexis and Alexandra came at her like the twin tornados that they were and wrapped themselves around her body.

She showered them with kisses and hugs, thankful that those two magical beings were always the highlight of her day; they were the spitting images of their dad, with their ink-dark hair, arresting blue eyes, and flawless skin that easily turned golden in the sun. They were destined to be heartbreakers.

"Hi, Mrs. Graham."

"Hey, Farrah," she said to her housekeeper and sitter. "They weren't too much of a handful today, I hope," she said with a smile.

"No more than usual. Your mail is on the counter. Homework is done. They've had their showers. There's chicken salad in the fridge, if you want. The girls said it was pizza night."

Kimberly grinned. "Yes, it is."

"Well, if you don't need anything else, I'm going to head home."

"That's fine. Please get going. Thanks for everything."

"See you in the morning." She hugged the girls and left.

As the elevator door closed behind Farrah, Kimberly realized yet again what her money afforded her, and she wondered how she would be able to do what she did without help. Yet that was the weight on the shoulders of thousands of parents and double the weight on single mothers.

She sighed. All she could do was the best she could.

"Okay, ladies, let's order that pizza before dad gets home "

"Yippee!"

<hr/>

"Still reading?" Rowan asked as he slid under the sheets next to his wife.

"Hmm." She closed the folder that held the information about the *Recorder* and Zoie Crawford. She placed it on the nightstand, then curled next to her husband. "Remember when I told you about that reporter who wants to shadow me during the campaign?"

"Hmm-umm. What about her?"

"Not about her specifically. It's the idea in general. Now I'm not so sure if I should go through with it."

"Why?"

"I don't know." She looked up at him. "It's so invasive. I'll have to be 'on' all the time."

Rowan chuckled. "Politics is an invasive business. You know that. Besides, isn't it better to have someone on the inside who gets to see the real you, rather than someone who is only out for the next salacious headline?"

She sighed deeply. "You're always so logical."

Rowan hugged her closer. "Sweetheart, this is your show.

Whatever you want or decide, I'm behind you. Our government needs someone like you, as long as it's what you want."

"That's why I love you," she whispered and leaned up for a kiss.

"And all this time, I thought it was my startling blue eyes and dashing personality," he said against her mouth.

"Hmm, maybe a little," she teased and ran her tongue lightly across his lips. She rose up and braced her body above his, straddling him. Her long blond hair cascaded around them, cocooning their faces.

Rowan groaned when she ground against him. He palmed her heavy breasts, teasing the pinkish brown nipples until they peaked and Kimberly whimpered.

In the beginning of their relationship, she was always tempted to turn off the lights when they made love, but Rowan wouldn't hear of it. He said he wanted to witness everything that happened to her when he was inside her. He wanted to see her face, watch her body flush, her throat clench, her breasts swell. How could she deny him? Now she wouldn't have it any other way.

Rowan clasped the back of her head and pressed her toward him. He kissed her long and deep to muffle the sounds of her cries when he pushed inside her.

CHAPTER 8

"How did the meeting go?" Gail asked when Kimberly entered the office.

"Pretty good. We made some progress. Of course, Donald Hayes had a laundry list of reasons why we should wait on the vote."

Gail shook her head. "What would politics be if everyone agreed?"

"True. Can you try to reach Ms. Crawford? I want to get some kind of timeline."

"Sure. Everyone on the team has confirmed for the planning meeting at noon. I've had everything set up in the small conference room, and I ordered lunch."

"You're the best. You do know that if I win the Senate seat I'm taking you with me."

"Not *if* you win, *when* you win."

"From your lips . . ." She walked into her office and settled in. She took the folder from her tote and placed it on the desk. She flipped open the folder.

From what she'd read about Zoie Crawford, she was a stellar journalist. Her exposé on the World Trade Center attack was outstanding. It was clear that she had the vision to look beneath the surface for the human side of the story. She was a craftsman and dedicated to truth. Kimberly liked that, respected it, even if she generally didn't hold the press in the highest regard.

Her intercom buzzed.

"Yes?"

"I have Ms. Crawford on the line"

"Thanks, Gail. Put her through." She waited a beat for the call to connect. "Ms. Crawford, thanks for taking my call. I want to discuss some of the particulars about your article and try to work out an amicable timetable."

"Of course."

"I've reviewed several of your pieces, and I'm very impressed with your work. May I ask why politics, when recently you were working on a Trade Center series?"

"It was an editorial decision. My boss believes that I'm the best one for this assignment."

"I see. Do you feel the same way?"

"Of course."

"I didn't see in any of your clips that you've done any prior campaign work, specifically what you plan to do with me—essentially embed yourself in my life."

"That may be true to a point, but I pride myself on being the best at whatever I do."

"Glad to hear it. Okay then, my assistant, Gail, will be in touch with you to work out the schedule. I do want to meet you first, before we get started officially. The two of you can discuss that as well."

"Um, Mrs. Graham, I don't want to start off on the wrong foot. But I do want you to know this upfront."

Kimberly braced herself. "Yes?"

"I'm currently in New Orleans. I recently lost my grandmother, and I'm here with my family trying to tie up some family business before I return to New York."

"Oh, I'm very sorry for your loss."

"Thanks."

"As I said, work out the details with Gail. The wheels of the campaign will keep turning. You join us when it's feasible."

"Thank you, Mrs. Graham."

"Enjoy your day." She disconnected the call.

———⟫⟨⟨———

Zoie put her cell phone down on the bed and expelled a sigh of relief. One hurdle was out of the way. At least Graham was still on board with the plan for her reporting, and although she didn't sound thrilled, she was good with her arriving in New York once her "family business" was settled.

She crossed the room to sit on the ledge of her bedroom window. *Kimberly Graham.* She'd seen photos, black and white, from different newspapers, but she didn't sound the way she looked. Her appearance was picture-perfect, flawless. She expected her to sound the same way. But there was no getting away from the Nawlins drawl in her voice, that lullaby tone. What was she really like? Who was the person behind the voice whom she tried to tamp down? She'd find out soon enough.

Zoie pushed to her feet and headed back up to the attic. She still needed to figure out how she was going to manage Nana's business *and* do her job. Maybe the answers were in that trunk.

Once again, she was hit with hot air, but at least this time she was prepared and dressed for the occasion in shorts and a tank top. She headed straight for the trunk.

The lid was heavy, and the hinges were stiff with age. It took a bit of elbow grease, but she finally got it open. She expected to find more old clothes and family heirlooms, but instead she found at least two dozen or more notebooks with flowered covers. Her brows drew together. She took out one and opened it.

The pages were in her grandmother's neat handwriting. It was some kind of journal. The first page was dated a year ago. She flipped through the pages. The book appeared to chronicle the last year. She took out another. Same thing, only this one was from five years earlier.

Her heart thumped. She had no business reading her grandmother's personal diary, but the investigator in her begged to differ. She began to take out the books and lay them on the floor. There were forty in all. If what she initially discovered held, then these books catalogued the past forty years.

The enormity of it shook her. Was there a story in one of them about her dad, an explanation for why her mother and her aunts resented her so much, and the real reason Nana had left everything to her?

Among the photos and journals were packets of letters. She untied the ribbon that held one packet together and gingerly opened the weathered envelope. The letter was dated 1942, the year that her grandmother had arrived from Barbados. It was a letter from her older sister Celeste . . .

> *Dear Claudia,*
> *I pray that you are well and arrived safely in the States. Mami and Papi send their love.*
> *It is usually the eldest that goes off to the States, but it was only right that it should be you. I need to stay and take care of our parents.*
> *I want you to take care of yourself, work hard, and be a good girl. You have a chance to make a wonderful life. Choose wisely in all that you do.*
> *The money in the envelope is from Mami. Hide it away and only spend what you need.*
> *The Maitlands are a good family. They made a good impression on Mami when they came down here, and that's why they agreed to let you live with them. So do as they ask.*
> *We miss and love you. Write to us soon.*
> *Love, Celeste*

Zoie dropped the letter as if it had caught fire. The Maitlands! She picked up the letter and read it again to make sure that she hadn't made a mistake. No. It clearly said Maitland. Her grandmother left Barbados to live with the Maitlands?

She frantically picked up one letter after the other and raced through them, trying to glean bits of information. For the most part, they were letters from home asking how she was, wishing her happy birthday, and merry Christmas. One letter among the many stopped Zoie cold. It informed her grandmother about the passing of her mother. Zoie's heart ached when she imagined how her grandmother must have felt, losing her mother and being so far away from home. It went on to say that there wasn't enough money to send for her to come home for the service, but to know that her mother thought of her to the very end.

Zoie held the letter to her chest, then reverently refolded it and returned it to the yellowed envelope.

She got to her knees, then stood, stiff from hours of sitting on the floor, and she'd barely scratched the surface of what lay in front of her. She randomly took two of the journals and returned the rest to the trunk.

Back in her room, she shoved the journals under her mattress and went to find her mother.

"Where you been?" her aunt Sage asked as she stepped out of the sitting room, cutting off Zoie's path to the kitchen.

"The attic."

Sage's odd-colored eyes flashed for a moment. She leaned on her cane. "Why?"

"When did Nana work for the Maitlands?"

Sage's nostrils flared. Her lips tightened into a bud.

"Aunt Sage . . ."

"That's no concern of yours!" She jammed the cane against the floor, making Zoie flinch. She flapped her hand in the air to push the conversation away. "Leave the past where it belongs, if you know what's good for you." She huffed loudly and walked away, the beat of her cane echoing her footfalls.

The worst thing you can tell an investigative journalist is that a story is off-limits. For Zoie, *no* was a shot of adrenaline. It fueled her.

Clearly, there was much more to the story of Nana working for the Maitlands. There was nothing odd about Caribbean families sending their children to the States for a better life. That wasn't the issue or what was gnawing at Zoie. The issue was what had happened all those years ago between her family and the Maitlands that rose to the level of a topic not to be discussed? Did Kimberly Maitland-Graham know what had transpired?

A thunderstorm of questions relentlessly pelted her, giving her no escape. She had to get to the bottom of things, pull the story out by the roots.

———⊷•⊶———

"What?" Miranda squealed into the phone.

"Yes. You heard me. My grandmother was sent from Barbados when she was about eighteen to live with the Maitlands as live-in help."

"Okay. But why is that a big secret?"

"That's what I want to find out. My Aunt Sage nearly snapped my head off when I asked about it."

"What about your mom?"

She groaned. "She's next. But I know my mother. She'll be on the defensive before I get two words out. And Aunt Hyacinth—well, you know the sad story with her and her health and memory."

"Then I guess you're going to have to do what you were trained to do, sis, which is investigate, sift through information, and put the pieces together. If you can't get assistance from your family . . ." She let the idea trail off.

"I know."

"On another note, how is this going to play out with your interviews of Kimberly Graham?"

"Girl, that's the question that has been running relays through my head. I haven't begun to crack the surface of how long my grandmother worked for the Maitlands, but from what I gleaned from skimming the letters, it was until she was at least well into her thirties, probably longer. I'm thinking Kimberly must have known my grandmother."

"And your Nana never talked about where she had worked?"

Zoie frowned, tried to recall. "I don't remember her ever saying anything in particular, just that she used to work as a live-in. That's about it. I was a kid and, sad to say, uninterested. And I'm positive the name Maitland never came up."

"Hey, maybe it's no more complicated than your Nana had a bad experience and quit. You know how the privileged folks can be, especially back then."

"Maybe," she said on a long breath.

"But your gut is telling you something different."

"Yep."

"What are you going to tell Mark tomorrow?"

"That I got this."

Miranda chuckled. "Of course you do, girl. If there is a rock to be turned over, you are the go-to."

They laughed.

"Anyway," Zoie said, "I'm going to read these journals. Hopefully the answers are in there somewhere."

"Keep me posted. But before I let you go, how long do you plan to stay down there?"

Zoie sighed. "At least another week. I have to meet Kimberly, and that can only be put off for so long."

"True. Okay, well, keep me posted."

"Will do."

"Love you, girl."

"Back at ya."

Zoie put the phone down and looked at the journals on her bed. She picked up the blue-and-red-flowered journal and began to read.

> *Diary,*
> *Today is master Kyle's birthday. Ms. Lou Ellen and Mr. Franklin done gone all out. I been cooking and cleaning since sunrise.*

All this fuss. Back home a birthday celebration was just family. Mami would bake a cake, and folks on the street might stop by and bring food or a small gift wrapped in brown paper. Some birthdays was nothing more than a good wish and a kiss on the cheek.

They spoil him rotten, and he ain't going to be no good husband material.

Diary,
I miss home terrible. The Maitlands are nice enough, but I'm lonely.

Diary,
When I went to town to do the shopping. I met some-one. He is so handsome. Tall and brown with pretty white teeth. His name is Duncan Bennett.

Grandpa! Her heart hammered. She flipped through the pages.

Diary,
Duncan met me at the park today. It was my day off. We been planning this day for weeks. I was so excited that I was sick to my stomach all morning. Ms. Lou Ellen told me I needed to stay in bed if I was sick. But I had to see Duncan since I didn't know when he'd back. He getting ready to ship out in the morning.
I pulled myself together and put on my best yellow dress and went down to the park, praying the whole way that he hadn't changed his mind.
He was as sweet and handsome as always, and I swear I don't know how I'm gonna make it with him gone for the next six months and me growing big. But we'd gotten the papers taken care of and took them right down to the Justice of the Peace today.

I came back home tonight a married woman. Least my baby will have a daddy's name on the birth certificate. I ain't never been so scared in all my life.

Diary,
Ms. Lou Ellen said I can stay here as long as I like when the baby comes. That's a blessing. But I don't think Mr. Franklin is too happy about it. Seems like the bigger I get, the more work he wants me to do. When Duncan comes home on leave, we need to find our own place as husband and wife.

Zoie continued to read through the journals. From what she gathered, her grandfather was a career marine, and each time he came home, he left Nana pregnant. Nana's entries were sporadic, without dates, but the more she read, the more she felt her grandmother's growing loneliness and the hard times she faced raising three little girls alone, working for the Maitlands and only seeing her own children on weekends and her days off. She used part of the money she made to pay someone else to take care of her children. Apparently, the birth of Hyacinth was acceptable, as Nana and her first baby continued to live in the house. But the births of Sage and Rose over the succeeding years put added stress on Nana and the Maitlands.

Why didn't Nana just leave? Why stay and not be able to take care of your own children? Zoie simply could not understand it. She knew that things were different in the forties and fifties, and opportunities for blacks were limited at best. It brought to mind the stories she'd read about the slave women who were confined to the "big house," charged with caring for the master's children while neglecting their own.

Zoie shoved the journals aside. She shook with anger. No wonder the Maitland name was reviled in the Bennett household. It stirred up a past of hurt and dependency that was best forgotten.

But even as she fumed about what had happened to her grandmother, something still nagged at her.

From everything that she knew of her grandmother, she was
not the kind of woman who settled. She always reminded Zoie
how strong and bright and independent she was, and that she
could be anything that she wanted. Claudia Bennett was a woman
who had launched a thriving business in her seventies. Those
weren't the qualities of a woman who would lose herself to a man
who wasn't as committed to her as she was to him, or who would
sacrifice raising her own children to raise someone else's. Nana always touted that family was everything.

This picture that was forming of her grandmother was not the
woman whom she'd known and admired and adored.

Zoie wanted to write it off as her grandmother being young
and naïve, but she still felt in her gut that there was more to the
story.

CHAPTER 9

Zoie avoided her mother and aunts and spent the morning sifting through the items in the trunk. She looked through the photographs, most of which were too faded to make out. Then she came across one that made her look closer.

It was a photograph of her grandmother. She must have been in her late thirties. Nana was seated in what looked to be a hospital or clinic waiting room, holding a baby in her arms. The imprinted date on the photo was October 10, 1954.

Zoie looked closer at the photo. The expression of love on her grandmother's face was unmistakable. But based on the date, if it was correct, the child could not have been her mother or her aunts. Her mother was about sixteen and her aunts older than that.

She turned the photo over. There was only one word—Kimberly.

Zoie's expression tensed. Even after years of being at the beck and call of the Maitlands, Nana still doted over their children. She tossed the picture aside and picked up one of the journals. The first entry froze her in place.

> *Diary,*
> *They buried Kyle today. I raised that boy from an infant, and I don't have the words for the pain in my heart*

for the family and for my Rose. I'm just happy that she's
off in New York and didn't have to see all this. I know she
never got over him, but what we did was the right thing.
I'll always be grateful to Ms. Lou Ellen. Kim will have
what is rightly hers, and my baby Rose will, too.

Zoie could not make sense out of what she was reading. She
skimmed some more pages, but they were random notes about
recipes and Bible verses, and the rest of the pages were blank.

She dug in the trunk and picked up another journal. This one
was from Nana's early years with the Maitlands; it recorded her
thoughts about the lavish parties they gave and tidbits about Kyle.

She went through every journal in the trunk, but nothing
linked to or explained the entry about Kyle's death or the cryptic
lines about Kimberly and Rose.

Her eyes stung from hours of reading, and her temples pounded.
When she looked out of the small attic window, she realized that it
had grown dark. It was only three in the afternoon. A storm was
coming.

Zoie picked up the photograph of her grandmother and baby
Kimberly and the journal with the entry about Kyle's death and
took them to her room. She switched on the light.

A high-profile death such as that of Kyle Maitland would easily
make the newspapers. She put the photo and the journal in the
top drawer of her nightstand. The library should have clippings,
and as soon as the weather cleared, that's where she was going.
She walked over to her window. That trip wouldn't be anytime
soon.

It was pitch black outside, as if all the lights in the world had been
turned off. She pushed the curtain aside. The strength of the wind
bent branches, and the fallen leaves swirled in a macabre dance.

The windows rattled, and the wind suddenly screamed. A chill
raced up her spine as childhood memories of hurricanes flashed
through her head.

She shook off the feeling of dread, made sure that her windows were locked and the shutters closed for extra security. Some of the major injuries during these kinds of storms happened because of objects and tree limbs crashing through windows and the flying glass hitting the occupants.

Her stomach growled, and she realized she hadn't eaten anything all day, which would explain her headache, which had intensified. She stuck her cell phone in her back pocket, switched off the light, and went down to the kitchen.

Rose and Sage stood at the kitchen sink, cutting and dicing vegetables and dropping them into a large pot. Hyacinth sat at the table, reading the Bible.

"Pretty bad storm coming," Zoie said, stepping into the kitchen.

"Bad one," Hyacinth murmured.

Zoie walked over and patted her aunt on the shoulder. "Can I help with anything?" she asked in the vague hope of getting her mother and aunt to at least acknowledge her presence.

Rose briefly glanced over her shoulder. "We're making stew in case we lose power, which is likely. Don't want too much going to waste."

"You can make sure all the shutters are latched tight," Sage said. "And I guess you need to check your garden—since it's yours now. Make sure the tarp is tied down tight."

"Oh. Okay. Sure." She went out back first. She'd never tied down tarp and had no idea what she was doing as she tightened the ropes around the stakes while battling the rising wind, which threatened to knock her off her feet. She finished as best as she could, checked that the storage shed was locked, then ran back inside, breathless from the force of the wind.

She started in the attic and was hit again with what she had uncovered. Now wasn't the time to dwell on it. There was nothing she could do with the bits and pieces of information, but at the first opportunity she intended to change that. In the meantime, she needed to make sure that everyone in the house would be safe.

After securing the windows and the hatch to the roof, she checked all the windows on the second floor and then the main level.

By the time she returned to the kitchen, the to-die-for aroma of simmering stew and fresh vegetables filled the air, which only reminded her of how hungry she was.

"This is going to take a while," Rose said. "You must be hungry. You missed breakfast."

"Starving."

"There're cold cuts and a block of cheese in the fridge to make sandwiches," Sage said. She wiped her hands on her apron and faced Zoie. "Find what you been looking for up in that attic?"

Zoie flinched. The penetrating look in her aunt's eyes unnerved her. She shifted her weight. "Just trying to get a handle on how Nana ran her business." She wasn't ready to divulge what she'd uncovered.

Sage folded her hands in front of her. "Maybe you should just ask one of us." Her lips tightened into a pout.

Zoie took a breath. "Fine." She shrugged. "Tell me." She rested her hip against the counter.

———✦———

Jackson switched the speed on the wipers as the rain, which had been no more than a drizzle moments ago, fell harder and faster.

This was turning into a really poor decision on his part. Today was not the day for construction site visits. His intention was to do a quick run-through on the progress of the work being done on the affordable housing complex that his company was in charge of. But the rapidly deteriorating weather nixed that idea.

He glanced in his rearview mirror. Going back was no longer

an option. Thick dark clouds loomed behind him. To go back would mean driving right into the storm. His only choice was to try and outrun it.

He turned up the volume on the radio. The announcer offered nothing good, but rather a strong warning to seek shelter; the meteorologist talked about the gale-force winds that would within hours be upgraded to a category-one hurricane, with sustained winds of 80 to 90 miles per hour. All cars were ordered off the roads unless they were emergency vehicles, and there were already reports of downed trees falling onto the roadways.

"Shit." He leaned forward, squinted at the windshield, and tried to follow the barely visible road. There was a faint glow of taillights up ahead. The next thing he knew, his car was careening nose-first into a ditch. The airbag deployed, knocking the wind out of him.

He wasn't certain how long it took him to grasp what had happened. It felt like hours but in fact was only minutes. He did a mental inventory of his body. Nothing seemed to be broken, but his chest felt like he'd been kicked. He punched down the airbag until it deflated enough for him to unfasten his seatbelt. If there was a silver lining in all this, it was that he didn't drive into the water and the car didn't flip over. *Small mercies.*

Jackson checked for his phone. No signal. He popped the trunk, grabbed his briefcase and car keys, and pushed open the door. He stepped out and sank almost knee deep in mud and was pummeled by wind and rain.

He'd lived in NOLA all his life and would swear that he knew every inch, but in the pitch blackness, made more ominous by the rain, he had no real sense of where he was.

His first challenge, however, was to climb out of the ditch. But he knew he'd never make it in his dress shoes. His boots and an emergency kit were in the trunk. After several failed attempts, he was finally able to get a good grip on the back wheel well and pull himself into a position to get into the trunk.

The blinding rain made every move an Olympics-level event. He managed to keep the trunk open, even as the now howling wind fought against him.

His work boots, a rain slicker, flashlight, and flares were in a crate in the trunk. He quickly donned the raincoat, pulled up the hood, and turned on the flashlight. Getting out of his mud-filled shoes was another challenge.

The wind grew stronger, and the rain slashed with the fierceness of tiny scalpels. It took nearly a half hour for him to crawl out of the ditch. For every inch gained, he slipped back by two. Finally, his head crested the top of the ditch. He dug his hands deep into the mud wall, pushed upward with his last ounce of energy, and dragged himself over onto the side of the road.

Jackson crawled to his knees and staggered to his feet. He swung the flashlight back and forth in the hope of getting a handle on where he was. As best as he could determine, he was well into the outskirts of downtown. His property was at least another three miles away.

As much as he wanted to simply crawl back into his car and wait it out, he knew that his car had a very good chance of sinking even further into the muck and that he had to get to safety. If the forecast was to be believed, this was not the worst of what was to come.

Jackson kept the flashlight aimed ahead and started walking.

———⊳•⊲———

The lights flickered. Zoie glanced up from eating her sandwich. The kitchen light went out, then came right back on.

"Gonna lose power," Hyacinth murmured.

"We don't have a generator?" Zoie asked.

"Mama never wanted one," Rose said while she stirred the pot.

"But now that everything in here is yours, I s'pose you can get one," Sage said.

"You know what, Aunt Sage, I think I will," she said, refusing to back down from the passive-aggressive comment. "It makes sense, especially with the kinds of storms we get down here. Then cooking everything in the house so that it won't spoil wouldn't need to be the response to a storm."

Sage sucked her teeth.

"Good idea," Hyacinth said, then went back to reading her Bible.

"What other changes you plan to make?" Sage challenged.

"I don't plan to change anything, Auntie. Why should I?"

"I would expect that once you get settled and see how things run around here, you'll find ways to *improve* things."

Zoie pulled in a breath. She pressed her palms down on the table. "Listen, I know that this is difficult for everyone, me included. This wasn't what I wanted. It's what Nana wanted. I don't know what her reasons were. All I know for sure is that I am going to do my best to honor her wishes."

"Well, I for one am glad you're home," Rose said softly. "Even if the circumstances aren't the best." She offered her daughter a tight smile.

Zoie didn't know what to make of her mother's comment. Should she take it at face value or prepare herself for the usual backhand? It was moments and statements like that one that kept Zoie off balance and in a constant state of being on the defensive.

She cleared her throat. "I, um, want to ask you all something. I ran across some letters and journals that Nana wrote." The room grew quiet. She looked from one to the other. Sage's expression had shifted to one of warning; her mother's was wide-eyed curiosity, and Hyacinth seemed to have tuned them all out. "How long did she actually work for the Maitlands?"

"Too long," Sage spat. She slapped a wooden spoon on the counter.

"Why?" Rose asked. "That was so long ago."

"From what I've been able to put together, she seemed very attached to the family, even when the three of you were older. What else makes no sense is that it seems that her parents actually sent her to them. Why would they do that?"

"Same reason all the parents back then did it, and still do," Sage said. "So the child could have a better life."

"I get that part. Sort of. But what I don't understand is that even after she married Grandpa she still took care of the Maitland children, and the three of you were with a sitter."

Sage and Rose wouldn't look at Zoie, as if suddenly ashamed of their past.

"How did Kyle Maitland die?" she asked, switching her approach.

Rose inhaled a sharp breath and visibly paled. Surprisingly, Sage reached out and patted her sister's arm.

"Head-on collision. He was on his way to some fund-raising thing. Running for some kind of office or the other." She slowly shook her head. "Shame."

But Zoie was focused on her mother's reaction, which seemed a bit extreme. She was biting down on her lip, and her fingers had curled into fists.

"Rose had a crush," Hyacinth said out of the blue. She laughed.

Rose pushed up from the table and went to the refrigerator.

"Oh, hush," Sage admonished her sister. She turned to Zoie and lowered her voice. "You know your aunt ain't quite right. Don't pay that no mind."

To Zoie, those were the magic words. The one thing you didn't tell her was to ignore something. That's when she latched on. She tucked that bit of information away to investigate more fully when she could get her mother alone.

"Did any of you ever meet Kimberly, the daughter?"

"Why?" Sage demanded.

"Actually . . ." She hesitated, then plunged ahead. "I'm doing an extensive piece on her since she's running for New York State Senate."

"Cute little thing," Hyacinth said. "She loved her brother, Kyle," she added with crystal clear clarity. "Followed him everywhere. Rose, too, once upon a time." She giggled.

"That's enough, Hy," Sage snapped. "Why they give that story to you? Need to leave those rocks right where they are."

"Why, Aunt Sage? What is it that you don't want me to know?"

"You can know whatever you want. Won't change nothing." She got up and went to stir the pot.

Zoie continued. "Jackson said the family is still here. I plan to interview them."

The stirring spoon clattered to the floor.

"I always liked that Jackson fella," Hyacinth said.

Sage pivoted. "Say what?"

"I plan on interviewing the Maitland family as part of my reporting on Kimberly's run for office."

Sage's chest heaved. She shot a glance at Rose, whose expression was frozen in alarm.

"Your aunt is right," Rose managed in a voice that was barely above a whisper. "Need to leave them people alone."

Zoie looked from her aunt back to her mother. "Leaving things alone is not what I do. And when you say to stay away, that gives me more reason to believe—"

"I don't give a hot damn what you believe, little girl," Sage railed, her face flushed with fury. "You turn over them rocks and you will regret it. Nothing good is going to come of it. You hear what I'm saying? Nothing!" She ripped her apron from around her thick waist and tossed it on the table before storming out.

Zoie's pulse thundered in her veins. Her hands shook. Never in her life had she heard her aunt speak that way, and neither had she ever seen the look of pure terror in the eyes of the always stoic Sage.

"Mama . . ."

Rose held up her hand. "If your work is more important than the wishes of your family . . . well . . . I just don't know what to say to you."

"All 'cause of that boy, that's all," Hyacinth mumbled.

"What did you say, Hy?" Rose asked.

"When the stew gonna be ready? I'm hungry. Mama probably hungry, too. Where is she anyhow? Ain't seen her all morning." She looked up at Rose and smiled.

"Auntie, what did you mean when you said it's all because of that boy?" Zoie pressed.

Hyacinth looked at her niece with emptiness in her eyes. "You look so familiar. You family?"

Whatever window Hyacinth had briefly glanced out of was closed and clouded now. Zoie sighed with resignation.

"Come on. Let's go sit in the living room while the food cooks." Rose helped her sister to her feet and ushered her away.

Zoie sat motionless, trying to process the rapid-fire chain of events. What did her aunt mean? Something had happened between her mother and Kyle Maitland. What? She would have been a teen at the time of his death, and he was much older than her—in his mid to late twenties. A crush? Or something more? Even so, after all these years, the animosity was alive and thriving in the Bennett household. Yet it appeared, from what she'd gathered from her grandmother's letters and journals, that the Maitlands were wonderful people. The two realities didn't make sense.

She was so immersed in the spinning of her thoughts that she mistook the banging on the front door for the wind doing its damnedest to get inside. She cocked her head to the side and listened again. She pushed up from the table and went to the front of the house. There it was again, and it wasn't the wind. She went to the window next to the door, opened the shutters, and peered out in to the darkness.

There was someone standing on the front porch.

"Who is it?" she yelled.

"Jackson!"

She jerked back in surprise, then opened the door. The instant she opened it, she was assaulted by a powerful blast of wind and slashing rain, and she found herself drenched in the time it took for Jackson to cross the threshold.

He was barely recognizable, dripping wet and covered in mud.

"What the hell are you doing out in this mess?" She helped him out of his raincoat. "Never mind. Don't move." She darted off to the laundry room and grabbed some towels and the mop from the kitchen. "Here." She handed him a towel and put another on the floor for his boots. "You have to get out of those things." She began to mop up the water. "A man hasn't lived here in decades, so there isn't much to offer in the way of a change of clothes."

He half-smiled. "I'm just glad to be indoors. Thanks."

She looked at the floor to make sure she'd gotten up the puddles of water. Her family would have a fit, and she didn't need another tongue-lashing. "Come on upstairs. You can get out of your clothes in my room and take a hot shower. I'll throw your things in the washer." She led the way upstairs. "Try not to leave too much of a trail," she said over her shoulder.

Zoie switched on the light in her bedroom. It flickered for a moment, then came on. "Lights have been acting up for the past hour or so," she sputtered, suddenly nervous about having Jackson in her bedroom. It resurrected too many memories. "I can't believe they don't have a generator. Things could go out at any minute, and then what?" she rambled.

"I'm sure your family has been through this enough times to be able to handle it."

She dared to actually look at him. Her heart pounded. "Um, the bathroom is right through there."

"I remember."

"Oh . . ." She folded her arms. "There are fresh towels on the shelf."

"Thanks." He walked off.

Zoie actually breathed. Her heart had been racing so fast she was short of breath. She turned in a circle. *Jackson in her bed-*

room. How many years had it been? How many secret trysts did they spend in this room, right under her family's noses? The excitement of possibly getting caught turned them both on, heightened the pleasure.

She sat down on the side of her bed. They were good together once. They'd been happy until they weren't. And as reluctant as she was to admit it, no man had ever made her feel the way that Jackson Fuller had. Ever.

How do you get beyond that? She knew she had played a major role in the demise of their relationship. But she wanted him to fight for her, make her stay. He didn't, and she took that to mean that he didn't care the way he claimed he did. She let her ego get in the way. She'd spent so much of her life and energy dealing with the chill of the Bennett household, her mother's clinging and nagging, that to discover or believe that the one meaningful person in her life, other than her grandmother, didn't seem to care in the way she needed him to care was more than she could handle. Why were his life and goals more important than hers? Why couldn't he simply pack up and follow her to New York?

She wanted to work herself up into an emotional frenzy again, dredge up the old hurts and miscues, so that when Jackson stepped out of the bathroom she could sit on her high horse of resentment instead of willing him to gather her close and tell her that everything was going to be fine. She could not let that happen. Too much time had passed. He had moved on, and so had she. Him turning up on her doorstep in the middle of a pending hurricane was no more than prevailing circumstances, not divine intervention.

She heard the water shut off in the bathroom. Quickly she jumped up to her feet. No need for him to walk in on her sitting on the bed, of all places.

The bathroom door opened, and Jackson stepped out from a cloud of steam. Her throat tightened, and her heartbeat escalated.

She'd tried to forget how gorgeous this man's body was, but now it was all in front of her in living, breathing color. If it was possible, he looked more chiseled and defined than what she remembered. She swallowed and forced her eyes away from the knot that held the towel around his waist.

He carried his wet clothing under his arm.

"I'll take those and put them in the machine. Um, can I get you anything?"

"A stiff drink." He shook his head. "I can't believe I was so stupid. I heard the forecast and went out anyway. Pretty sure my car is up to the windshield in mud and water by now."

"Oh no! Wait. Let me get these clothes washed. I'll see what the folks have around here to drink and be right back."

"I would go with you, but . . ." He extended his arms in explanation.

Zoie chuckled. "Yeah, I don't think they're ready for all that. Be right back." She went out and shut the door behind her.

Her thoughts spun as she dumped the clothes in the machine, added detergent, and turned on the machine. Jackson in her bedroom. Storm raging outside. Secrets stowed away in the attic. Family that resented her inheritance. All the makings of a *Lifetime* movie.

She went to check on the stew and found her mother in the kitchen.

"Oh. I was going to check on the food."

"No need." Rose kept her back turned.

"Mama, did something happen between you and Kyle Maitland?" she asked as gently as she could and saw her mother's body stiffen.

"Nothing more than a schoolgirl crush. That's it. Nothing to tell, so let it go. Please," she added and turned to face her daughter. "Please, Zoie, for once in your life do what I ask, not what you want." She turned and put the lid back on the pot. "Another half hour," she said and walked off.

Zoie blew out a breath. Something had happened. If she doubted it before, she didn't any longer. But it was so long ago. There was no reason not to talk about it. Sure, things were very different back then. Not only was her mother the daughter of the Maitlands' employee, she was young and black. She could see the Maitlands wanting to erase that mark, but why her family? Yet, as much as she wanted to dive right in, she couldn't erase the look of hurt and pleading on her mother's face when she asked her to leave it alone.

She replayed her mother's words. Had she always been bull-headed and difficult? Was it always her way or none at all? Jackson had said as much to her the night they broke up for the final time. She didn't want to hear it then, and she didn't want to hear it now.

She went in search of her grandmother's stash of liquor. Nana usually kept a bottle of bourbon tucked away on the top shelf of the bookcase.

Bingo! It was right where she remembered. She took the bottle, went back to the kitchen, grabbed two glasses, filled them with ice, and swiped the plate of cold roasted chicken from the fridge. Loaded with her booty, she hurried back up to her room. She knocked on the door with her foot, and when Jackson pulled the door open, her breath hitched in her chest.

"Hey, let me help you." He took the platter and bottle and set them down on the nightstand.

Zoie stood in the center of the room. When Jackson turned toward her, she held up the two glasses to take his attention away from the fact that she was a basket case with him half naked in her bedroom. As much as what went wrong between them continued to rise to the surface and remind her of why they'd parted ways, she could not deny the pull that Jackson still had on her.

He grinned. "Bourbon, huh? You planning on taking advantage of me?"

"Not hardly. And from what I remember, you are pretty good at holding your liquor."

"True." He took the ice-filled glasses from her and splashed them both with bourbon. He handed her a glass and raised his. "To those who come to the rescue of others." He winked.

Zoie couldn't help but smile at the reference to the last time they'd seen each other.

"We have to stop meeting under traumatic conditions," she quipped and took a short sip of her drink. She screwed up her face. "Whoa, definitely has a kick."

"That it does." He took a deep swallow, crossed the room, and sat in the chair by the shuttered window.

Zoie felt safe enough to sit on the bed. "So, what were you doing out there, and how did you wind up on my doorstep?"

Jackson rested his forearms on his thighs. "My intention was to check out the development I'm working on before the storm really hit." He went on to describe what happened and ultimately his decision to walk to her house in the storm.

"Jackson, you could have been killed!" The reality of what could have happened to him rocked her in a way that she did not expect. Regardless of what had happened between them, the thought of losing him, really losing him, shook her to her center. She took a swallow of her drink and allowed the burn to sear away the feelings that had ignited just beneath the surface.

He looked directly at her. "The only thing I kept thinking about was that if I could make it here, everything would be okay."

The pulse in her throat quickened. "Well . . . you're safe now," she said on a breath. "Damn, I didn't bring plates for the chicken." She jumped up and started for the door.

"Don't worry about it. Let's pretend we're having a picnic. Eat with our fingers. I don't mind. Do you?"

She swallowed. "Sure. Fine." She walked over to her closet and pulled out a quilt from the top shelf and spread it out on the floor. "Waa-laa, instant picnic."

Jackson chuckled, got up from the chair, and retrieved the plat-ter of chicken and the bottle of bourbon. He set them on the center of the blanket, then lowered himself to the floor. Zoie took a moment before she joined him.

"So how are things going here?" He ripped off a wing.

Zoie shut her eyes for a moment and sighed. "The usual times ten." She looked into his eyes, and in that instant, she remembered that, no matter what was happening between them, Jackson could always be trusted to be the rational one when she went off the deep end.

"Whatever it is, you know, you can tell me, right?" he said as if reading her thoughts.

Zoie dug out a piece of white meat from the chicken. "I found some things . . . letters, journals, pictures in my grandmother's trunk up in the attic."

He looked at her from the side. "And . . ."

Between bites of chicken and sips of bourbon, she told him about what she'd found, what she'd pieced together, and her family's irrational response.

"Wow." His brows lifted, then lowered. He draped his arm across his bent knee.

"I'm thinking that both families wanted to avoid a scandal," Zoie said, "especially with Kyle Maitland being primed for politics. That kind of scandal with an underage black girl would probably have ruined him."

"Makes perfect sense *if* that's what happened. It's still all speculation on your part, Z. Your mother hasn't admitted to anything more than a crush. What young woman or man hasn't had a crush on someone that went nowhere?"

She was thoughtful for a moment, allowing the information she'd found, her family's response, and Jackson's sobering words to marinate in her head. She looked at him. "That may all be true, but my gut tells me that there is much more to this, and I'm going to find out what it is."

"Even if it opens old wounds and could potentially hurt a lot of people?"

She leaned forward to press her point. "This is what I do, Jax. This is what I was trained to do . . . investigate until there is nothing left to find. It's why I'm good at my job, why I was assigned this story," she said with the gravitas of one who had come to believe the hype.

Jackson let his gaze move slowly across her face. "You really have changed," he said softly.

Zoie jerked back. "We all have. It's part of the process." She took a sip of her drink and held her glass out for a refill. Jackson obliged her.

"All I'm going to say is this, and then I'm going to leave it alone." He reached out and took her hand. "Don't let your drive for glory run you off a road that you can't ever come back from. You may have a fucked-up family, but they're still family, Z." He released her and held up both hands. "That's all I have to say on the subject. "

She tugged on her bottom lip with her teeth, then got to her feet. "I'd better check on your clothes and get them in the dryer."

"Yeah . . . then maybe you can show me what you found."

Zoie stopped, looked at him over her shoulder. He always gave her a way out. "Sure." She walked out and shut the door.

Chapter 10

Jackson looked around Zoie's bedroom. He'd tried to tamp down the bubbling memories while they sat together talking, eating and drinking, but it was impossible. They'd spent many nights in this room, afternoons too, when they thought they could get away with it.

From the moment they'd met years ago at that café, Zoie Crawford had gotten under his skin, and no matter the distance between them or the women who'd come and gone from his life, he had not quite gotten over Zoie, and now he didn't think he ever would.

Until he saw Zoie again, he'd wanted to believe that maybe Lena was finally the one. She was intelligent, sexy, caring, and a savvy businesswoman. And he did care about her. But the truth was, he hadn't given her a second thought all day. It didn't occur to him to try to call her, even though he knew she would be worried. Fortunately, he could use the excuse of no phone signal to buy some time because him being at Zoie's home was the last thing he wanted Lena to know about.

Maybe the storm, getting stranded, and winding up on Zoie's doorstep was a blessing in disguise. Maybe this is the time they needed to figure out what had really gone wrong between them and if there was any way to fix what they'd broken.

Zoie returned. "The natives are moving about. Stew is ready."

"That's what I smelled."

"Hmm. I guess as soon as your clothes are dry, you can come down and say hello."

"Yeah. Cool. Listen, like I said I can take a look at some of the stuff you found . . . if you want a second opinion. I meant that."

"Oh, you sure?"

"Yeah, since I'm here, I might as well make myself useful. Truth is, I have so many other things I want to do with you that reading old letters will take my mind off of them."

"Jackson . . ."

"Don't worry. I'm not going to jump your bones . . . unless you want me to," he added with a smirk.

Zoie lowered her head to hide her smile. She looked at him. "Be like old times: house full of wide-awake people while we were in here doing all kinds of things to each other and trying to keep quiet."

"You were always the noisy one," he reminded her as the sounds of her moans and cries of his name exploded in his head.

"With good reason."

She took a step toward him, and he became very aware of the rise happening beneath the towel. Zoie noticed it, too. She ran her tongue along her bottom lip. "I have one of the journals in my nightstand and a couple of letters."

Jackson heard the slight tremor in her voice and her innocuous words, but the dark look in her eyes, and the way her body seemed to have softened from the stiffness of earlier, told a different story.

"We can't, Jax," she whispered. "It would be wrong on so many levels."

"I don't agree," he said and stepped closer. He put her hand on the knot that held his towel together. If she did what he knew she wanted to do, then . . .

Her gaze dropped. After a moment, she looked up at him. He watched her chest rise and fall as her breathing escalated. She pressed a hand against his bare chest, and the softest moan escaped.

"Jax—"

He cut off her excuse, covering her mouth with his. Her brief instant of resistance quickly vanished as she melted against his body. He looped his arm around her, pulled her close. She fumbled with the knot of the towel, just as the lights went completely out.

The strident voice of her aunt Sage rang out in the hallway. They sprang apart. "Lights out! Hurricane lamps in the pantry. Zoie, did you find those candles like I told you?"

"Coming!" She stroked Jackson's face in the dark. "Be back."

"Good time to eat," she heard her mother call out.

"Just like old times," he quipped.

"Almost." She leaned up and kissed him lightly on the lips, then darted out.

Jackson expelled an expletive, but then he had to laugh at the irony. The lights went out just in time. It gave them both the time to let reality strike and to avoid raging hormones and unresolved feelings. If the lights hadn't gone out when they did, he knew for sure he would be in the throes of making love to Zoie, and that wouldn't be fair to Lena. She didn't deserve that.

He tightened the knot on the towel.

———※◆※———

"Is Grandma okay?" Kimberly's daughter Alexis asked.

"I'm sure she's fine, sweetheart. She's used to bad weather."

"Can we call her?" Alexandra asked.

Kimberly draped her arm around her daughter as they sat on the couch, watching the news of the storm. "As soon as the phone lines are working, we'll call. Okay? But I'm sure she is just fine." She hid her worry behind a smile.

Her mother and father were pretty much alone in that big house and had refused over the years to relocate with their daughter to New York. Her mother insisted that the only way she was leaving her home was feet first. Lou Ellen had unintentionally in-stilled her rock-solid determination into her daughter, a determi-nation that had set the course of Kimberly's life and career.

From the time Kimberly was a little girl following tight on the heels of her older brother, Kyle, Lou Ellen insisted that her daugh-ter needed to find her own place in the world as a woman and a wife. Her mother was set in her ways and worldview, believing that a true woman's place was at the side of her husband, a role that she played to the hilt.

Lou Ellen was ruled by protocol, social etiquette, and appear-ances. She sat on every board, accompanied her husband to every event, leaving little time to nurture her family, Kimberly in partic-ular. What attention she did pay was showered on Kyle. Had it not been for Ms. Claudia, Kimberly would have wallowed in lone-liness. It was Ms. Claudia and her brother who reminded her how special she was, how worthy of love she was. But it was her mother's love that she sought and never truly found. She never understood her mother's seeming detachment, especially when she became a mother herself. Her children were her world, and she vowed that she would never be the kind of parent her mother had been.

"Here are my beautiful girls," Rowan said as he entered the liv-ing room. He held out his arms.

His twin daughters jumped to their feet and wrapped them-selves around their father.

"The best part of my day," he said, kissing them both on the head. He crossed over to his wife and leaned down and kissed her, to the giggles of their daughters. "How's my favorite girl?" he said against her lips.

Kimberly cupped the back of his head. "Better now," she said and smiled.

Rowan's dark brows drew together. He sat down next to Kim-berly. "What's wrong? Is it the campaign?"

"No, just a little worried about my mother." She ignored his slight groan. His ambivalent feelings about her mother were no secret between them.

"The storm?"

She nodded. "The lines are down, and I can't reach her."

"She's a tough one. I'm sure she's fine."

Kimberly offered a vague smile. "You're probably right."

He patted her hand, placed a quick kiss on her cheek, and stood. "I'm going to take a shower. How about we go out to dinner tonight? I know the girls would love it, and you could use it."

"You know me so well."

"Great. Give me a half hour." He walked out.

Meeting Rowan had changed her life on so many levels. They met nearly fifteen years earlier while she worked at a small law firm that handled violations of civil liberty. It had been the path of her brother, Kyle, that she had followed, mostly because she believed in justice and partly because, with her brother gone, it was her hope that if she picked up his mantle, perhaps she would finally earn her mother's love.

She often wondered, and maybe now more than ever, how different her life would be if Kyle had not been killed. Would she have chosen the life of her mother—socialite and wife—or would she still have followed in his political footsteps?

Although she was only in second grade at the time of the accident, she would never forget the emptiness that filled the house like an unwanted guest after his death.

Kyle was much older than she was, and she often heard herself referred to as a "change of life baby." But to Kyle, the age difference didn't matter. He never dismissed her or made her feel that she was in the way. More often than not, he took her everywhere that was feasible and sat with her at night before bedtime and talked with her about his plans to change the world, emphasizing that she could, too.

"Our family is a family of privilege," he'd said one night during their talks.

"What does that mean?"

"It means, pumpkin, that we are a little different from a lot of other families. We have money and position in our community. And because of that, people tend to listen to what we say, and we have the money to make a difference in people's lives who are not as lucky as we are."

She frowned as she tried to grasp what her brother told her. "Are we different from Ms. Claudia and Sage, and Hy and Rose?"

She seemed to remember an odd look in his eyes that made her palm his cheek, the secret "handshake" they shared if something was wrong. He held her hand against his cheek.

"Yes, we're different. So it's important that we do good things with our privilege. We have a responsibility."

"Should we give our money away to those people, like Ms. Claudia?"

Kyle laughed. "Not exactly. But we can use our money to help. And we can use our voice to talk about what is important for all people. That's why I want to run for office, so that I can work to help people."

"Me too!"

He leaned down and kissed her forehead. "Maybe one day you will. But right now"—he pulled the sheet up to her chin—"I want you to get some sleep."

She yawned. "Can I have some water?"

"I'll ask Ms. Claudia to bring it to you."

"Okay."

He kissed her again and left.

That was the last time she saw her brother. He went out that night to an event but never made it home.

"Ready?"

Kimberly blinked to see her husband standing in front of her.

"Oh, goodness. Daydreaming." She forced a smile and stood. "About?"

She shrugged slightly and slid her arms around his waist. "A little melancholy. Thinking about my brother for some reason."

Rowan hugged her. "It's good that you haven't forgotten him

and that you're keeping his dream alive. He would be proud of you. I know I am."

She lifted her head and looked into his dark-blue eyes. "I love you."

"Keep that kind of talk up and we'll never make it to dinner." He stroked the cleft in her chin, then took her hand. "Girls! We're ready. Let's go."

———◆———

"Good morning," Gail greeted as Kimberly entered the office.

"Morning." She stopped at Gail's desk. "Haven't been able to reach anybody back home."

Gail's expression softened. "Oh, yes, the storm. Hopefully, everything will be up and running today. I heard on the news this morning that the storm had passed."

"I know. A lot of damage."

"I'm sure your mom is fine."

Kimberly pushed out a sigh. "Anyway, I guess a silver lining is that it has slowed Zoie Crawford down for a minute."

Gail laughed. "But you know reporters. They always find a way."

Kimberly groaned. "Unfortunately."

———◆———

Zoie slowly opened her eyes. The first thing she noticed was the silence. The rain and howling winds had ended. She stretched her long limbs beneath the patterned sheets and turned her head to see Jackson fast asleep in the overstuffed armchair by the window.

The prior evening resurfaced in her head, but she was still unsure what had gone wrong so quickly. The pull between them had been unmistakable, the brief kiss a prelude to more until the clarion call to come and eat put what she thought was a temporary hold on what was to come.

When she'd returned to her room with their dinner and his dry clothes, the atmosphere was decidedly cool. Jackson's entire demeanor had changed from hot and ready to standoffish and all business, as if what had transpired between them only moments earlier had never happened.

"Did I do something?" she asked in confusion.

Jackson didn't look directly at her. "No. You didn't do anything."

She dropped the clothes on the bed and set down the hurricane lamp. "So why do I feel like I left one person in the room and came back to find someone else?"

Jackson looked at her in the dimness. His voice was low. "Z, as much as I want to reclaim every inch of you, we gotta be real. Jumping into bed isn't going to fix what we broke. You're going to be back here for a while . . . let's take it slow . . . see what happens. If you really want to."

Her back stiffened. Her brows rose and fell. "Wow." She never felt so stupid. She lifted her chin. "Hey, you're right. Bad storms do things to folks." She snorted a laugh. "Anyway, here's your bowl of stew. It's pretty good." She placed it on the blanket.

"Thanks. Z, look—"

She held up her hand. "If you're going to give me the 'let me explain,' don't. I'm a big girl, and what you said makes perfect sense. So let's move on."

Jackson slowly nodded his head.

They spent the rest of the evening in the semi-dark room, reading Claudia's journal and letters by the lamplight. Many of the notes talked about her baby girl, Kimberly, and the good life she would have and how she prayed for forgiveness.

"I have to agree with you, Zoie; there is definitely more to this. What that is I'm not sure." He paused. "If I didn't know better," he said slowly, "I would believe that your grandmother had another child—Kimberly."

Zoie's heart felt like it stopped. In the back of her mind, she thought the same crazy thing. "I've been scared to say that out loud," she confessed. "But it doesn't make sense."

"Yeah," he said. "Crazy."

"It would explain Nana's attachment to the family if she gave her child to the Maitlands to raise," she said, tentatively easing down a dark road. "It would mean she would be doing for her child exactly what her parents had done for her. I guess . . ."

"Things were different for us back then. We're talking about the fifties in the South."

"I know. I mean, I get it on some level, but my heart won't accept that. Not Nana. She drilled into us the importance of family."

"If the sketchy time frame is near correct, your grandfather was dead by then."

"Meaning that if Nana had another child, it was by someone we know nothing about." She vigorously shook her head. "Nana having a child by some unnamed man and then giving her over to another family to raise while she what . . . pretended to be the housekeeper! I can't wrap my mind around it, Jax. I mean, if I do, then everything I've been told and felt and believed about my grandmother is a lie. She's not the woman I thought she was."

She moved away from him and paced the dimly lit room, then suddenly stopped. "If any of this craziness is true, that would make Kimberly Graham my aunt. An aunt who was raised as and clearly believes she's a white woman. Damnit, that sounds like some mess out of *Imitation of Life*. She shook her head. "No. Can't process that."

"Then I guess this is where your investigative skills come in. If it's there, you'll find it. If you want to. But if you do go down that path, there might not be a way to come back from it."

"Maybe that's what my Aunt Sage meant when she said to leave it alone." She was quiet for a moment. She looked at him. "But I can't."

Jackson shifted his position in the chair and groaned. His eyes flickered open, and his gaze landed on Zoie, who sat on the side of her bed.

"Hey," he said, his voice still thick with sleep. He rotated his neck and groaned again.

"You could have slept in the bed, you know."

"Yeah, right. We know where that would have gone." He yawned, stretched, and stood. He turned around and went to the window and opened the shutters. The room flooded with light.

Fallen branches and debris covered the front yard, but the sky was crystal clear. He could feel the rising heat through the window.

Zoie got up and joined him at the window. "What a mess. Oh no! The garden." She scrambled around for her shoes.

"I'll go with you."

"If you run into anyone on the way, act like you just got here," she said, looking up at him from tying her sneakers. "No point in putting ideas in their heads."

"Like what?"

"Like something going on between us that isn't," she said, with more bite than she intended. She saw him flinch slightly, but she didn't care. He'd led her to believe that maybe there was a chance of reconciliation, and she'd been foolish enough to open her heart to the possibility. Then the moment of truth arrived, and he jammed on the brakes. Fine. Jackson Fuller was not the reason she'd returned to New Orleans, and he certainly wouldn't be the reason she stayed.

Zoie opened her bedroom door, and much like they'd done in their early days together, they tiptoed down the hallway to the stairs, concentrating hard to avoid the telltale squeaky floor planks.

Fortunately, her mother and aunts were not up and about. Zoie stopped in the kitchen and put on a pot of coffee, then they went out back.

Miraculously, there was not as much destruction as she'd imagined. The tarp had held, and only minimal damage was done to several tomato vines. The grounds, however, remained saturated, and that did not bode well for the vegetables.

"I have no idea what to do about all the water," she said, looking out at the rows of vegetables that lined the garden.

"Well, if Louisiana holds true to form, it will be hot enough to dry out this water in no time." Jackson gingerly walked along the rows, testing the sturdiness of the root vegetables and the vines. "I think you're in good shape. Your grandmother had a really good drainage system. The entire plot is angled for runoff. What we do now is get rid of any debris and walk as carefully as possible so we don't pack down the wet soil. Anything that's ready, we need to go ahead and harvest."

Zoie stared at him in wide-eyed amazement. "Wait." She propped her hand on her hip. She pointed the index finger of her free hand at him. "Since when do you know so much about gardening?"

He chuckled and shrugged. "Just know stuff."

"Really? Just know stuff?"

He hesitated. "Alright. I didn't want to say anything, but when I heard that your grandmother had gone into business . . . I stopped by. We talked, and she gave me a tour. I asked a bunch of questions, and she was happy to answer every one."

Zoie didn't know what to say or think, and worse, she didn't know how to feel about Jackson remaining connected to her family without her.

"Oh" was all she could manage. A part of her was jealous of the time Jackson and her grandmother had shared, and another part was guilty because she hadn't been there for her grandmother when she was dying.

"Her big dream was turning this all over to you."

Now she really felt guilty. "So . . . will you help me . . . with the garden?"

When he smiled at her, the butterflies in her belly broke free.

"No problem."

She remembered to breathe. "Great. We should get something to eat first."

"I do have a favor to ask."

"What?"

"Give me a lift to see about my car?"

"Oh, God." She slapped the heel of her palm against her forehead. "Your car! I totally forgot. We should do that first. Let's get some food. Hopefully whatever is in the freezer didn't defrost and spoil." She breezed around him and walked back to the house.

When they reached the kitchen, three pairs of gray-green eyes landed on them in a combination of surprise and suspicion.

"That you, Jackson?" Hyacinth exclaimed.

He grinned. "In the flesh." He walked over to where she was seated and kissed her cheek.

"Always liked that boy," Hyacinth said.

"I didn't hear you come in." Sage looked Jackson up and down and offered her cheek for a kiss.

Jackson sidestepped the statement and kissed her cheek, then stepped over to Rose and did the same.

"How are you, Ms. Rose?"

"Maybe not as good as you," she said softly and winked.

He squeezed her shoulder and took a seat at the table.

"Checked on the garden. Jackson is going to help me clean up."

"Hmm." Sage murmured. "You planning on spending time here, young man?"

Jackson cleared his throat and shot Zoie a quick look. "Only to help out. I do have a business to run," he added.

"That's your project up the road," Rose stated. "The Horizon Housing Complex."

"Yes, it is."

"Good thing you doing for the community," Sage said. "Poor folks need housing too."

Zoie listened in silence. She'd been so wrapped up in her own issues that she hadn't really registered or asked any questions about what Jackson was involved in, but clearly her family was aware and thought highly of him as a result. Had she always been so self-absorbed?

Jackson's cell phone rang. He pulled it from his back pocket.

Zoie watched his expression when he looked at his phone.

Jackson glanced up. "Excuse me."

Zoie could hear him talking as he walked away but couldn't make out the words. What she did know was that it was definitely a woman. She'd know that look anywhere.

CHAPTER 11

"Hey," Jackson said into the phone.

"I've been so worried," Lena said on a breath. "Where are you? Is everything okay?"

"Yeah. Everything's fine. I had some car trouble, trying to be superman," he tried to joke.

"What kind of car trouble? Do you need me to pick you up? Where are you?" she asked again.

He tried to keep his voice light. "Missed the road and drove off into a ditch."

"What! Oh my God. Are you sure you're okay?"

"I'm fine. Really. Actually, I'm heading over to see what condition the car is in now."

"Heading over from where?"

"I'm here at the Bennett's house."

Silence.

"Oh," she finally said. "What are you doing there?"

Even as the words flowed from his lips, he knew he was doing a piss-poor job of explaining. He wasn't exactly lying to her, but the guilt of what almost happened danced in his head.

"So . . . you spent the night there? Is that what you're telling me?"

"Listen, it's no big deal. I'm lucky someone was home."

"Humph, I'm sure." She paused. "Is Zoie still there, too?"

"Yes, she is. You know she came back for the funeral."

"Extend my condolences to her."

"I will."

"Jackson . . . I'm not generally the possessive or jealous type. I don't want to be that kind of woman. But you and Zoie—"

"Babe, nothing is going on with me and Zoie. We were a long time ago." That much was true.

She sighed into the phone, and he could almost see the expression of doubt on her face, the look of worry in her eyes. Lena knew all about him and Zoie. When they got together and he saw that the relationship was getting serious on her part, he was upfront with her. He tried to make it clear that he'd been rocked by their breakup and that it would take him a while to wrap his mind around being that involved again. But Lena was willing to hang in there. She literally nursed his heart and spirit back to health. With Zoie living hundreds of miles away, the idea of reconciliation was not on the table. But Zoie was back, and feelings he'd thought were dead and buried were being dug up by the hour.

"When will you be home?"

"As soon as I can. Gonna take care of the car and check in with the team at the development site. Why don't you come by tonight, or I can come to you?"

"Let's talk about it later. I've got to go. Staff meeting."

"I'll call you."

"Sure."

The line went dead.

Jackson gripped the phone in his hand and pressed his lips tightly together. He had a bad feeling about all this—a really bad feeling.

"Everything okay?"

He turned in surprise. Zoie was standing in the doorway.

"Yeah." He grinned and shoved his phone into his back pocket. "I need to get rolling. Look, I'm sure you have stuff to do around here. I can call one of my guys to come and pick me up."

She shrugged. "Up to you, Jax. It's not a problem, but you do what you think is best."

Why did her words seem to have a double meaning? "Cool."

They stared at each other for a moment before Zoie turned and walked away. Jackson shut his eyes. "Damnit," he muttered. He took out his phone again and called Lennox. Although he wasn't in the mood for an interrogation or for any of his buddy's unwanted words of advice, Lennox was his go-to guy.

———⊱•⊰———

"On my way over here, I kept tellin' myself, don't say shit. Be cool," Lennox said as they drove along the watery roads. "Just pick your boy up and take him to see about his ride." He snatched a look at Jackson. "But the hell with that. What were you doing at Zoie's house, of all places? And what went down?"

As much as he tried to convince himself that he didn't want to hear what Lennox had to say about the whole scenario, underneath he did want to talk about it, and maybe try to sort out the conflicting emotions that plagued him. If nothing else, Lennox never pulled any punches with him, and his friend made him hear what he needed to hear, whether he wanted to or not. He braced himself for the cold truths and laid out the events that led up to him arriving on Zoie's doorstep and everything that followed.

It was longer than he expected before Lennox said a word.

"Man, I'ma be honest with you," he finally said. "There were at least a half dozen other places you could have gone last night, but you went to her. Gotta be a reason, and it sure as hell wasn't proximity. You went 'cause you wanted to. That whole thing coulda gone sideways." He pushed out a breath. "But, hey, I get it. I do. You never got over her. We both know that. But I've never known you to play games with women. Me, that's another story," he joked. "You have a good woman. You don't know how long Zoie is going to stay, and even if she does, then what? Toss Lena to the curb? Has Zoie changed that much that you would risk a good thing for a maybe?"

"Same questions I've been asking myself, man. It ain't cut and dry, ya know."

"Well, you're gonna have to make a decision one way or the other."

They pulled up to where Jackson's car had gone into the ditch. Lennox put the car in park. He turned to his friend. "At least you had sense enough to keep it in your pants." He chuckled.

"Very funny."

They got out of the car and walked around to look down into the ditch.

"Damn," they said in unison.

———❖———

Finally, back home after waiting for nearly an hour and a half for a tow truck, Jackson changed clothes and called his foreman, Mitch to check on the status of the project. Thankfully, according to Mitch, there wasn't too much damage, at least nothing that couldn't be taken care of without setting back the timeline or effecting costs.

With that bit of business out of the way, his next call was to a car rental agency. They'd have a car for him by mid-afternoon and even offered to have someone bring it to him.

His next call was to Lena. The call went straight to voice mail. He debated about leaving a message but finally did. To his surprise, she called back moments later.

"Sorry, was finishing up with a class," she said. "Did you get your car?"

"Lennox drove me over. Got it towed. But with it sitting in all that water and dirt . . ."

"I'm sorry, baby. Hopefully, it won't be too bad."

"Yeah. Anyway, enough about that. What about us? How does me fixing us dinner at my place tonight sound?"

"You sure?"

"Why wouldn't I be?"

"What's on the menu?"

"Hmm, whatever you want."

"You."

His stomach knotted. "That can be arranged."

"Seven?"

"Sure. Seven is fine. See you then."

"Need me to bring anything?"

"Nope. I have everything we'll need."

"Ahh, nothing like a confident man," she said, and he was relieved to hear lightness in her voice.

"See you tonight. Plan to stay."

"I do. See you later."

Jackson rested the phone on his desk. He'd hoped to feel some sense of relief that he and Lena were on track. But he knew he was fooling himself.

———————

"Mark, I promise you, everything is under control. I've already spoken with Ms. Graham, and I plan to interview her family this week to get the ball rolling," Zoie said into the phone as she paced her bedroom floor. "Yes, things were a bit touch and go with the storm, but we're in good shape down here. Thanks for asking. Yes, I will keep you posted. I got this, Mark. Stop worrying. Fine. We'll touch base at the end of the week. Thanks. Take care."

She blew out a breath. That was one obstacle down. At least Mark was placated for the time being. She checked the time. It was nearly noon. She wondered if the library was open. She still needed to do some background research on the Maitland family before she contacted Lou Ellen Maitland. Maybe some of the old news clippings would shed some light on her grandmother's cryptic notes and letters, and hopefully they would allay her simmering belief that Kimberly Maitland-Graham wasn't who she thought she was. Now *that* was a story. Her pulse quickened. If any of the crazy assumptions were true, her articles would be a game changer. At its least, her investigation would put her suspicions to rest.

She bent down to fold up the blanket she and Jackson had used for their faux picnic. As she held it against her chest, she closed her eyes, and vivid images of Jackson bloomed behind her lids. Even right at this moment, she struggled with what it was that she wanted from him. Had she really wanted to have sex with Jackson? For what purpose? To see if she still turned him on, or to prove to herself that it was really over—or not? In the light of day, she was no longer sure. At the time, everything seemed so clear. The desire was there, the feelings were there. She knew that. She saw it in his eyes and felt it in the way he held her and the way she responded.

It was purely physical, she reasoned. She'd certainly been on a serious dry spell for months, and maybe the idea of Jackson, someone familiar and still so incredibly sexy, was the attraction and nothing more.

If that were true, then why did it bother her so much when she thought he was speaking to another woman?

CHAPTER 12

"I've been trying to reach you all day," Kimberly said to her mother. "Are you alright? Is everything okay? How's Dad?"

"I'm right as rain, and your father is the same." Lou Ellen said. "I've been through more of these Louisiana storms than you have age on you. No need for your concern."

"I can come home—"

"Child, please. I don't need you here."

The innocuous words stung. Kimberly cleared her throat. "Well, I simply wanted to make sure you and Dad were okay, Mother, and to say that I can come down if you need me."

"I just told you I don't need you. Everything is fine."

Kimberly steeled herself. Her mother's dainty, ladylike qualities and that soothing southern twang belied the fierce, calculating woman that she was; her simple declarations were generally laced with arsenic.

"Mother, I was contacted by a reporter. Her name is Zoie Crawford. She will be with me during my campaign."

"Please get to the point, Kimberly."

Kimberly gripped the edge of her desk and shut her eyes for a moment. "She will be calling you."

"Me! What in heaven's sake for?"

"Her paper is doing an ongoing series on my campaign, and she wants some background about my life at home."

The stretch of silence was so long that Kimberly thought they'd been cut off.

"Mother . . ."

Lou Ellen cleared her throat. "I don't have time to deal with reporters. I fail to see what I can add. I would think that your PR person would have everything that this reporter will need."

"Mother, she wants more than pieces of papers. She wants to personalize the story." She heard the pleading in her voice. She knew how much her mother disliked weakness, but she couldn't help herself.

"Well, I'm sorry. I don't have time."

"No, you're not."

"What did you say to me?"

"I said you're not sorry. You would have done it for Kyle." She heard her mother's sharp intake of breath.

"That was an evil, hurtful thing to say to me! I have given you everything. You went to the best schools and had the nicest clothes; you belonged to the best clubs; you traveled the world. Your life has been one silver spoon after another. You chose your life in New York and still you act as if I owe you."

Kimberly fought back tears by sheer will. "I'm sorry, Mother," she whispered. "That's not what I meant."

Lou Ellen sniffed with indignation. "Well, that's the way it sounded."

"Will you at least think about it?"

"I rarely change my mind." She paused. "How are my grand-children?"

"The girls are great."

"Shame that I only get to see them once a year."

Kimberly took the sarcastic comment in stride. "I'll have them call you this evening."

"Fine. Is there anything else?"

"No, Mother, nothing else."

"Alright then, good-bye."

Kimberly's hand shook as she put down the phone on her desk. Her mother possessed the singular ability to carve a person to shreds with her rapier tongue, which delivered her assaults with milk, honey, and a smile.

Over the years, Kimberly had managed to erect temporary façades to ward off her mother's verbal attacks. Most times, she was well protected, but there were other times, like now, when she already felt weak and vulnerable that the façade would collapse. Her father, for most of her life, had been so involved with building his fortune that he'd paid little attention to the dynamics between her and her mother. Then he became ill.

"Kim! What's wrong?"

Kimberly sniffed and tried to stop the tears with her fingers but failed.

"Is your family alright?" Gail hurried around the desk and knelt beside Kimberly. She covered her hand.

"I'm sorry," Kimberly managed. She reached in her desk drawer for a tissue and wiped her face. "This is so unprofessional. The office isn't the place . . ."

Gail got up, closed the office door, and returned to Kimberly's side.

"Kim, whatever it is, let me help."

Kimberly lowered her head and slowly shook it from side to side. "Thank you, really. I'll be fine. Momentary meltdown." She offered a shaky smile and dabbed at her eyes. She patted Gail's hand as if it was she who needed consoling.

Gail got to her feet. "I'll give you a few minutes."

"No. It's fine." She looked across at Gail and blinked rapidly to clear the mist from her eyes. "What's up?"

Gail laid the folder that Kimberly hadn't noticed on her desk. "It's the agenda for your sit-down tomorrow with the fund-raising committee."

Kimberly pulled the folder toward her and flipped it open.

"Do you get along with your mother?" Kimberly asked, catching Gail off guard.

"Um, yes," she sputtered a laugh. "Why do you ask?"

The weight of Kimberly's sigh spoke volumes. She leaned back against the thick leather of her high-back chair, a gift from Rowan when she first opened her office. "I've always wondered what that was like," she said in faraway voice. Her gaze roamed the room as if searching for an answer in the stack of law books that lined the bookshelves or the plaques and degrees that adorned the off-white walls. She returned her focus to Gail.

"Every family is different, and some are better than others," Gail said.

"It's what I tell myself, what Rowan tells me. I guess a part of me always wanted a TV mom." She laughed. "Silly."

Gail pulled up a chair and sat down opposite Kimberly's desk. "I'm not going to pretend to know the ins and outs of your relationship with your mom, but what I do know is the great mother that you are to your girls, the take-no-prisoners attorney you have been for your clients, the rock-steady wife you are to Rowan, and the amazing state senator you'll become. Not for nothing, as the kids would say, but all that heart and grit come from somewhere."

Kimberly's cheeks flushed crimson. "I'd like to think so. Hard to imagine sometimes."

"Imagine it, because it's all true." She tapped her hand on the desktop, then stood. "Look over the agenda, and let me know if you want to change anything."

"I will. Thank you."

"And Kim . . ."

Kimberly glanced up. "Yes?"

"I meant what I said."

⇒•◦•⇐

Zoie was escorted by a librarian to the archive room and set up at one of the computers. She began her search using the keyword *Maitland*. Several dozen news clips were listed. Most of them were only mentions of the Maitland family at various social functions. She finally ran across the articles about Kyle Maitland's rise in the political arena at such a young age, his death and funeral, and the court case that followed. There was a grainy photograph of the family at the service and a picture of a little girl tossing a rose on the casket at the gravesite. It had to be Kimberly. She printed that one out and continued her search, but stopped cold when she landed on a headline touting the Maitland family as one of the main benefactors of the Horizon Housing Complex, via the Kyle Maitland Foundation.

She poured over every word, especially the quote from Jackson that spoke about how the project would not have been possible without the support of the Maitland family.

Zoie flopped back in her seat. Jackson hadn't said a word about his connection to the Maitlands, even after all the things she'd told him. Why? She printed out that article as well.

For the next hour, she continued to see what other tidbits she could uncover, specifically anything relating to her grandmother. But as with most wealthy and powerful families, whatever the Maitlands didn't want in print didn't get into print. From what she was able to find, the Maitland family was above reproach. She found that hard to believe but could find nothing to the contrary.

Not much of what she'd hoped for was found in the clips that she'd located, and then she ran across a photograph nearly forty years old. MAITLANDS WELCOME BABY GIRL. It was only a photo with a caption: "Franklin and Lou Ellen Maitland welcome baby Kimberly." Zoie searched for at least another hour, but that one photo was the only reference to the arrival of Kimberly Maitland.

Zoie pressed her fingertips to her burning eyes and rocked her neck from side to side. She arched her back to relieve the stiffness, then gathered her sparse notes and the printouts of the articles, stuck them in her tote, and headed out, with more questions than answers.

When Zoie returned home, her mother was sitting in the rocker on the front porch, snapping green beans. Zoie climbed the two steps and took a seat.

"Have a good day in town?" her mother asked.

"I went to the library."

"Oh?" She dropped a handful of snapped beans into the aluminum bowl at her feet.

"I was trying to find some background information on the Maitland family."

Rose's long, nimble fingers stopped their work. "For your story?"

"Yes."

Rose nodded slowly.

Zoie drew in a breath of resolve. "Mama, please tell me what you know about Nana and the Maitlands."

Rose folded her hands on her lap. "I don't have much to tell you, really. She worked for them for years, the early part of my life. She'd take me over there sometimes. I filled in for her a few times when she wasn't feeling well."

"Is that how you got involved with Kyle Maitland?"

Rose's eyes flashed at her daughter. She pushed up from her seat and turned her back to her Zoie. "It was nothing more than a girlhood crush. Kyle was . . . he was charming and handsome and much older than me." She shrugged, then turned to face Zoie. "That's it." She pressed her lips tightly together.

"Did you ever meet Kimberly?"

"No. I was away in school in New York." Rose leaned her hip against the railing. "Why?"

Zoie switched topics. "Why did you go away to school instead of staying here?"

"Does it matter?"

"Does it?"

Zoie watched the nerve beneath her mother's eye flutter.

"Why are you doing this? What does my going to school in New York have to do with your article?"

"Nothing," she said on a sigh. "I'm curious, that's all."

"I guess you forgot that you left and went to school in New York," she said with a lift of her brows. Then suddenly she smiled. "You were always curious. From the moment you could put words together, you asked questions. Most babies, the first word they say is ma-ma or da-da, or no." She shook her head at the memory. "Not you. Your very first word was 'why.'" Rose laughed.

Zoie lowered her head and chuckled. "I always thought that was a story everyone made up about me."

"Nope. You were about eighteen months old. We were sitting out back. It was Hyacinth's birthday. I had you all dressed up in a frilly yellow dress." She smiled. "Couldn't do much with that hair of yours. It was all wild curls even then."

Zoie reflexively patted her mane of auburn curls.

"We sang 'Happy Birthday.' You were sitting on your father's lap." Her voice hitched for a moment. "When we were done and Hy had blown out the candles, you said as clear as water, 'Why?'"

Zoie grinned. "What did everyone say?"

"We were stunned. Sage said, 'Did that baby just say why?' And you looked around at all of us, propped up on your daddy's lap like the Queen of Sheba, with this big old grin—you only had about six teeth. Your daddy said, 'What did you say, pumpkin? Say it for Daddy.' You looked up at him, and plain as you please, you said. 'Why?' and flashed that grin. We all burst out laughing and clapping, and you've been asking why ever since."

Rose's shoulders shook with her laughter, and Zoie realized it was the first time in longer than she could recall that her mother had actually laughed, that she had looked happy and not simply content. But what really gave her pause was that she and her mother were having a real conversation, and not a debate or a volley of barbs.

Rose sobered by degrees, but the gleam didn't leave her eyes. "I'm so glad that you're home, Zoie. The circumstances aren't ideal, but you're home. That's what's important." She stretched out her hand to her daughter.

Zoie walked over to her mother and took her hand.

"Sit," her mother said. "Tell me about your life in New York. Seeing anybody?"

Zoie ducked her head. "No. Too busy with work."

"Hmm. Work can't keep you warm at night."

"Mama!"

Rose grinned. "It's true." She paused. "What about Jackson?"

Zoie flinched, shook her head. "It's over. We've both moved on."

"Probably best since you won't be here long after your sentence is over."

Zoie rolled her eyes. *Too good to be true.* "Can I take those inside for you?" she asked in an attempt to ward off any impending verbal sparring.

"No, I can take care of it."

Zoie started to walk away then stopped. "Mama . . . did Nana have any other children beside you and my aunties?"

"What? No." She sputtered a laugh. "Why would you ask something like that?"

Zoie shook her head. "Nothing. Silly question." She opened the screen door and went inside.

CHAPTER 13

Lena picked up her glass of wine. "What did the shop say about your car?"

Jackson turned the steaks on the grill.

"Those smell great. I'm starving."

"Few more minutes." He closed the hood of the grill. "Car is totaled." He wiped his hands on a towel and picked up a beer from the table.

"Sorry."

"Yeah. Shit happens. I can always get another car."

Lena stretched her bare legs out on the striped lawn chair and crossed her ankles. "So do you want to tell me what happened with you and Zoie?"

He knew the questions would come, but he'd hoped to have a couple of beers and some food in his belly first.

Jackson sat on the side of the opposite lawn chair. He rested his forearms on his thighs and looked directly at her. "Nothing happened. It could have, but it didn't."

The muscles in her throat worked for a moment before she spoke. "Why not?"

He heaved a breath. "Because I thought about you—about us."

Her mink-brown eyes studied his face. "I want to believe you. I . . . do believe you. It's . . . Zoie." She said the name as if it explained everything. She reached for her glass. "There's history between the two of you. More than you and I have had a chance to build." She sighed and looked upward. "Of all the places that you could have gone, Jackson, you went there, to her." Her brows drew close, and she turned to look at him. "That bothers me, and if I sound silly or petty or whatever, then so be it. And what am I supposed to think when you tell me something 'could have happened'?"

He shifted his jaw. "Lousy choice of words."

"Really?" Her voice rose with incredulity. "A lousy choice of words? You wouldn't have that to say if there was nothing between you two that 'could have happened,' Jackson. Don't you see that? Because I sure do."

Jackson lowered his head. This was not going well, and knowing Lena, who knew what went down between him and Zoie, she wouldn't let him dance around the truth. It was a promise they'd made to each other when they both realized that simple dating and casual sex had turned into something more.

Jackson folded her hands into his and ached at the sadness in her eyes, knowing that he had put it there. "I don't know what I feel about Zoie." She flinched. "I thought she would stay in my past. When I saw her again . . . it stirred up feelings, and I don't know what those feelings are. That's the truth. Regret, nostalgia . . . But," he held her hands tighter, "I thought about us—you. And I knew that I didn't want to hurt you trying to figure it out."

Lena blinked back tears. "I love you, Jackson." She swallowed. "And I love you enough to let you go and find your way."

"Lena—"

"I can't and I won't compete with the ghost of your relationship with Zoie Crawford. I deserve better than that." She eased her hands away. "You need to figure it out on your own." She leaned close and kissed him, then stood. "Good-bye, Jackson."

The steaks sizzled and burned.

⇒•⇐

"Damn, man, I'm sorry," Lennox said as they walked into the locker room of the gym. "Lena is a great girl."

"Yeah," Jackson said, somberly.

Lennox clapped Jackson on the shoulder. "Now what?"

Jackson scrubbed his damp face with a towel, then tossed it over his shoulder. "There are no guarantees with Z. It was a moment. We haven't talked about all the crap that went down between us back then."

"Not talking is what got you into this shit in the first place."

"Yeah, who you tellin'?" He opened his locker and took out his shower slippers and body wash.

"On you, man. At least whatever you decide to do, you can do it with a clean conscience."

"I can't get the look in Lena's eyes out of my head." He slammed his locker door shut. He faced his friend.

"Not supposed to, bro. That's what keeps us human."

<hr />

Zoie sat on the floor of her bedroom with the journals, letters, photos, and articles from the library spread out in front of her. Even though all of the pieces didn't quite fit, a picture was forming. But until she was certain . . .

She gathered up all the materials, put them in a box she'd taken from the attic, and tucked it on the top shelf of her closet.

Over the past few days, she'd been so immersed in her shaky family tree that she'd neglected to follow up on what she'd been called upon to take care of—her grandmother's business. The truth was that she had not a clue about how to run a business. Sure, she knew how to plant, knew when fruits and vegetables were ripe, but anything beyond that was up for grabs. What had her grandmother been thinking?

Nana. She was much more complicated than she had let on— the whole thing with the Maitlands, the odd letter about Kimberly, the fact that her family went postal at the mere mention of the Maitland name. And then starting a business and leaving it all to her.

Zoie shook her head in frustration. Her grandmother was a real-life Pandora, and the more that fell out of the box, the more confused Zoie became about the image she had of her grandmother.

In the meantime, she needed to establish a list of priorities. Although she was good at multitasking, that didn't extend beyond lining up interviews and meeting deadlines, which reminded her that she needed to put in a call to Lou Ellen Maitland and then figure out the next steps for her grandmother's business.

———⟩•◦•⟨———

Aunt Sage was in the sitting room reading the paper. She glanced at Zoie over the top of her glasses.

"Stash any more ex-boyfriends in my house?"

Zoie fought between laughing and rolling her eyes. She opted for neither and went to sit next to her aunt.

"Auntie, can we please talk, or at least let me talk and just hear me out?"

"Fine. Go 'head."

"I know this whole thing with Nana's will is upsetting. It's not what I expected." Her aunt huffed but didn't interrupt. "And I want to be sure that her legacy lives on—for all of us. But I can't do this by myself, no matter what Nana might have thought. I need your help and Mama's."

Sage shifted her shoulders, and Zoie watched her tight demeanor loosen. The need to be needed could melt the hardest of hearts.

"Well," Sage dragged the word out. "Don't know how much help I can be. I know the folks she did business with, but that's about it."

"That's definitely a help," she said to encourage her aunt.

"Mama kept a tight rein on the business. We each had a tiny part to play, but no one person knew everything 'cept Mama."

She lowered her voice and looked around as if someone might be listening. "You'd think Mama was runnin' some kind of cartel or somethin'."

Zoie burst out laughing and couldn't stop. She kept seeing her grandmother as the head of a vegetable business cartel. Sage caught the contagious laughter, and before long they were slapping thighs and leaning on each other as they rocked from side to side.

"Whew!" Sage exclaimed and wiped tears from her eyes.

Zoie hiccupped.

"Chile, chile, I ain't laughed that hard since Reverend Earl tripped on his way to the altar and split his breeches. Didn't have on no drawers!" She slapped her thigh. "Lawd Jesus, forgive me." She fell into another fit of laughter. "Humph, humph, humph."

Sage looked at her niece, and Zoie wanted to believe with all her heart that what she saw in her aunt's eyes was love or, at the very least, acceptance and forgiveness.

Sage patted Zoie's hand. "Like I said, I don't know much, but I'll do what I can to help."

"Thank you, Auntie. That means a lot to me."

Sage shooed off the thanks. "Look here, this ain't none of my business." *Since when?* "But what you should do is ask Jackson for some help. He knows a thing or two about running a business."

Zoie leaned back shaking her head. "I . . . couldn't, Auntie."

"Why not. Just cause you two stop sleeping together don't mean you can't ask him." Zoie nearly choked. "Jackson is a good man. Shame things didn't work out. Always did like him."

Zoie's head snapped back in disbelief. She was beginning to think that maybe during the storm—like Dorothy from *The Wizard of Oz*—she'd been tossed into some alternate universe. First her mom and now her aunt.

"Are we talking about the same Jackson that you practically

ran out of the house every time he came here? The one you always gave the side-eye to?"

Sage folded her arms beneath her heavy breasts and puckered her lips. "That's what I was s'pose to do. Look out for you. Keep that boy on his toes." She looked at Zoie. "Sometimes you ain't got the sense you were born with."

Zoie's throat tightened.

"Every time I seen him, he asked about you. But it ain't none of my business."

She blinked back tears.

Sage patted Zoie's hand. "Go on now. You got work to do." She picked up her newspaper and resumed reading.

———————

Zoie was so overcome by the conversation with her aunt Sage that she literally ran right into her aunt Hyacinth, who was ambling down the hallway.

"Oh! Auntie, I'm so sorry." She gripped her aunt's slim shoulders to keep her from tumbling backward. "Are you okay? I'm sorry."

Hyacinth looked into Zoie's eyes, but it was immediately clear to Zoie that Hyacinth was not really seeing her, and Hyacinth confirmed her suspicion with the outlandish thing she said next.

"I'm so sorry about the baby." Her eyes teared up. She patted Zoie's hand. "You'll be fine."

"Aunt Hy, what baby? It's me, Auntie. It's Zoie."

Hyacinth blinked in slow motion, then a smile of recognition spread across her mouth and lit the dull light in her eyes. She cupped Zoie's cheek in her palm. "Zoie, chile. Spitting image of your mother. Can you fix me some tea? I'm gonna sit out back."

"Of course, Auntie. Let me help you." She put her arm around her aunt's waist and walked with her to the back of the house.

"Too young for a baby anyhow," she muttered.

Zoie's heart thumped. "Who, Auntie? Who's too young?"

"Would have been nice having a baby in the house."

Zoie's pulse raced. She opened the screen door. Her mother napped in the rocker.

Hyacinth inched over to the swing bench, and Zoie helped her to sit. She looked at her sleeping sister. "Gave her everything to make up for it." She made a sound with her teeth, then looked up at Zoie. "You seen Mama?"

Zoie's stomach tightened. "No, Auntie, I haven't," she said gently. "I'm going to fix your tea. Okay?"

She glanced for a moment at her mother, who stirred but didn't wake. Dozens of thoughts twisted in her head. She opened the screen door and went inside.

It was clear that Aunt Hyacinth was a bit detached from reality. She shouldn't take what she babbled to heart. That's what Zoie kept telling herself while she prepared the tea.

Hyacinth proved Zoie's conclusions to be accurate. When she returned with the cup of tea, Hyacinth wanted to know why anyone would drink tea in all this heat and proceeded to fuss and complain.

Rose, fully awake, looked at her daughter with sad acceptance in her eyes. "I'll take care of her," she mouthed to Zoie and shooed her away.

Zoie wanted to question her aunt, but she knew it would be a waste of time. Hyacinth had already moved on to another corner of her mind.

Zoie went back inside with the intention of going to her room when her cell phone vibrated in her back pocket. She pulled the phone out. *Jackson*. She debated whether or not to answer but gave into her baser instincts.

"Hey, Jackson."

"Hi. How are you making out?"

"Busy. Had an enlightening day, to say the least."

"Oh? Want to talk about it?"

She reached her room, went in, and shut the door behind her. No matter what she might think or feel about Jackson, he was rational and levelheaded. He thought things through, when she was always ready to dive in blind.

"There are a few things I could use an objective opinion on," she said with slow determination. "*Not* advice, Jax. Just an opinion."

Jackson chuckled. "I've been duly warned. So . . . you wanna get together for dinner? We could meet up in town."

"What about your car?"

"Got a rental. Car's totaled."

"Ouch. Sorry."

"Seven? Eight?"

"I have some calls to make before the end of the business day, and then I'd need to get ready. So . . . seven?"

"Cool."

"I'll meet you. Pick a spot and let me know. Nothing fancy. I have one decent dress and two pairs of jeans."

Jackson chuckled. "No worries. I can swing by and pick you up."

"Um, I like to have my own getaway."

"Yes, ma'am. I'll text you with the spot."

"K."

"Later."

Zoie paused for a moment. Her face cinched in consternation. *Was this a date?*

CHAPTER 14

The private dining room at the Hilton Hotel was set up for thirty special guests and their plus ones, who had begun to arrive.

Kimberly had attended a number of fund-raisers—as a child with her parents, and various events as part of her job—but this was the first of many for her.

"You look as if you are going in front of a firing squad," Rowan whispered in her ear. "Relax."

"I'm trying. I don't know why I'm so nervous."

"It's natural, babe. But it's all part of the dog and pony show." He kissed her cheek. "Just remember that everyone is here for you because they want to be, and they want to get to know their candidate. Be your fabulous self."

Gail approached. "Sorry to interrupt lovebirds, but I have to steal Kim for a few minutes. Some people you need to meet."

Kimberly squeezed Rowan's hand and walked off with Gail.

"Mr. and Mrs. Halstead, Kimberly Graham," Gail said.

Kimberly extended her hand. "Thank you both so much for coming."

"I've followed your legal career. You have an impressive record in and out of the courtroom."

"Thank you. I'm very committed to my work and my clients."

"Then why politics?" Mrs. Halstead asked. "It seems that would take you away from the very things that got you to where you are." Her smile was benevolent, but the hard edge in her green eyes was most telling.

"I know it will be a big transition. However, I believe that as a state senator I can effect change on a much larger scale. As an attorney, I'm relegated to one case, one client at a time."

"If I have my facts correct, your older brother was making some political inroads before his untimely death," Mr. Halstead said.

Kimberly tensed. "Yes. You have your facts correct."

"Following in the family footsteps," Mrs. Halstead commented.

"You could say that. I believe my brother would have made an outstanding politician, and I promised myself that I would one day fulfill what he began."

"And with your support we can make that happen," Gail cut in. "So please enjoy the evening, and if you need anything, please let me know." She took Kimberly's arm.

"Thank you again for coming," Kimberly said before she was skillfully ushered away by Gail.

"That wasn't so bad," Gail said under her breath.

"I'd rather stand in front of a courtroom full of jurors and a judge," she half-joked.

"Well, get used to it. When people are giving you their money, they want to feel connected to the candidate. Political ideology is one thing, but if you can reach them on a personal level, come across as human and accessible, they will stick with you . . . and bring friends," she added with a laugh. "Come on, let's make the rounds before dinner."

Kimberly never thought of herself as a master of small talk, unlike her husband, who could strike up and hold a conversation about a piece of paper and make it seem like the most important topic on the planet. The hour of introductions before dinner was more taxing for her than when she finally addressed the gathering before dessert.

Kimberly stood at the podium and gazed out at the glitter and glamour of the room. Crystal goblets sparkled on white linen tabletops, silver gleamed, and the floral centerpieces all competed with the glitz of diamonds and pearls, evening dresses and tailored suits.

"Good evening. I hope each of you have enjoyed our little gathering tonight. Thank you so much for being here and lending your support." She pulled in a breath. "As you all know, my run for State Senate is both personal and political. Personal because it is the legacy that my brother, Kyle, began many years ago. I believed then that public service was a duty and a responsibility, and I believe that even more now. My work in the Public Defender's office has provided me with insight into the plight of so many of our fellow citizens, those whose circumstances don't provide them with the same safeguards as those with means." She scanned the group to push her point home.

"My vision and my platform are to ensure the fair and equal distribution of justice for everyone. That includes pressing forward with prison reform and sentencing criteria, a ban on the sale of assault weapons, and instituting comprehensive measures to provide real affordable housing for the residents of our city.

"These, I know, are lofty goals, but they are goals that I know can be achieved with the support of people like you and the countless others who seek equity for us all. We each want to feel safe and to live in a decent community, and when things go wrong and we are faced with the justice system, we want to be treated fairly, no matter where we live, how much money we have, or what we look like.

"This is only the beginning of a long and uphill fight to the State Senate, but with your support, it can be done, and I will do everything in my power to live up to all that I aim to achieve. Thank you all for being here tonight and for your generous support. Please enjoy dessert and the rest of your evening."

Kimberly stepped away from the podium to a round of applause and into the warm embrace of her husband. They turned to the crowd and waved their thanks before walking off to their table.

"You were fantastic," Rowan said in her ear. "They love you." He helped her into her seat.

Kimberly looked up at him. Her eyes glowed as her veins were fueled with adrenaline. She beamed at her husband. "Damn, that felt good."

"You're a natural. Just think of all of this as a great big jury to whom you are presenting your arguments."

She nodded and reached for her glass of wine.

Gail came over and stooped down to Kimberly's level. "Great job. You'll probably want to seal the deal with personal good-byes as folks are leaving," she advised. "You should be there at the door as well, Rowan."

"Not a problem."

Kimberly took a quick sip of her wine, and she and Rowan, along with Gail, went to the door to say good night to the guests.

⸻

"Very successful night," Rowan said as he slipped under the sheets next to his wife.

"Yes, it was," Gail said we garnered a total of fifty thousand dollars tonight. I can't believe it." She turned on her side to face her husband.

"This is only the beginning, babe. Tonight was a small gathering. Your next event is a much bigger venue."

"I know. Gail said the RSVPs are already up to three hundred. But I'm ready."

He kissed her forehead. "That's my girl." He pulled back the sheet and eased on top of her. Kimberly looped her arms around his neck. "I'm looking forward to finding out what it feels like to make love to a state senator."

Kimberly giggled. "For the time being," she whispered against his mouth, "you'll have to settle for a lowly attorney."

"I can do that . . ."

<hr>

Zoie flipped open her notebook and searched for the number of Lou Ellen Maitland. She needed to nail down a date and time for this interview before Mark went ballistic and pulled her off the story. The last thing she needed was for him to turn it over to Brian. It still stung that it was Brian, of all people, who got to pick up her mantle and run with the 9/11 series.

Mark knew about her imploded relationship with Brian. He knew how competitive they both were, which was the root of their problems. It was a slap in the face, which was all the more reason why she must knock this story out of the park. She picked up her phone to call Lou Ellen Maitland, and it rang in her hand. She groaned. It was her office, and she was sure it was Mark, demanding an update. She pressed the talk icon.

"Hey, Mark, before you get started I'm on it, I was—"

"Whoa, whoa, it's Brian."

"Brian?"

"Don't sound so appalled. You used to love hearing from me."

"*Used to* are the operative words. What's up?"

"Tsk, tsk. You still have that bite. Anyway, I wanted to run a few things by you regarding the series."

"Oh. Okay." She settled down in her chair by the window.

"I want to move forward with the interviews with the first responders. I have your list of contacts, but I wanted to clear it with you since you made the initial connections."

Her brows rose in surprise. Since when did Brian ask permission from anyone, especially her? She was momentarily speechless.

"Hello?"

"Oh, sorry. Um, sure. Is there anything specific that you need from me?"

"I'll give you a few of the names, and if there is anything you can share, that would be helpful. I know you don't have your notes, but your memory for details is as tight as the Pentagon," he teased.

Her ability to remember and hold onto even the smallest detail had always been a running joke between them. For work purposes, it was an amazing talent, but in her personal life, it posed the a major problem for the same reason. She tended not to forget anything.

"Shoot."

Brian went down the list, and one after another, Zoie relayed personal details she'd pulled together when she'd planned the series—things like where the first responders had grown up, how they'd come to work in their chosen fields, information about their families and friends.

"Wow," Brian said. "Impressive as always. I see why Mark admires your work, Z, . . . and me too."

She didn't want to go down this road with him.

"I want this to remain a joint effort, with you still calling the shots."

"I appreciate that."

"So how are things going down there? Have you gotten stuff settled with the family?"

"Long story. I had a few surprises, to put it mildly. But everything is coming together. "

"I didn't get a chance to tell you how sorry I was about your grandmother. I know how close you two were."

"Apparently not as close as I thought."

"Should I even guess what that means?"

"It's all part of a long story. Basically, she left everything to me."

"That's a good thing, isn't it?"

"It's complicated, but I'm trying to work it all out."

"You will. If there's anything . . . that I can do, you can always ask. I hope you know that."

"Thank you."

"Well, I'll let you go." He paused. "Good hearing your voice. I . . . we miss you around here."

Her heart jumped. "Uh, hope to be back soon."

"Maybe when you get back we could have a drink, catch up, and maybe if you feel like talking about the complications . . . we can do that, too."

Damn.

"No strings. Anyway, think about it. Okay?"

"Sure."

"Take care."

"Yeah, you too. Bye, Brian."

Zoie put down the phone and replayed the conversation in her head. It had been a while since she and Brian shared actual pleasantries. It wasn't so much what was said, but Brian's underlying tone, the vague attempt to take them back to where they once were. Did he really think that they could rekindle what they once had?

Her relationship with Brian was built on their mutual passion for journalism, a passion that was combustible in the bedroom and lethal in the office. They were competitive on every level and never truly allowed each other to fully let down their guard to be able to connect emotionally.

Brian was the distraction that she needed after Jackson. He was able to blur the lines of her past. As a result, what could have been a strong, meaningful union remained superficial.

She could have loved him and been loved back if she'd wanted it, allowed it. But always beating in the back of her heart was Jackson. In the quiet hours of the night, she could admit that she'd never stopped loving him. In the light of day, she worked to deny it, pouring herself into her job and keeping any other meaningful intimacy at bay.

When she saw Jackson again, every emotion she'd cast aside was tossed back at her. That "almost" moment between them the other day was what she'd wanted. It was Jackson who did not seem to feel the same way. That became her hard reality. While she'd pretended to move on, Jackson had succeeded.

But if nothing else, she was pragmatic, never one to wallow in something as mysterious as feelings. She operated with facts, and the fact was that Jackson didn't want her anymore—and maybe that was the wake-up call she needed that could finally quell the whispers of possibility that lurked under the cover of night.

She picked up her phone and blinked away the water that pooled in her eyes, reached for her notebook again, then dialed the number for Lou Ellen Maitland.

The phone rang several times. Zoie was prepared to leave a message when the call was answered.

"Maitland residence."

"Good evening. This is Zoie Crawford from the *National Recorder*. I would like to speak with Mrs. Maitland."

"One moment please."

Zoie experienced that familiar rush while she waited. Gearing up for a story gave her a physical response. Her senses heightened, her heart beat faster, and the world became crystal clear. She equated it with a hunter going after its prey.

"This is Lou Ellen Maitland."

Zoie snapped to attention. The voice was pretty much what she'd expected: cultured with a splash of southern comfort.

"Hello, Mrs. Maitland. I'm doing a series of articles on your daughter, Kimberly's—"

"As I told my daughter, I do not have the time nor the inclination to deal with reporters. I'm quite sure that there is nothing for me to add that is not available to you otherwise."

"I'm sure you have so much to contribute from a personal perspective. What I'm looking for—"

"Apparently, you didn't hear me. I've taken time already to accept this call, and that is all the time I plan to give you. Good luck with your story, Ms. Crawford."

Click.

Zoie snapped her head back in disbelief. Well, damn. She didn't know if she should be amused or pissed off. She opted for pissed off. If there was one thing that set her on a quest, it was to find a way to get what she wanted after being denied. Denial made her tenacious.

Mrs. "High and Mighty" Maitland could continue to sit on her pedestal, but that only slowed Zoie's forward momentum. It didn't stop it. However, she did have to come up with something to tell Mark. No way was she going to lose this story because of a glitch like this.

Zoie checked the time on her phone; she had barely an hour to get ready and drive into town. She got up and headed to the shower while contemplating the difficult designer decision of which of her two pair of jeans to wear.

While she was washing off the sticky vibes of her abbreviated call to Lou Ellen Maitland, an idea clicked in her head. Even though he hadn't seen fit to mention it, Jackson had some level of relationship with the matriarch, which she'd discovered at the library.

Smiling to herself while she dried off, she padded into her bedroom and began to formulate her "casual" approach to elicit Jackson's help when her phone chirped with a text message. She picked up the phone. *Le Grille.* "Very funny, Jackson," she groused. She tossed the phone on the bed and finished getting dressed.

CHAPTER 15

Jackson figured he was taking a risk by inviting Zoie to the place where they'd met. His hope was that maybe, surrounded by the good memories, they could find their way back. He wasn't naïve enough to believe that Z would miss the irony of his choice, but he hoped she would see it as his clumsy way of saying he was sorry for being an asshole and letting her go in the first place. But, with Zoie, anything was possible.

She did say that she didn't have much in the way of clothing, so he toned down his usual suit and tie to black denim and a fitted black T-shirt. He considered a sport jacket but decided against it.

———⟡———

Driving over to Le Grille, he had a serious bout of nerves, as though he was going on a first date with the high school prom queen. His palms were damp, and his stomach was in a knot. The first thing on his agenda when he hit the restaurant was to get a quick drink.

He pulled up on the street next to Le Grille, then drove behind the building to the parking lot in back. When he'd walked around front, he checked the time. He was ten minutes early. Rather than stand outside and look as anxious as he felt, he went in and headed to the bar. He ordered a Jack Daniel's straight up and slowly began to unwind while he listened to the live band.

As he sipped his drink, his thoughts ran through a montage of outcomes for the evening. Knowing Zoie the way he did, the night could go in a variety of directions. She could be indifferent, or she could be open to possibilities. His goal was to lay everything on the table, up to and including his relationship with Lena—well, now the lack of one. He needed Zoie to understand that while he was committed to Lena, he could not betray her trust.

"You started without me."

Jackson turned on the barstool to see Zoie standing behind him. Seeing her in all her lushness sent a jolt of electricity through his system. Even in a pair of jeans and a T-shirt she was fine.

"Hey." He stood and without thinking went to kiss her on the cheek, but she turned her head at the last second, and their lips met instead.

Zoie smiled, walked around him, and eased onto the stool next to him. She placed her purse on the bar. "Jack Daniel's?" she asked knowingly.

"You remembered."

"I remember a lot of things, Jax."

"Not all bad."

"No. You're right. Not everything that I remember about us was bad."

"I hope you don't mind that I picked Le Grille."

She laughed lightly. "If nothing else, Jax, you're transparent."

When she looked at him, the light caught her eyes, and they seemed to actually sparkle. This was the Zoie he wanted to remember. The one who laughed and teased and was so totally unaware of how crazy sexy she was.

"You want to order something or get a table?"

"Let's get a table."

"Cool." He looked around, signaled one of the passing waiters, and asked to be seated.

The waiter got them seated and placed menus in front of them, detailed the specials for the evening, then took Zoie's drink order.

"I'm glad you said yes," Jackson said. He leaned back in his seat.

"I do have an ulterior motive," she hedged.

"Oh?"

She linked her fingers together on top of the table and leveled him with her gaze. "I ran across a bunch of info today on the Maitlands."

So this was going to be a business dinner. "Helpful?"

"Curious is more like it." She went on to tell him about the articles and ended with her tidbit about him being in business with the Maitlands.

He gave a slight shrug. "The Maitlands are very wealthy and very tied to the community. The foundation they started after Kyle was killed has always contributed to development. It was a no-brainer to get their support."

"But why didn't you say anything?"

"One thing doesn't have anything to do with the other," he said in an offhand way.

Zoie sighed. "Maybe, maybe not. But you still could have told me. You knew what I was up against. Why keep that a secret? It seems everything about the Maitlands is under wraps for all kinds of reasons."

"Maybe I had my reasons, Zoie." He felt himself getting annoyed at once again being cast as the bad guy.

The waiter appeared with Zoie's margarita.

"Are you ready to order?" the waiter asked.

Jackson looked at Zoie.

"I'll have the seared salmon, yellow rice, and a side salad." She handed over the menu.

"And for you, sir?"

"Steak, medium well, baked potato, and string beans—and a refill," he added, holding up his near empty glass.

"I'll put your orders in right away."

Jackson turned his attention back to Zoie. "Look, maybe I should have said something. I didn't. Like I said, I didn't see it as relevant."

Zoie pursed her lips. "Anyway, I called the head lady in charge today."

Jackson's dark eyes widened with curiosity. "And?"

"She pretty much told me to get lost." She went on to recount the brief conversation

"Hmm, unfortunately, that sounds like Lou Ellen. She's . . . difficult at times and very private. As much as the foundation does, she rarely, if ever, talks about it. The article in the paper should have never happened. She went ballistic—in her way— and even threatened to pull out of the deal until I promised that it wouldn't happen again."

"So that's the *real* reason why you didn't say anything, not that it wasn't relevant."

He ran his tongue along his bottom lip. "Yeah."

"What is it with those people—that they can wield that kind of power over everyone? Clearly, they had some kind of hold on my grandmother, and they can even black out information with the press and hold you to some kind of pact." She slowly shook her head. "Unreal," she murmured, then lifted her glass to her lips. "She totally refused to talk to me—period."

"No way that you can do your story without her?"

Zoie pushed out a breath of annoyance. "Probably, but it'll miss the flavor I wanted. Not to mention that landing an interview with Lou Ellen Maitland would get my butt out of a sling with my boss."

Jackson bit back a sardonic smile. She was good, really good. He knew exactly what she was doing. "Maybe I can try to talk to her," he offered, knowing that's what she wanted in the first place.

Her expression bloomed. "Could you do that?"

"No promises."

"I totally understand," she said with wide-eyed enthusiasm. "Really. Whatever you can do."

The waiter arrived with their meal.

"It's what you'd planned all along," Jackson said once the waiter had left.

She looked at him, the picture of innocence. "Planned?"

"How 'bout this."

"What?"

"How 'bout from here on out, we're up front with each other, no matter what?"

Zoie speared a piece of salmon. She tilted her head to the side. "You sure about that?"

"Don't think you can handle it?"

"I always know what I can handle."

The corner of his mouth curved up in a grin. "So do I."

She popped the piece of fish in her mouth and chewed slowly, without taking her eyes off of him. "There's more to the Bennett-Maitland connection," she finally said.

"Meaning?"

She told him of the entry about Kimberly that she'd found in her grandmother's journal, how it read that they "did the right thing," and then the odd remarks made by her aunt Hyacinth. All the cloak and dagger surrounding the Maitland family was beginning to come together like the pieces of a puzzle.

"So you *really* think that your grandmother had another child?" he asked in disbelief. "Why would she lie about it?"

"That's the only thing that made sense . . . at first"—she reached for her drink—"until I really paid attention to what Aunt Hyacinth said."

"Z, you know you can't rely on your aunt . . ."

"I know. But like babies and drunks, people who are a little removed from reality have real moments of clarity and speak the truth."

He studied her for a moment, even as the path she was leading him down was becoming clear. "You're not saying—"

"Jackson . . ."

He glanced up. His eyes widened for a moment. "Lena. Hi." He got up from his seat.

Lena slid a glance at Zoie while her friend threw daggers at Jackson.

He placed his hand lightly on her arm. "Lena, this is Zoie Crawford."

Lena's eyes flashed for a moment. She lifted her chin. "Nice to meet you," she said, barely moving her lips. She focused her attention on Jackson. "You remember Diane."

"Yes. How are you, Diane? Good to see you again."

Diane murmured something in her throat.

"I'll let you two get back to what you were doing," Lena said. "We were just leaving. Too crowded tonight." The two women walked off before Jackson could respond.

He slowly sat back down.

"That was clearly awkward," Zoie said.

He studied the table for a minute, then looked across at Zoie. "That was Lena Fields."

"Okaaay . . . I hear an *and* or a *but* in there."

Jackson wrapped his hands around his glass. "We . . . me and Lena—"

Zoie held up her hand. "I get it. You don't have to explain."

"I do. We said we were going to be straight with each other."

Zoie heaved a sigh. "Fine."

Jackson paused for a moment. "Lena and I have been seeing each other for quite a while. She's a teacher at the college. Lena was the reason why I backed off the other day. We were still together."

"Were?"

He nodded. "I broke it off with her because of you."

Zoie opened her mouth, but nothing came out.

"I still care about you, Z. And I couldn't keep seeing her. She always knew about you, about us, from the beginning."

"I don't want to be the reason—"

"Too late for that." He reached across the table and covered her hands. "Too late." He squeezed her hands. "I want to try again. With us."

"Jax, I don't know how long I'm going to be here. I have a life in New York."

"I know that."

"And you're good with that? You weren't before."

"That was then. I should have done a lot of things differently back then. I want to see how things go with us now for as long as we have."

Her brows drew together. "You're sure?"

"Yes."

"Jackson, it's not that simple."

"It's only as difficult as we make it."

"You really mean that?"

"Yeah, I really mean it."

"Jax, I have all kinds of stuff going on in my life—my grandmother's business, this whole weird Maitland connection, my job . . ."

"We'll work it out."

"I'm not the easiest person to get along with."

Jackson snorted a laugh. "No kidding."

Zoie smiled.

"Are you seeing anyone?"

"No. Not anymore."

"Good. So . . . what do you say? Try again?"

She looked into his eyes. "I'm fresh out of excuses."

"That's what I wanted to hear." He lifted his glass. "To new beginnings."

Zoie hesitated. She touched her glass to his. "To new beginnings."

"Now let's eat before our food gets cold, and you can tell me everything."

———————

"I know it all sounds like some movie of the week, but my gut tells me that I'm right," she insisted.

"So what are you going to do . . . especially if it's true?"

"I haven't figured that part out yet. But I plan to speak with my mother. Lay everything out to her and see what she says."

"You do realize that if you're right and you put it in print, the blowback will implode a lot of lives."

"I understand that. Believe me. I don't want to see anyone hurt; that's not what this is about. I'll do everything I can to protect everyone's feelings. But the truth has been buried too long. We deserve to know."

He saw the old fire in her eyes and knew that no matter what the cost, she would get the answers she wanted. How many lives would become casualties was the only question up in the air.

CHAPTER 16

Zoie hadn't wanted to allow herself to fall into the trap of thinking that she and Jackson would ever be together again. The moment she did, back in her bedroom that night, her faint hope had been shot down. Now Jackson had set the table for a whole new agenda. She was excited and terrified.

"Where'd you park?" he asked when they stepped outside of the restaurant.

"In the lot out back."

"So did I." He slid his arm around her waist.

She glanced up at him and smiled. It felt good, and she knew how easily she could get used to his hands on her again.

"There is something else I wanted to run by you," she said as they entered the lot.

"Anything."

"Be careful what you wish for," she teased. "I'm totally in over my head with the business, and my Aunt Sage, of all people, suggested that I ask you for some help."

Jackson tossed his head back and laughed. "Sage Bennett! The same woman who would have as easily had me in front of a firing squad as say good morning?" he joked.

"I thought the exact same thing." They stopped in front of her car. She faced him. "Come to find out, she said she acted that way because it was her duty to protect me." Her throat tightened. "And that she wanted you to stay on your toes." She swallowed. "I never knew she cared—not like that."

He cupped her cheek. "I think," he said softly, "if you give people half a chance, you'll be surprised at how much they care. Folks show affection in all kinds of ways. I kinda knew she wasn't for real." He half-grinned. "That's why I still went around to check on them from time to time after you left. They were supposed to give me a hard time. That's what families do."

She studied the ground. So much was happening, so many changes and new feelings and shifting relationships. She needed some time to process it all.

"Anyway, I'd be happy to see how I can help. You said your grandmother kept records."

Zoie snapped back. She looked at him. "Yes. In the attic. I went through some of the files, but . . ."

"I can take a look."

"Thanks," she breathed. "And thanks for tonight."

"I'm glad you said yes."

"So am I."

He took a step closer, dipped his head, and covered her mouth with his.

She felt her heart slam against her chest, and a rush of heat jettisoned from the soles of her feet to the top of her head. She moaned against his warm lips and nearly wept when the tip of his tongue dipped into her mouth.

Jackson pulled her tight against him, and her mind flooded with memories of just how well they'd always fit together and still did. He eased back, but didn't let her go.

"Listen, I'm gonna be honest."

Her heart thumped.

"I'm not up for playing hide and seek at your house. I want to take you home with me so we can make love like grownups and I can see if I can still make you holler." He waited a beat. "So . . . what do you say to that?"

She ran her tongue across her bottom lip and tasted him again. "I'm feeling very grown up this evening."

Jackson's eyes crinkled at the edges. "You remember the way?"

"Yep."

He gave her a light kiss. "See you there." He walked off to his car, which was parked two rows away.

Zoie got in her car and realized that her hands were actually shaking. She drew in a long, steadying breath and gripped the wheel. Her thoughts spun. Was this really going to happen? *She and Jackson?* Tonight?

She stuck the key in the ignition and turned on the car. She glanced in her side mirror and saw Jackson pulling out of the lot. She put the car in gear and followed him out.

———◆◆◆———

Zoie pulled into the driveway, parking behind Jackson's rental. He came to open her door.

"Still have a hot foot, I see," he teased.

Zoie laughed, gripped his hand, and stepped out. "Have to keep up with you."

Jackson angled his head toward the house. "Driving was the fastest thing I plan to do all night. From here on out, we're gonna take it real slow." He pecked her on the lips and led her inside.

———◆◆◆———

The house was very much as she remembered. The furnishings were basically the same. He had purchased some new paintings, as art was one of his passions. It was Jackson who'd gotten her to begin to appreciate art, and she'd collected some pieces of her own back in New York.

"This is new," she said of the Basquiat that hung over the mantle.

"Yeah, I picked that up at a gallery opening about six months ago." He came to stand behind her.

She looked closer. "This is an original," she said surprised. "Must have cost a pretty penny."

"That it did." He lifted her hair and kissed the back of her neck, right on the spot that drove her crazy. He hadn't forgotten. She squeezed her eyes shut to contain the shiver that scurried down her spine.

"You do well for yourself," she managed.

"I can't complain. I do what I enjoy, and it happens to pay well." He slid his arms around her waist. "But things are tough at times, with the housing market being what it is. And after the Trade Center bombings, investors are holding onto their purses more tightly."

"How is that going to affect you?" She turned in his arms to face him.

He half-shrugged. "It's going to make any new financing for projects more difficult. For the ones in the works, the money is already committed." His eyes moved slowly over her face. "Worried about my fate?"

"I think you can take care of yourself. You always have."

"Things are always better with a partner." His hand stroked her back, and he exhaled. "You feel good, girl." He kissed one cheek and then the other before seeking her mouth.

Zoie welcomed him, melted into his body, and relished the hard feel of him against her. So many of their days and nights together rushed through her, one explosive image after another.

"I want our reunion to start off right," he said against her lips.

"Meaning?"

"We'll have some wine, listen to some music, talk, strip, and find our way to my bedroom, make some long overdue love, sleep, do it again . . . and breakfast in the morning."

Zoie giggled. "Have it all figured out, huh?"

"I never have it all figured out when it comes to you, Z." He moved away. "Red or white? Luther or Kem?"

"White. Luther."

He winked, went to the sound system and found the Luther CD, then got two glasses and the bottle of white wine. He poured a glass and handed it to Zoie, then poured his. He lifted his glass. "To putting the past in the rearview."

Zoie tilted her head and pursed her lips. After a moment, she clinked her glass to his and took a sip to seal the pact.

Jackson took her free hand and led her down the short hallway to his room. His bedroom, like the rest of the house, was much the same. He always had a habit of taking off his slacks and tossing them on the chair by the window. Zoie smiled when she saw two pairs, one over each arm. The dresser top was lined with loose change, two bottles of his favorite cologne, and a random CD. One black sneaker peeked out from under the foot of the bed, and its mate was by the closet door. A lone white dress shirt was tossed across the bottom of the bed, along with a navy-blue tie. But the bed, as always, was made. The hardwood floors gleamed, and the room held his scent. Her tummy fluttered.

Jackson walked over to the bed, picked up the shirt and tie, and tossed them onto the chair with the jeans. He grinned at Zoie.

"Some things don't change," she teased with an expansive wave of her hands.

He shrugged. "Gives me a sense of normalcy." He sat on the side of the bed and took off his shoes.

Zoie made a show of taking off hers. Jackson got up and walked over to her. He threaded his fingers through her hair and pulled her to him.

"Jax," she whispered.

"No more talking. Not now."

She remembered a lot—the rooms, the scent, the clothes on the chair. She thought she'd committed to memory how Jackson made her feel. She imagined his touch every time she was with Brian, the way he tasted, and the way he moved inside her. But now in the real world, it was not what she remembered at all. It was different, hotter, more urgent.

Every nerve ending sparked. Every inch of her body that he touched or kissed ignited. She wanted to scream when he spread her legs and ran his tongue along the insides of her thighs, then suckled her swollen clit until her entire body vibrated. But the sound clung to her throat, unsung. Yet when he eased inside of her and her body opened in welcome, like a door for an old friend, she found her voice and sang his name to the new rhythm between them.

———————————

Spooned against him, she listened to the soothing beat of his heart, which soon became unified with hers. She closed her eyes and let herself enjoy the moment, the feel of having Jackson in her life again, even if it was only temporary. She had no immediate plans to stay in New Orleans. Once her year was up—her "sentence," as her mother called it—she would go back to New York and continue where she left off. Her job gave her the ability to go and come as she pleased, but she'd made New York her home. That had to count for something. Would it be enough?

She kissed his hand, which possessively cupped her breast. Could she pick up and leave him again? Jackson stirred against her. What choice did she have? The only thing she could do is enjoy the time they had together and try to keep her feelings under control.

He kissed the back of her neck and brushed his knee along her thighs. She sucked in a breath. Keeping her feelings under control would be easier said than done.

She'd lost count of how many times they made love throughout the night, in every position and combination. But Jackson was true to his promise. He took his sweet time with everything, which drove her nearly out of her mind with lust.

Maybe they slept at some point, off and on, between sessions. She wasn't sure. When she was able to open her eyes against the sun that streamed in from the skylight and stretched beneath the sheets, she moaned in a good kind of pain. Her muscles ached. Her nipples were sore, and her vajayjay throbbed. She had been worked out. It had been a long time since she'd been with anyone, and her body was testifying to that fact.

She turned onto her back and realized she was alone in the bed. She stretched toward the nightstand for her phone, held it up, and squinted at the face. 9:30. Damn! She pushed up onto her elbows. When was the last time she'd slept until 9:30? There were a million things she had to take care of. She tossed the sheet aside and jumped out of bed. Why the hell did Jackson let her sleep like that? Where were her clothes?

"Morning."

Zoie stopped in mid-rant. Jackson was standing in the doorway with a towel tucked around his waist and two mugs of coffee in his hands. His body still glistened from his recent shower. The scent of his freshly washed body, the sight of his rippling abs, and the aroma of coffee instantly calmed the savage beast.

She ran her hands through her hair. "Morning."

"It could get really easy waking up to *that* every morning," he said, stepping into the room and hungrily eyeing her nakedness.

Zoie flushed and eased her way over to the chair, where their discarded clothes had been tossed. She plucked her bra and panties from the pile and put them on.

"How'd you sleep?" he asked as he set the mugs down on the nightstand.

Zoie secured the hooks of her bra and turned to him. "Good question. I guess I must have slept at some point," she said with a grin. She cat-walked across the room, then sat next to him on the side of the bed. He handed her a mug.

"Thanks."

"About last night," he said in a bad British accent, and they both burst out laughing.

Zoie looked at him. "We can't do strings, Jax."

"I get that."

"And no promises."

"We do have one promise: to be upfront and real with each other."

She nodded in agreement.

"I was gonna fix some cheese grits, scrambled eggs, and fried fish. You good with that?"

"Do you see my mouth watering?"

He chuckled and kissed her forehead. "Everything is where it's always been in the bathroom. Help yourself. I think there's an extra toothbrush in the basket under the sink with the soap and stuff." He pushed up from the bed, took his coffee, and walked out.

"See, if you'd let me pick you up last night, I'd be driving you home this morning instead of you pulling out of my driveway alone," Jackson said as they stood by her car.

"Maybe next time." She winked.

He pulled open her door, and she got in. "I'll stop by Mrs. Maitland's later today and see if I can get her to change her mind about talking to you."

"What about Mr. Maitland?"

Jackson slowly shook his head. "The old man is pretty sick. She watches over him like a hawk. No one gets near him. In the times that I've been to the house, I may have seen him once."

"Okay." She stuck the key in the ignition and turned on the car. "Call me later."

"Will do." He leaned down and kissed her long and slow. "Drive safe," he said, then stepped back and shut her door.

Zoie finger-waved and drove off.

She turned on the radio, but she wasn't really listening. She tried to process the events of the past twenty-four hours. One fact stood out the most. When she'd come back for her grandmother's funeral, the last thing she'd ever imagined herself doing was driving home in the morning from a "sleepover" at Jackson Fuller's house. But then again, since she'd arrived, nothing had turned out the way she'd expected.

CHAPTER 17

"Girl, are you gonna make me come down there and get your crazy behind?" Miranda yelled into the phone.

Zoie giggled, leaned back against the headboard of her bed, and tucked her feet beneath her. "Randi, relax. I know what I'm doing."

"No, you don't. Not when it comes to Jackson. Your feelings are all over the place. You hate him, you love him, you never want to see him again, he broke your heart, he's the only man you'll ever love. You have no clue how you feel. And now in the middle of everything you need to focus on, you sleep with him!" She paused for a breath. "So . . . how was it, girl?"

They burst out laughing.

Zoie shared with her friend everything that led up to her and Jackson's night together, and brought her up to speed on what she'd shaken loose from her family tree, along with her growing suspicions.

"I'm telling you, sis, this needs to be a made-for-TV-movie. You can't make this stuff up. So when are you going to meet with Kimberly?"

"I still need to set that up. My hope was to talk with her mother first. We'll see. In any event, I'm going to have to get back up to

New York. But I still have to deal with Nana's vegetable business. Oh, guess what?"

"What?"

"Aunt Sage said she'd help me."

"Get the hell outta here. For real?"

"Yep. Couldn't believe it myself. But, Randi, ever since I got back, I've been hit with one unbelievable event after the other."

"I hate to say I told you so, but I did!" She chuckled. "Give folks a chance, Z," she said softly.

"I'm trying. But when you've been at the short end of everyone's pissed-off list for so long, it makes you wary."

"I hear ya. But they say folks mellow with age. That's what's happening with your family."

Zoie sighed. "I guess . . . anyway, I need to get myself in gear. I'll call you in a couple of days."

"Okay. Take care, and good luck with everything. Oh, one last piece of advice."

"What?"

"Eyes open, legs closed!"

"Girl, bye!"

Just as she was about to hop off the bed, her phone rang. It was a New York number, but at least it wasn't her office.

"Hello?"

"Good morning. May I speak with Zoie Crawford?"

"Speaking."

"Good morning, Ms. Crawford. This is Gail Sorensen, Mrs. Graham's assistant."

"Yes, good morning. What can I do for you?"

"I'm calling to extend an invitation to you and a guest for the upcoming fund-raising dinner for Mrs. Graham."

"Oh! Okay. Thank you."

"I will send you an email with all of the particulars."

"I'll keep an eye out for it. What is the date?"

"Two weeks from this Friday."

"Alright. Thank you."

"Enjoy your day."

The call disconnected.

Humph. Well, one way or the other, she was going back to New York. She had two weeks to get her ducks in a row. A fund-raiser? This would certainly give her an opportunity to see Kimberly Graham in action and to observe how a crowd reacted to her. She smiled. Hopefully things were starting to fall into place. At least she could tick this off as a tidbit to keep Mark pacified.

Her phone chirped with a text message.

I'LL STOP BY LATER AND TAKE A LOOK AT THE FILES. ABOUT FOUR. J.

Her heart thumped.

K. CU THEN.

⟶⋗⋅⋖⟵

"Mr. Fuller, would you care for some sweet tea?" Mrs. Maitland's housekeeper asked.

"That would be great. Thank you."

"Sure you don't want something a bit stronger, Jackson?" Lou Ellen coaxed.

Jackson chuckled. "No, thanks. I still have some more work to put in today."

Lou Ellen pursed her thin lips. She looked up at her housekeeper. "My usual, Margaret."

"Yes, ma'am."

They were seated in the enclosed veranda, which looked out onto the sprawling estate and the lake beyond. Overhead fans moved lazily, cooling the humid air.

"So, what can I do for you? I hope it's not more money," she said, half in jest.

"No. Nothing like that. The project is on schedule and on budget. Thankfully the storm didn't cause much damage."

She peered at him with her penetrating green eyes and folded her liver-stained hands on her lap. Even though she was petite in stature, there was an imposing presence about Lou Ellen Maitland that could not be denied. Everything about her was impeccable, from her perfectly coiffed gray hair, to the pearl studs in her ears and the rope of pearls around her neck, to the stylish coral-colored dress that was fit for a luncheon at the country club and not a simple chat with a business associate. But that was Lou Ellen Maitland. She was all about appearances.

"I'm listening."

"I was hoping that you would reconsider talking with a colleague of mine."

Her thin brows rose. "Who might that be?"

"Zoie Crawford."

Her cheeks flushed, and her body grew rigid. "And why would I do that? More important, why are you interceding when I already told that woman no?"

"I hoped that if you did talk with her, you could lend some insight into your daughter. I know how important the family image is to you." He watched her visibly relax. "If you control the message, you can shape it to cast the best light."

She lifted her chin and sniffed. "I never wanted that life for Kimberly, you know. It was Franklin who thought that somehow she could miraculously step into Kyle's shoes. He was the one who put those ideas in her head from the time she was a teenager. The Maitland legacy, he said." She flicked her hand as if to toss aside the absurdity of it. "I never agreed."

"With Kimberly being . . . your only child," he hedged, "I can understand your husband's reasoning."

Her thin nostrils flared. "I don't have any idea what I can say that would make a difference one way or the other."

"I know that anything you could offer would be important," he said, continuing to stroke her ego.

She sniffed again.

Margaret appeared with their beverages in glasses on a tray, along with one carafe of mimosas and one of sweet tea.

"Thank you, dear," Lou Ellen said and took a sip of her mimosa. "Perfect." She turned her attention back to Jackson. "I have a distinct dislike of the media. They have an almost sinister way of bending the facts. I've made it a point, since Kimberly's birth, to keep them out of our lives."

"That's why it's important for you to be able to tell your side."

"Dig, dig. That's all they do. Dig to try to find something unpleasant. That's what sells," she insisted in her lofty tone. She took a long swallow of her drink, nearly finishing it off.

Jackson held his tongue. The last thing he wanted to do was set her off. He knew how she was, and once she dug her heels in, there was no wrestling her free.

Lou Ellen set down her glass just as Franklin's nurse pushed open the door and wheeled the patriarch in.

Franklin Maitland, even in his illness, was still regal, though frail. He sat ramrod straight in his wheelchair, and his thick shock of silver hair brought to mind movie-star royalty. His white shirt was starched stiff, the crease in his black slacks was sharp enough to slice bread, and for an added touch, he had a red ascot tied around his neck. This was maybe the second time Jackson had seen him up close. The only thing that hinted at his illness was the slight yellow tinge to his otherwise pale skin.

"Hello, sweetheart," Lou Ellen greeted. She patted his hand.

"Needed some air," he said, his voice surprisingly deep and strong. He looked Jackson over.

"You remember Jackson Fuller, dear. He's—"

"Of course I remember him," he said, sharply cutting her off in mid-sentence.

Lou Ellen flushed.

Jackson extended his hand and was taken aback by Franklin's powerful grip. "Good to see you, Mr. Maitland."

"And what brings you here? Problem with the development?"

"He came to ask about—"

He threw a look at Lou Ellen that stopped her cold. "I'm talking to Mr. Fuller."

The muscles in Lou Ellen's throat flexed, and her face flamed. She reached for her glass and finished off her drink, then quickly refilled it from the carafe, took another long swallow, then pressed her lips together into a tight thin line as if to permanently seal them.

Franklin looked at her with what Jackson perceived as disdain. He might be wrong, but the vibe he got from these two was anything but loving. Maybe they were having a bad day, something any couple went through even after decades of marriage. But he had to admit that, in all of his dealings with Lou Ellen, he had never seen her flustered until now.

"You were about to say, Mr. Fuller . . ." Franklin said.

"I have a very good friend, a colleague of mine," he qualified, "who is working on a story about your daughter Kimberly's run for the New York State Senate. She would really like to have an interview with . . . you . . . both"—he looked from one to the other—"about your daughter to give the article a more humanized perspective."

"Humph. I see." He worked his mouth for several moments. "That might be a good thing for Kimberly."

"Franklin!"

He reached over and patted her hand, which held the arm of her chair in a vice grip. "It will be fine," he said, in an almost consoling tone. He turned his focus on Jackson and nodded his head. "I take it that my dear wife gave your 'friend' a hard time."

"No. I wouldn't say that."

"Of course you wouldn't. But I know my wife. Tell this reporter that she can stop by. We'll give her one half hour."

"Thank you, sir."

Franklin glanced over his shoulder at his nurse, who stood dutifully behind him. "I'm ready for lunch, and we can escort Mr. Fuller out."

Jackson stood. "Thank you for your time, Mrs. Maitland." She shook his hand, and Jackson would have sworn that she fought back tears by sheer will.

He followed Mr. Maitland out and, as promised, was shown the front door.

"Enjoy your day, Mr. Fuller."

"Thank you, sir."

———≫•◦≪———

"Gave me a whole new perspective about the Maitlands," Jackson said, while he looked through Claudia's files.

"Wow. I thought for sure that Lou Ellen ran the show."

"So did I. Maybe she's just the front, and Franklin is pulling the strings behind the scenes."

"It would actually make sense," Zoie said.

"Meaning?" He made some notes.

Zoie leaned her hip against the side of her grandmother's desk and folded her arms. "Well, with the family in general being all about appearances, maybe they decided that Lou Ellen would be the face to avoid Franklin looking weak."

"Hmm, maybe," he said without much conviction. "The man I saw today was still a force to be reckoned with, wheelchair or not. And he definitely has Lou Ellen on a short leash."

"Hey, rich folk have a whole other philosophy about the world," Zoie said.

"I wouldn't know," he joked.

"Me neither."

He leaned back in the chair and took off his reading glasses.

The glasses were a new addition, and noticing that made Zoie realize how time was flying by and changing everyone in the process.

"From what I've determined, your grandmother had five steady clients that she provided product for at given times. Looks like every six to eight weeks. She alternated the products with each delivery. I guess that has to do with when things were ripe and ready. Then there were periodic customers who put in special requests. Now she also has a contract with a boxing company that packaged the merchandise, and it looks like they were responsible for delivery as well. And according to this schedule, there are delivery dates coming up in the next two weeks."

"So now what?"

"Now we need to go through the lists of customers, see what their orders are, and get the products prepared."

"Aunt Sage said she would help with the clients, and my mom has been tending the garden. I've really got to stop calling what's out there a garden. It's field. It stopped being a garden a long time ago," she said with a tone of awe.

"There ya go. It'll be fine." He closed the files and checked the time on his phone. "Listen, I gotta run. I need to get over to the site."

"Sure. I'm sorry I'm taking up so much of your time, like you don't have enough to do."

Jackson stood. "I don't mind." He smiled at her. "It's not a problem."

"Thank you anyway."

He took his jacket from the back of the chair and slipped it on.

"Oh, I got an invitation to Kimberly Graham's fund-raiser."

"Great."

"I was wondering if you would like to go with me. My plus one."

"To New York?"

"Yeah. It's in two weeks. I can get everything on track here, fly out, and come back."

"Let me look at my schedule, make sure everything is in order, and I'll let you know."

"Sure."

They walked to the stairs and started down.

"So, uh, where will I be staying if I go?"

"We can stay at my place. It's not the Ritz, but it'll do."

"I'll let you know as soon as I can."

She walked him outside. "Jackson, there's one more thing I want to run by you."

"Shoot." He shoved his hands in pockets.

"You've pretty much seen what I found in my grandmother's journals and letters."

"Yeah." He dragged out the word.

"There's something about the timeline that's been bugging me."

He frowned. "What timeline?"

"Why did my mother leave New Orleans in her last year of high school to go to school in New York?"

"I don't know. Why?"

"That's what I don't get, and when I asked her, she got all defensive."

"Where are you going with this?"

"Think about it. My mother was sixteen, almost seventeen. She leaves home, and in the same year Kimberly Maitland is born, yet there is no record that I could find that even remotely indicates the Maitlands were expecting another child, only her birth."

"And . . ."

"Don't you think that's odd?"

"Only to a point. You see for yourself how the Maitlands control their message and their image in the press."

"Exactly, but only since Kimberly was born."

"Are you thinking that your mother . . ."

She nodded. "It would explain so much. It would explain the secrecy, Lou Ellen's unwillingness to talk to me, even Aunt Hyacinth's ramblings."

"Z, be careful. That's a heavy accusation. The ramifications . . ." He shook his head. "Why? It makes no sense."

"It would if Kyle Maitland was the father."

"What?"

"Think about it. My mother was a minor, black, housekeeper's daughter who got pregnant by the heir to the Maitland fortune and a rising political star. The scandal would have ruined them, especially back then."

"So, what, you're thinking that Kimberly is your mother's daughter and the Maitlands have been passing her off as theirs?"

"Yes. Kimberly Graham is my sister, and I'm going to prove it."

The screen door swung open. Rose stepped out. "What are you saying?"

CHAPTER 18

Jackson couldn't shake from his head the look of shock and pain on Rose's face. He'd wanted to stay and maybe be a buffer between mother and daughter, but Zoie insisted that he leave and she'd call him later. That had been nearly four hours ago. He'd been tempted to call her but opted against it.

What Zoie had culled together was crazy, but in the back of his head he could see how easily it could be true. From what he knew of the Maitlands, they set themselves up as above reproach. They were revered in the community and always had been, and became even more beloved after the untimely death of their son. There had never been a hint of scandal connected with the Maitland name.

Now Zoie had her teeth sunk into this story, and he knew that she wouldn't let go until her appetite for the truth was satisfied.

———✦———

Zoie took her mother to her bedroom, sat her down, and then went to take the box of her grandmother's journals and letters from the shelf in her closet.

"What the hell were you talking about out there? I need you to tell me right now what's going on, Zoie!" her mother demanded.

"I will. I will. There are some things that I want you to see. Then we can talk."

"Talk now!"

Her mother was visibly shaking.

She pressed her hand to her mother's shoulder. "Mama, please," Zoie said, trying to soothe her. "I'll explain everything."

Zoie opened the box and placed the journals on the small round table.

"What is all this?"

"Nana's journals." She took out the letters and placed them on the table as well.

The nerves in Rose's face fluttered. She reared back in the chair. "Where did you get these?"

"In the attic. They were in a trunk tucked away behind some boxes."

"You ain't had no business going through Mama's things."

"I had every right when she left everything to me. I wasn't looking for them. I was looking for anything to help me with the business."

"So . . . what's in them to make you say such crazy things?"

She'd marked the pages that were important and flipped to them in each of the journals. "Read them for yourself, Mama," she said gently.

Rose huffed and with reluctance pulled one of the journals toward her. She cast Zoie a doubtful look, then began to read.

Zoie sat with clenched fists and listened to her own heart thudding in her chest as she watched her mother's expression shift from outright denial, to confusion, pain, fear, and acceptance. Her mother's sharp gasp confirmed to Zoie that what she suspected was indeed true.

Rose pressed her fingers to her chest as if to contain the flood of emotions that ran through her. Her breathing stopped and started as her eyes moved over the words her mother had written long ago.

Zoie couldn't begin to imagine what her mother must be thinking and feeling. The enormity of the lie spanned decades, and her grandmother was complicit in its execution. That part she was still trying to wrap her mind around. This conspiracy between Nana and the Maitlands was inconceivable to Zoie—no matter what the circumstances were. And the fact that her grandmother, whom she adored, had been part of it tore away pieces of Zoie's heart.

Tears slid from Rose's eyes, even as her lips remained tightly sealed. Finally, she folded the last letter and slid it back into its envelope. She wouldn't look at her daughter. Without a word, she got up.

"Mama . . ."

She brushed by Zoie and walked to the door.

"Mama . . . We need to talk."

Rose turned, and the pain and disillusionment that haunted her eyes and weighed down her shoulders pushed back against Zoie with such force that she gasped for air.

"No. We don't," she said simply. She closed the door quietly behind her.

<hr />

After a day filled with meetings and phone calls, Kimberly had never been more grateful to be home. There was a press conference scheduled for the morning, and Gail had set up a time with the local television station for her to do a public service announcement. She'd spent several hours fine-tuning what her message would be and several more reviewing a pro-bono case that she'd taken on. To say that she was exhausted would be an understatement. But the sound of her daughters' welcoming voices gave her the shot of adrenalin that she needed.

At twelve, Alexis and Alexandra were on the cusps of teenhood. One minute they were little girls who couldn't find their favorite socks or finish their homework without her help or refused to go to sleep unless she sat on their beds and listened to every minute of their day. At other times, they were aloof and self-contained, and insisted that whatever it was, they could do it themselves, and why did she have to treat them like babies all the time?

Alexis, three minutes older than her sister, was the most outspoken and spontaneous of the two. Alexandra was the thinker and often had to rein in her sister's ideas for pranks, which were many.

Together they were her heartbeats, and she would move heaven and earth to keep them safe and happy.

"Evening, Mrs. Graham," Farrah said. "Dinner is in the warmer. Homework is finished." She smiled at each girl in turn. "So I'm going to head home."

"Thanks so much, Farrah."

"Oh, Mr. Graham said he should be home by nine. Meeting."

"Thanks."

"Night, girls. See you tomorrow."

"Bye, Farrah," they said.

She waved good night and let herself out.

The moment the door closed, Alexis announced with wicked glee, "Mom! Sandi has a boyfriend."

"Oh, God, I hate you. Mommmm!"

Alexis giggled.

"What did I tell you about ratting out your sister, Lexi," Kimberly teased. She cast loving eyes on her mortified child. "Is he cute?"

Alexandra beamed. "Yes." She stuck her tongue out at her sister.

"Oh, big deal," Alexis said. "He has zits."

"Does not!"

"Does too."

"Girls! Can I at least get in the door and take off my shoes before we have a war of words? Please."

"Sorry," they harmonized.

"Thank you."

They trailed behind her to her bedroom and plopped down on the area rug while she got out of her work clothes and changed into yoga pants and a T-shirt.

"How was your day?" she asked.

Miraculously, they were back on friendly territory and took turns talking about their day. Their change in attitude had as much to do with their raging hormones as it did with the house rule of no arguing in bedrooms. Bedrooms were safety zones, off-limits to feuding and arguments, and it was a rule that Kimberly and Rowan would not allow to be broken.

"Okay, let's eat."

"We're not going to wait for Daddy?" Alexandra asked.

"Daddy has to work late. By the time he gets in, you two will be fast asleep."

"Is he still working with the rescuers?" Alexis wanted to know.

"Yes. His company is helping to fix a lot of the equipment that was damaged."

"But what if more buildings fall?" Alexandra said, the anxiety clear in her voice.

"That's not going to happen, sweetheart."

Both she and Rowan had spent days talking with their daughters about the tragedy of the World Trade Center. She wanted to shield them from the horror of what happened. Rowan believed that they needed to understand, as much as possible, what had happened to remove their fear rather than increase it. They met on middle ground, giving the girls the basics without going into depth about what had happened.

Kimberly still experienced nightmares about that day. She could have lost her husband. For more than a day she thought she had, and any time Rowan was late or unreachable, she had flashbacks to that horrific morning.

Rowan's company InnerVision Technologies, had secured a contract to overhaul the computer routing systems for the Hanover Corporation, whose offices occupied the eighty-eighth to the ninety-first floors of Tower Two. He and his team were working in the building when it was hit.

Kimberly was in her Midtown Manhattan office, reviewing a

case, when frantic shouts filled the corridor. Panicked, she ran out of her office and collided with Felicia, one of the legal assistants.

"What's happening?"

Tears filled Felicia's eyes. "My God, the World Trade Center . . ."

Kimberly's breath caught. "What? What happened?"

"They were just hit by airplanes!"

"What!"

Staff ran past them toward the conference room. Kimberly ran down the hallway, and when she got to the packed room, her colleagues stood frozen in fear and disbelief as they stared at the television screen.

The images were unreal. Smoke, plumes of white dust, running and screaming people, fire and police tore through the decimated streets in what looked like a war zone. The television reporter tried to maintain his composure even as explosions and fire engines screamed in the background.

He reported that two airplanes had stuck Towers One and Two in what was deemed a terrorist attack. And then the unthinkable happened. Tower One collapsed, as if it had imploded.

A gasp of horror reverberated in the packed room. The reporter became covered in soot and ash, and the screams from those on the ground swelled to a roar of sound.

Kimberly ran from the room back to her office to retrieve her cell phone. Her hands shook as she hit the speed dial for her husband, only to get an automated message stating that all circuits were busy. She tried repeatedly for more than an hour, alternating between attempting to reach her husband and Farrah as the chaos in Lower Manhattan grew. Then reports came in that the Pentagon was hit and another passenger plane had gone down in Pennsylvania.

She managed to drive home, using pure instinct as her guide because her mind was on finding her children and husband. The twenty-minute drive took more than two agonizing hours, and she literally collapsed in relief when she burst through the doors of her condo and found Farrah and her children. She hugged her daughters for so long that they finally wiggled away.

"Any word from Mr. Graham?" Farrah mouthed over the tops of the twins' heads.

Kimberly shook her head no.

As the hours ticked by with no word from Rowan and the devastating news from the site grew more grim, Kimberly's fears of the worst escalated. The girls constantly asking for their father only made the interminable wait that much more unbearable.

At some point, pure exhaustion kicked in, and she passed out on the couch with her daughters. Her cell phone finally rang at about three in the morning, jerking her awake.

The call was from a nurse at St. Luke's Hospital. Rowan had been admitted. He was stable but had suffered a mild concussion and would be discharged later in the day.

For weeks after, they clung to each other more than ever, bound together in ways that they hadn't experienced before. The tragic event brought them closer as a couple and a family.

It was also how Kimberly first became aware of Zoie Crawford. She religiously followed Zoie's in-depth series on the attack on the Towers that infamously became dubbed 9/11, which was why she was surprised to open the paper one day and see someone else's byline. Not long after, she understood why. The very thorough and tenacious reporter had been assigned to her.

When she heard the keys in the front door, the tension that stiffened her limbs and pounded in her temples eased, and she took a deep breath for what felt like the first time in hours. She got up from the couch and met Rowan before he had a chance to shut the door. She wrapped her arms around him and rested her head on his chest.

"What is it, babe?"

She shook her head and held on tighter. "Just glad you're home," she said on a shaky breath.

Rowan took a step back and held her at arm's length. He dipped his head. "Look at me, babe."

Hesitantly, she lifted her gaze.

"Another episode," he asked softly.

"Not quite. Just feeling . . . I don't know—vulnerable, I guess. Momentary panic attack when I heard you'd be late. Silly."

"Kim." He looped his arm around her waist, and they walked together inside. "I went to see someone after . . . It helped. It really did. It's been months now, and you're still struggling with this. You need to talk to somebody."

They sat down on the couch. Kim curled into the sanctuary of her husband's body. "I can't. Not now. Not in the middle of running for office. With all that we have going on, the last thing the people want is someone they think is unstable. I mean, let's be for real, I wasn't even there."

"That doesn't mean it wasn't traumatic. Shit like this hits people in different ways."

"I know. I know. I promise that as soon as this campaign is over, I'll see someone." She lifted her face to him. "In the meantime, just keep coming home for dinner."

Kimberly closed her eyes and listened to the soothing, steady heartbeat of her husband. As long as she had Rowan and her children, everything would be fine.

CHAPTER 19

For more than an hour, Zoie drove through the streets of her neighborhood, looking for her mother. After Rose left Zoie's room, she'd gotten into her car and taken off. It was getting dark, and even though Zoie had grown up on these streets, they seemed suddenly unfamiliar, and she found herself driving in circles. Finally, she pulled over at a curb, took out her phone, and dialed the one other person she knew—Jackson.

"Z, what's up?"

"I can't find my mother . . ."

Twenty minutes later, Jackson pulled up behind Zoie's car and got out. She opened her passenger door, and he got in.

Zoie wiped away tears. "Thanks for coming."

"No problem. Tell me what happened."

Zoie sniffed and told him what she'd revealed to her mother. "She just left. Wouldn't talk to me."

For several moments, Jackson remained silent.

"Say something."

Jackson blew out a breath. "Look, don't take this the wrong way, but how did you think she was going to react? Of course, she was upset. Wouldn't you be? All these years, she thought the child she gave birth to was dead, only to find out that her own mother was involved in the cover-up."

"I get that, but we were all duped. Don't you think it messed me up, too? My grandmother? This is the woman that I trusted, adored. Why would she do something like that?"

"You may never know."

"Oh, I'm going to know," she said, the fire reigniting in her belly. "There's no way I'm going to let this go."

"Zoie . . ." He shook his head vehemently. "You will destroy too many lives. What about Kimberly? She has a life, a family, and a career. Are you willing to ruin that just to get a story?"

Zoie nearly leapt out of her seat. "Just to get a story? Are you kidding me? This is more than a story. This is my fucking life, Jax!"

"It's not all about you, Z."

Her expression softened. "I know it's not all about me. I understand that. I do. But I also care about the truth. Sometimes the truth hurts." She turned her head away and stared out the window.

Jackson heaved a sigh. He reached for the door handle. "Looks like you have it all figured out. Like always." He opened the door. "I'm sure your mother will come home when she's ready. And when she does, I hope you will consider how she feels." He got out.

Jackson shut the door and strode to his car.

Zoie sat in aching silence while she watched him drive away.

⎯⎯●◄●⎯⎯

She drove around for another half hour or so before finally giving up and returning home, relieved to see her mother's car parked at an angle out front.

Zoie ran inside. The house was quiet. She walked through the ground floor and found it empty. She hurried out back and pushed through the screen door to find her mother and aunts sitting on the veranda sipping sweet tea.

"What are you in such a hurry about?" Sage asked. She brought the glass to her lips.

Zoie looked from one to the other. Her mother kept her focus on the newspaper on her lap.

"Where's that cute Jackson fella?" Hyacinth asked. "Always did like him."

"You just gonna stand there?" Sage asked.

"I, um, wanted to talk to Mom."

"Can't you see I'm relaxing?" Rose said, her tone flat. "Heard enough from you to last me a lifetime." She snapped open the paper and held it up to her face.

Sage's thick brows rose. "Humph. What's this all about?'

"Nothing," Rose said and threw Zoie a warning stare.

Zoie swallowed. "I'm going to take a shower. Can I get anyone anything first?"

"Dinner's on the stove," Sage said. "Figure everything out with Mama's accounts? You was up there a long time today."

"Um, pretty much. Jackson was very helpful."

"Always liked Jackson," Hyacinth said again.

Zoie took a final look at her mother, who still refused to meet her gaze. She went back inside.

The journals, still open and spread on the table, stared accusingly back at her. She slammed each book shut, gathered the letters, and put them all back in the box. She didn't want to agree with Jackson—or her aunt Sage, for that matter, who said early on that some things needed to be left alone. Maybe it would be best to leave the past buried, but that thing inside her, that thing that drove her, wouldn't allow her to leave it alone, and that part of her would never be satisfied until she knew the truth.

As far as she could determine, the Maitlands weren't the benevolent souls that they presented to the world. They used their money and their position to manipulate a young girl and her entire family in order to save face and their precious reputation. Not to mention the deal they had made to take in her grandmother as a young girl. Those truths left a really bad taste in her mouth. And she intended to show the world who the Maitlands actually were.

She opened her laptop to check her email, and the first message was from Mark, who wanted to check on her progress and get some assurances that she was still on track for the story. He went on to remind her how important this story was to the paper.

She quickly shot off a response, letting him know that she would be meeting with Lou Ellen Maitland in the next day or two and that Kimberly Graham had invited her to the fund-raiser.

If she had any moment of hesitation about proceeding with this story, it went out the window as her determination was reignited with Mark's message.

It was too late to call the Maitland home, but she would do that first thing in the morning and lock down a time and day with the matriarch.

She took her shower, went to get a plate of food, and returned with it to her room, but even as she worked at convincing herself that her quest was in pursuit of justice and truth, she couldn't shake the sound of utter disappointment in Jackson's voice or the look of anguish in her mother's eyes.

———— ❧ ————

"Maybe Jackson is right, Z," Miranda said.

"Et tu, Brute," Zoie said half in jest.

"I'm serious. Some things aren't worth it."

"Okay. What would you do if you found out what I did about *your* family; wouldn't you want to know the truth? Tell me you wouldn't."

Miranda was quiet for a moment. "What I believe is that you should seriously think about the *real* reason this is so important to you."

"The real reason? What's that supposed to mean?"

"For years, you and your family have been at odds. Deep in your heart, you want them to embrace you, love you the way you think you need, even as all of you play this crazy game of emotional roulette. I think that underneath it all, you think that bringing this dark past to light will somehow prove to them all your worth, validate you, show them the you that has been there all along."

"That's not true," she said unconvincingly.

"Okay. That's all I have to say on the subject. So when will you be coming home?" she asked, switching subjects.

"Sometime next week. Since I clearly won't be going to the fund-raiser with Jackson, you wanna go?"

"You're going to need someone to whisper in your ear to keep you from doing something crazy. So yeah."

Zoie laughed. "Cool. Anyway, I need to head out to the Maitlands. She was very clear that I had exactly a half hour."

"Get going. Let me know when you're ready to come back. I'll book the flight and meet you at the airport."

"Thanks."

"And, Z . . . I know you don't want to, but think about what I said. Okay?"

"I will. Bye, Randi."

"Love you, too."

Zoie gathered her things and got her tote.

———— ✦ ————

Zoie pulled up to the ornate gate that shielded the Maitland mansion from the world. The home, which sat on several acres of lush land that butted against their own private lake, was once a plantation. She'd spent the better part of the evening reading everything she could find on the history of the property. Much to her disgust but not surprise, the original owners, the Maitlands' ancestors, had enslaved hundreds of Africans over several generations. The land that was now green grass, towering magnolia trees, and perfectly manicured hedges was once covered with rows of cotton, sugarcane, and corn tended to by men, women, and children brought there against their will. It was no wonder that the generations after the emancipation had worked to distance themselves from the family's ugly past. But as far as Zoie was concerned, no matter how much money they had—which they'd earned on the backs of slaves—or how much charitable work they engaged in, it would never be enough to make restitution for what the family had done. Because no matter what, they still continued to benefit from the atrocity.

She lowered her window and reached out to press the button on the intercom.

"Who is it, please?" came a disembodied voice.

"Zoie Crawford. I have an appointment with Mr. and Mrs. Maitland."

There was a faint whirring sound, and the gates slowly opened inward. Zoie eased the car down the long, winding driveway. She finally pulled to a stop in front of the palatial estate, whose grandeur remained reminiscent of *Gone with the Wind*. She was momentarily intimidated by the looming white pillars and wraparound balconies, the pristine shrubbery, and the sense of immense power that lurked behind the massive doors. She drew in a breath of resolve and reminded herself of her intent.

She grabbed her tote from the passenger seat and got out in concert with the opening of the front door.

An older woman, complete in black dress and white apron, stood in the doorway. Zoie climbed the three steps.

"Ms. Crawford, Mrs. Maitland is waiting for you on the back veranda. Follow me, please."

Zoie fought to keep her mouth from dropping open as she was led through the sprawling main level. The marble flooring, gleaming wood furnishings, sparkling chandeliers, and eye-dropping winding staircase took her breath away. The artwork that hung on the walls was worth a fortune, and even her amateur eye could detect that the paintings were all originals.

The housekeeper opened the back door to the enclosed veranda, which looked out onto a magnificent display of the lake. Ducks floated regally in the water.

"Mrs. Maitland, Ms. Crawford is here."

Lou Ellen Maitland was adorned in a pale green suit that matched her eyes. Every inch of her was perfectly detailed as if she were preparing to sit for a portrait. She sipped from a tall glass of clear liquid, and Zoie got the sense that it wasn't water.

Lou Ellen barely looked up. "Please sit, Ms. Crawford."

"Thank you for seeing me."

"Let's not waste time on small talk."

Zoie bit her tongue and moved to the empty white wicker chair opposite Lou Ellen. She settled down and took out her notebook and phone to record the conversation.

"No notes. No recording," Lou Ellen said.

Zoie started to protest but knew that it would be pointless. She drew in a breath and returned her things to her tote.

"Now what exactly do you want to know about my daughter?"

Zoie folded her hands on her lap to keep from reaching over and strangling the smug look off of the face of Lou Ellen Maitland.

"Will Mr. Maitland be joining us?"

"No."

Zoie cleared her throat. "Why don't we start with the kind of child she was, the kinds of things you noticed about her at a young age."

Lou Ellen pursed her lips. "She was no different from any other child. Kimberly walked and talked about the same age as any child her age. There was nothing particularly remarkable."

This was going to be difficult. "I read in an article that she was considered a 'change of life' baby." It was the first time that she got a reaction from Lou Ellen. Her cheeks flamed, and her lips tightened into a pucker. Zoie felt a moment of glee. "How did her birth later in your life effect the household?"

Lou Ellen lifted her chin and leveled Zoie with a hard look. "Kimberly's arrival . . . was a joy to all of us. Her brother celebrated his nineteenth birthday when Kimberly was born. Things were certainly different in the house, hearing and caring for a baby after so long. I suppose Kim's arrival made us all feel young again. Her brother absolutely doted on her."

Zoie made a mental note about Kyle's age. "I'd like to hear more about Kim's relationship with her brother. I would think that a young man would have much more on his mind than spending time with an infant."

"That was the kind of man Kyle was," Lou Ellen qualified. "He was giving and had no problem devoting his time to people and causes and especially his family."

"When Kimberly was growing up, was there ever an indication that she was interested in politics?"

"She loved whatever her brother loved."

"Even with so many years between them?"

"Kyle was a charismatic young man. He spent a lot of time with his sister. When she was old enough, he would take her places. They were very close. I'm not at all surprised that she sought a career in law and now politics."

"Did Kimberly have a lot of friends growing up? Was she interested in sports or the arts?" she asked, switching gears.

"Kim had friends, of course. She didn't engage in sports." She said the word as if it was hot sauce on her tongue. "She was much more interested in her studies and playing piano. She graduated at the top of her class in high school and college."

"Um, I see you have a housekeeper. What about when Kimberly was a child?"

Lou Ellen's nostrils flared.

"What I mean is, I know that you and your husband did a lot of . . . work in the community with committees and such, so I was wondering what role the staff may have had with Kimberly's upbringing."

"My staff did what they were paid to do, Ms. Crawford. If you are trying to imply something else, I suggest that you quickly rethink it."

Zoie swallowed and tried a different approach. "Was Kimberly born here in New Orleans? I didn't see any hospital records."

Lou Ellen blinked rapidly. Her thin lips flickered. "She was not."

"Oh. Where was she born?"

"In New York, actually. I, we were visiting there at the time."

It was the first time Zoie saw a crack in the veneer.

"I believe your time is up, Ms. Crawford." She pushed to her feet.

Zoie clasped the strap of her tote and stood. She extended her hand. "Thank you for your time."

Lou Ellen briefly shook Zoie's hand but did not return a response other than, "My housekeeper will see you out, Ms. Crawford."

Zoie forced a smile. "Enjoy your day." She turned and was surprised to see said housekeeper standing in the doorway.

She was hoping to get a glimpse of Mr. Maitland, but he was nowhere to be seen. When she got to the door, she turned to the housekeeper.

"Do you remember a Claudia Bennett who worked for the family?"

"Before my time." She opened the door and held it, waiting for Zoie to walk out.

"Thank you."

She was offered a tight, practiced smile, and the door closed before she hit the first step.

CHAPTER 20

On the ride home, Zoie replayed the very stilted interview. She was accustomed to manipulating her subjects into telling her what she wanted to know. Lou Ellen Maitland was not a typical subject. The only real time she faltered was when she was asked about where Kimberly was born. That tidbit of information was key. If it put her in New York at the time her mother was there, she was sure that was a major piece of the puzzle that she needed.

When she pulled up in front of the house, her pulse kicked up a beat when she spotted her mother sweeping the front porch. Zoie drew in a breath and climbed the steps. "Hey, Mama."

Rose glanced up from her sweeping as if she hadn't noticed that her daughter was standing there. "Hi."

"Mama, I never meant for this to hurt you."

Rose rested the broom against the side of the house. "But it did," she said as if all the vitality had been sucked from her. "Can't put the genie back in the bottle." She lowered herself into a chair in a way that was reminiscent of a woman twice her age.

"I was sweet sixteen," she began, in a voice weighed down by the burden of the past. "Mama would take me to the Maitlands' house from time to time to help out when they were hosting one of their big parties." A faraway look filled her eyes, and a story-telling quality laced her voice. "Walking through those doors opened a world I'd only seen on television and in the movies. I was mesmerized by everything in that house, and whenever I could, I would sneak and touch the soft sheets in the linen closet, the figurines on the tabletops. I could spend hours just staring at how the light danced on the crystal of the chandeliers. And I could get lost in the wonder of their library. My God, I'd never seen so many books in a house."

A wistful smile tugged at her lips. Zoie, not wanting to break the spell of her mother's story, very slowly eased into a chair opposite her mother. "Kyle Maitland fascinated me, too." Her eyes flicked for a moment at Zoie, then glanced away. "He was like a movie star, a perfect addition to the magical world he lived in. He was always sweet to me, answered all my questions, and never got annoyed at having me around." She linked her fingers tighter together. "He found me one day in the library . . ."

———————

"You know my mother has a fit if anyone is in here."

Rose turned, terrified. "Ohh, Mr. Maitland, I . . . I'm so sorry. Please . . . I'll leave."

Kyle chuckled. He held up his hands to halt her hasty escape. "It's okay. Really. I always thought it was silly to have a room full of books and no one is allowed to read them. Too many things around here are only for show," he added, and Rose heard the slight edge in his voice. "Kyle. Call me Kyle. The 'Mr.' is reserved for my father." He walked fully into the library. "So, what do you like to read?"

Every coherent thought flew from her head. Standing in front of Kyle Maitland was like looking into the sun. "Everything" was the first word that came to her mind.

Kyle walked over to a wall of books. He reached up to the third shelf and plucked out a book. It was *Narrative of the Life of Frederick Douglass*. Rose couldn't have been more surprised by his choice. Even she knew the book was about the life of a slave.

"Did you know the original Maitlands were slave owners?"

Rose swallowed. "No."

He slowly nodded. "Yes. The upstanding pillars of society played a part in the ugliest period of American history. That's our real legacy, how we built our fortune," he added. His jaw tightened, and he exhaled a breath of regret. "Anyway"—he leaned his long frame against the wall—"I must have been about twelve or thirteen, and I snuck in here." He looked at her and winked, and Rose felt her heart tumble in her chest. "I found a book about our family." He moved over to another wall of books and removed a worn leather-bound volume and came to the rectangular cherrywood table that took up the center of the room.

"Come. Sit."

Rose snatched a quick look at the open door.

"Don't worry. They've gone out for the morning. Some charity event. Sit."

Hesitantly, she obeyed.

The gold lettering on the front of the volume was faded but clear enough to make out the title *Maitland 1840–*.

Kyle opened the heavy cover. The first page was the Maitland family tree, which traced back to the origins of the family in England and continued on to their arrival in New Orleans in 1840 and right up to the birth of Kyle.

He flipped through the pages, stopping at times to elaborate on a particular family member. He finally stopped on a page that looked like an invoice. What it happened to be, however, was an itemized list of Africans that had been purchased by Aaron Maitland. There were several more pages of "invoices" that detailed the purchases of human beings.

Kyle turned to another page, and there were several grainy sepia-toned photographs of rows of shacks fronted by lines of black men, women, and children. "These shacks used to be out back. Since torn down." He heaved a sigh. "Doesn't erase what once stood there."

Rose felt such a tightness in her chest that she could hardly breathe. She wanted to get up and run away from this man who had a legacy of brutality and lack of regard for human life running through his veins. But then he said something that held her in place.

"The day I found this book, it changed my life, my entire outlook on the world, my family. I knew I couldn't erase what my family had done to generations of innocent people, but I could at least try to set a new direction, and hopefully one day the legacy that I leave behind will somehow dim what came before me."

"How can you do that?" she asked, finally finding her voice.

He closed the book. "Community work, getting involved in furthering the equal rights of everyone, voting rights in particular." He paused. "Getting into elected office."

Rose's eyes widened. "Like a senator?"

Kyle chuckled. "Not right away. I'll start off local."

He went on to tell her of his plans, the vision that he had of making life better. Rose wasn't sure if it was then or during the many talks they continued to have that she fell in love with him.

"It was naïve, you know," Rose said, looking at her daughter. "He was a man already, a white man, son of one of the wealthiest families in New Orleans. But I couldn't help how I felt. Whenever I was at the house and could slip away, we met in the library and would talk and laugh, and he wanted to know everything about me and my family. When we . . . for the first time . . . it seemed like the most natural thing in the world."

Rose lowered her eyes, suddenly ashamed. "It was only one time. How cliché. I was terrified and excited all at once. I was in love with this wonderful progressive, color-blind man, and I knew he would do the right thing, but that didn't stop me from hiding it from Mama, until I couldn't."

Rose blinked back tears as she recalled the day Claudia pushed open the bathroom door and saw her daughter's protruding belly.

"I'll never forget the look on her face—the horror, the shame, the knowing." Rose slowly shook her head. "I insisted that we loved each other, and it was the first and only time Mama ever hit me." Reflectively, she cupped her cheek.

"You silly little girl. That white boy don't love you, and even if he swears by all the saints that he does, he cain't. You think that family gon' smile and grin about having a colored daughter-in-law and a half-breed baby? Kyle is dey golden boy, and dey ain't gon' let nothin' tarnish that gold. Nothin'!"

Rose twisted and untwisted, between her fingers, a piece of fabric from the skirt of her floral dress. "Mama did what folks did back then when a girl winds up in 'the family way.' She sent me away. No conversation. No tears. Put me on a bus to New York. Went to live with 'cousin' Phyllis. At least Mama said she was a cousin. I never asked from which side of the family. Cousin Phyllis got me into a special Catholic school for girls in . . . my situation."

Rose sighed deeply. "I was alone, away from everything and everyone that I knew. I was so scared. Instead of those days being happy, they were some of the worst days of my life. I couldn't enjoy the life growing inside me because of the uncertainty of my future and the fact that I was alienated from my family."

"Mama, I'm so sorry."

"Nothing you did. All started long before you."

"Did you try to stay in touch with Kyle?"

"I wrote letters, but I never heard a word from him ever again."

"I don't understand. Nana sent you away to have the baby, so what happened when you gave birth?"

"My last month was really bad. I was so sick, big as a house, feet so swollen I could barely walk. The school was affiliated with a Catholic hospital. I was admitted, and to tell you the truth, those days in the hospital are still a blur. I was on so many medications, I didn't know if I was coming or going. I vaguely remember the sound of buzzers going off and bodies rushing around my bed.

Then nothing. I guess they must have given me a sedative. When I came to, Mama was sitting at my bedside . . ."

———————

"Mama . . ."

Claudia reached over and covered her daughter's hand with her own. "You gon' be alright. You just need to rest."

"My baby . . ."

Claudia lowered her eyes then looked at her daughter. "I'm sorry, chile. Yo' baby didn't make it."

"There are no words to explain the pain I felt in my soul." She pressed her fist to her chest. "To lose a child . . ." Her eyes filled. Tears slid down her cheeks.

Zoie's heart twisted in her chest. She could not begin to imagine what her mother had endured or the emotional scars that she still carried.

"So they told you the baby died," Zoie said softly, as she tried to process the enormity of the lie.

Rose nodded. "I had no reason not to believe my mother. And I had no reason not to believe her when she told me that going back home would not look good, that I was to stay in New York, and that the Maitlands had generously agreed to pay for my college. I figured, at the time, that it was their way of paying us off for what happened.

"Mama insisted that going to college in New York was a wonderful opportunity, and I now had a chance that none of her other children had."

The screen door opened, and Sage stepped out, followed by Hyacinth, who was leaning heavily on her cane.

Sage glanced from one teary-eyed face to the other. "Guess she told ya," Sage said to Zoie.

Zoie sniffed and nodded her head.

Sage heaved a heavy sigh before helping her sister into a cushioned chair. "That family done caused so much hurt," she said stoically. " 'Bout ruined this family, caused a rift between us sisters for years."

Zoie frowned, not understanding.

"Resented Rose. Didn't understand why it was her that got the glory for doing wrong."

Rose's gaze jumped to her sister.

"I knew you was knocked up. Could see it in your face long before Mama found out. Humph. Then you get sent away." She shook her head and puckered her lips. "What else could it be? Just never figured it was that Maitland boy."

"No one ever questioned Kimberly's birth, her mother's pregnancy?" Zoie asked, amazed that a secret that big could be kept.

"There might have been someone who knew or suspected. *We* never knew. We didn't travel in the same circles."

"Grease the right hands," Hyacinth said and chuckled. "Make things go away."

Zoie knew that to be true. But were they powerful enough to make records disappear? "There has to be some record of the birth," Zoie said.

"There is. I was given a birth and death certificate when I left the hospital. Unnamed baby girl."

Zoie squeezed her eyes shut in disbelief.

"Now maybe you understand why we was so hard on you," Sage said to her niece. "Why your mama held on so tight."

Zoie looked over at her mother and reached out for her hand. Rose slipped her hand into her daughter's. "I'll make this right, Mama."

"Best leave it alone. It's enough to know the truth," Sage advised.

"That family has gotten away with too much, hurt too many people, and it's time the world saw them for who they really are."

CHAPTER 21

Zoie pulled her rollaboard behind her as she wound her way around the disembarking passengers at LaGuardia Airport, all headed for the exit. She pushed through the revolving doors and stepped out to the passenger pickup section. She walked to the curb, took out her cell phone, and dialed Miranda.

"Hey, girl. I'm here."

"Be there in a minute. Had to drive around in circles. You know they don't let you sit and wait. Coming back around now."

"See you in few." She disconnected the call and waited, taking in the hustle and bustle of being back in New York. The energy was palpable, and the presence of armed military and patrolling police were vividly evident and would be much the same when she got back to Lower Manhattan, where she lived.

Since 9/11, as it was now officially called, security had been tightened almost to a point of suffocation. But the country was willing to relinquish levels of its privacy and freedoms in order to feel safe again.

A short horn blow drew her attention, and she waved when she spotted Miranda pulling up to the curb in her white Lexus. The trunk popped open, and then Miranda got out and came around to meet her friend.

"Welcome home," Miranda greeted, and the friends embraced in a tight hug.

"Good to be back."

Zoie loaded her bag in the trunk, and they got in the car.

"So how was the family when you left?"

Zoie blew out a breath. "Taking it in stride. My Aunt Sage had an idea of what had happened but never knew for sure. My mother is still numb with the idea that the child she thought was dead isn't."

"Hmm, I can't even imagine."

"If I wasn't in the middle of it, I wouldn't either. But I swear, you can't make this stuff up. Bottom line is that the Maitland family used their wealth and position to manipulate my family, rob my mother of being a mother, and who the hell knows what else—all to save their family name."

Miranda shook her head with sadness. "Now what?"

"The family basically wants me to leave it alone. Too many years have passed. Too much loss and hurt."

"But of course you don't feel the same way."

"I want to get to the bottom of it. I want them to own up to what they've done, and I want Kimberly Maitland to know who she really is."

Miranda was quiet as she maneuvered along the Grand Central Parkway.

"What? Say what's on your mind," Zoie said, reading her friend's silence for what it really was.

Miranda snatched a quick look at Zoie. "Fine. I have to agree with your family, Z. I really don't think any good can come of it. And telling Kimberly Graham . . ." She shook her head. "You could ruin her entire life."

Zoie defiantly folded her arms. "How about the lives that her family ruined?" She huffed. "It just makes me so angry."

"I get the anger. But I think part of that anger is that you feel personally deceived by your grandmother," Miranda said softly.

Zoie tightened her lips. She stared out of the passenger window. "There's that, too," she quietly confessed. "The woman I thought I knew would never take a payoff for her own child."

"You don't know all of the circumstances. You need to remember when this was, what the climate was in the South. I mean, let's be for real: mixing the races was actually illegal in parts of the South."

"I know . . ."

"Maybe your grandmother did what mothers have been doing since the beginning of time, protecting her young." She offered Zoie a tight-lipped smile.

Damn, she hated it when Miranda was right.

⇒•◄

Jackson hung up the phone. His conversation with Lou Ellen Maitland had been anything but cordial. In essence, she'd threatened him. True, she'd done what she'd agreed, but now it came with a price. She made it perfectly clear that if Zoie printed one disparaging word about the Maitland family or anything at all that could potentially hurt Kimberly, not only would she sue, but she would pull her funding from the Horizon Housing Complex project. Then, in true Lou Ellen Maitland fashion, she pleasantly wished him a good day.

He flopped back in his seat and ran his hand across his head in frustration. He knew that once Zoie dug her heels in, there was no pulling her out. Their last conversation had made that clear, and he had no doubts whatsoever that Lou Ellen would make good on her "promise."

No good deed goes unpunished, as his mother always said. He didn't quite know what that meant until now. He'd thought he was helping when he stepped in and put in a word with Lou Ellen on Zoie's behalf. Truth was, he was angling for points with Zoie. Now that had all backfired, and he was caught in the middle.

He had a more immediate problem, because he knew Zoie would press forward. But the Maitland money was the cornerstone of the project. Without their funding, the development would come to a standstill, and all the promises made to the community would be broken and lives thrown into chaos. To complicate matters further, if the Maitlands pulled out, it would make it that much harder or impossible to get another backer of their caliber.

"Can't be that bad."

Jackson looked up to see Lennox standing in the doorway. "Hey, man," he said half-hearted.

"What's up?" Lennox stepped in.

"Close the door."

"That doesn't sound good," he said while closing the door.

"It's not. We have a problem."

Lennox sat down, and Jackson went on to explain the untenable position they were in.

"Shit," he sputtered. "We can't let that happen."

"That I know. But at the moment I have no clue what to do about it."

"I do. You need to tell Zoie to back off."

Jackson shot him a look. "We're talking about Zoie, remember."

"What choice do we have? We can't let her implode this project. We have too much on the line—the buyers and not to mention the crew. If Maitland pulls the money, we are royally screwed."

"We're going to have to look for new investors."

"Easier said than done. The whole country is still reeling from the Trade Center attack, and money is tight all over. Investors are scared."

"I know," he said on a breath. "But we have to try."

"You need to talk to Zoie. Make her understand what's at stake here."

"She's back in New York."

"For good?"

"I don't think so. She's there for a fund-raiser for Kimberly Maitland."

"Right. The event you were *disinvited* to."

"You're making me feel better by the minute," he snarked.

"Being real, brother. But the fact remains, we can't let her mess this up for us. Simple as that."

"Yeah, if only it was that simple."

—————

Kimberly stood in front of the full-length mirror and slowly turned to see how her cocktail dress fit. The sleeveless, teal-colored dress, which brought out the gray-green of her eyes, had a tight bodice that dipped just enough in the front to be alluring without giving too much away, then gently hugged her hips and stopped just above the knee. But it was the detail on the fabric that was the real showstopper. Hand-sewn rhinestones encrusted the bodice and made the dress shimmer in the light.

"You look stunning."

Kimberly whirled around with a bright smile. "I have to keep up if I'm going to be with the most handsome man in the room." She walked over and into Rowan's embrace.

"This is your big night. I'm just arm candy," he teased.

Kimberly laughed. "Candy that I wouldn't mind having a taste of," she cooed.

Rowan stroked the faint cleft in her chin. "I'm going to hold you to that," he said and kissed her lightly on the mouth. "When we get home. Now we need to get you to your event. The car is waiting, and Farrah said the girls are ready."

"Promise me one thing," she said, gripping his large hand.

"Anything."

"Don't leave my side."

Rowan winked. "You got it."

They walked to the door.

"You know, it almost feels . . . sacrilegious having this big swanky event when mass destruction is only a few miles away," Kimberly said.

Rowan slipped his arm around her waist. "That's even more reason why tonight is important. We get to remind people that we will not be intimidated and that we are resilient. Most of all, that you are the person who will be there for them."

She glanced up at him with love flowing from her eyes. "You want to give up that technology stuff you do and be my front man?" She adjusted his bow tie.

Rowan chuckled. "Never in front, baby. Always at your side."

She linked her arm through his and said a silent prayer that the anxious sensation that continued to bubble in her stomach was only a sign of nervous excitement and nothing more.

CHAPTER 22

"I know you're not going to walk right up to her and say, 'Oh, by the way, did you know that you have a half sister—me?'" Miranda said as she leaned toward the mirror and applied her lipstick.

"I am a bit more subtle than that," Zoie said, wiggling into the black dress that she'd borrowed from Miranda.

Miranda peeked her reflection in the mirror. "Fits perfectly."

"Yeah, and a good thing, too. You know this"—she ran her hands down her sides—"is so not my thing."

"Every now and then, a girl needs to dress up." She turned away from the mirror.

"In my line of work, casual works best."

"But doesn't it feel good?" Miranda said. "Look at yourself. I mean the only semi-fancy thing you had in your closet was the dress you wore to your grandmother's funeral. That. Is. Sad."

"Very funny." She smoothed the dress along her hips and looked at herself from the side, and for a hot minute, she wondered what Jackson would think if he saw her. She inhaled deeply and pushed thoughts of Jackson aside. "Ready?" Miranda asked.

"Yes." She picked up her—also borrowed—rectangular, beaded

clutch from the dresser and dropped her cell phone inside, along with a pen and mini notepad. She snapped the lock shut. "Let's do this."

———❖———

There was a line of cars in the queue to be parked when Zoie and Miranda pulled up in front of the Grand Meridian Hotel.

"Fancy," Miranda said, adding a bit of spice to the two syllables.

The Lexus was met by a red-jacketed valet who helped them from the car, handed them a ticket, took Miranda's keys, and pulled off in a flash.

"Fancy," Zoie repeated, mimicking her friend.

They followed the flowing crowd along the short path into the main lobby of the hotel and were met at the glittering entrance by one of several hostesses who directed them to the ballroom. Their names were checked at the door, and they were directed to their table.

The ballroom was nearly full, complete with a Who's Who of the Manhattan elite—Wall Street tycoons, political figures, socialites, and several faces that Zoie recognized from television—and, of course, there was the press.

"I feel like a stepchild," Miranda whispered. "Did you see Hamilton Forster and his wife? He was just in the last *Furious* movie."

"There is definitely some of everybody here tonight," Zoie said while slowly scanning the crowd. "I don't see the lady of the hour."

"Probably waiting to make an entrance. Oh, look there's Congressman Reynolds, and isn't that the anchor from NBC talking to him?"

"Yes. Stephanie Voss. Excuse me for a minute. I'm going to say hello." She pushed her chair back, stood, and began to wind her way around bodies and tables—and nearly ran into a waiter when she spotted Jackson standing by the entrance.

Her body vibrated. She tried to remember what they'd argued about, and why he wasn't on her arm tonight. But she couldn't get her thoughts in order. The shock of seeing him unraveled her resolve. He was simply gorgeous.

Jackson turned his head, and his gaze landed right on her. Air stuck in her chest.

A waiter passed, and she snatched a glass of champagne from the tray, took a sip, and walked straight for him.

Zoie stood solidly in front of him. She lifted her chin and looked him right in the eye. "What are you doing here, Jackson? How . . ."

His dark eyes roved over her like the hands of a masseuse and set off every nerve ending in her body. She concentrated on breathing.

"You look . . . incredible," he whispered in awe. He reached out and stroked her bare arm.

Electricity shimmied down the curve of her spine. She ran her tongue across her bottom lip. "You didn't answer me."

"I came for you."

Her breath hitched. "How did you even get in?"

"Pulled a few strings. Z, we need to talk."

"I kind of thought you didn't have anything else to say to me after our last conversation," she said, her tone tinged with a sprinkle of hope.

"Some things have happened."

"Like what?"

"I need you to really think about what you're doing, Z. I'm asking you to let this go."

"Did my family send you?"

"No. They don't even know I'm here."

"I'm doing my job. Being here is part of that job, Jax."

"Z, all I'm asking is that you let go of your theory."

"Theory!" Her voice rose and caught the attention of several guests nearby. She lowered her head. "This is not a theory, Jackson. You saw what I saw. I put the pieces together. My mother and my aunts confirmed everything. What they did, what those people did to my family . . ." Her voice cracked.

Jackson put his arm around her waist and ushered her out of the ballroom.

Zoie rapidly blinked away the tears that threatened to overflow.

Jackson ushered her down the hall and away from prying eyes and ears.

"You don't understand, Jackson." Her voice wobbled with an emotion that she couldn't identify.

"Then explain it to me, baby. What do you hope to accomplish?"

She pressed her lips tightly together. "The truth. It's as simple as that. The truth."

A flurry of activity at the ballroom entrance drew their attention. Kimberly Graham and her family had arrived.

When she turned to smile and greet a constituent who had come up to her, Zoie caught her first real look at Kimberly, and the effect was surreal. The eyes, the shape of her face, the dimple in her chin. She was the image of her mother—her *real* mother, except that her skin was the color of vanilla bean, instead of cinnamon. Zoie's hands shook.

Jackson caught the look of shock that had frozen Zoie's expression. He glanced over his shoulder. All he caught was Kimberly's back. Her husband, flanked by their children, escorted her inside.

"That's . . . her," Zoie whispered. "She looks like a young version of Mama," she said in awe.

"Zoie . . ."

She brushed past him and went inside.

Jackson slid his hands into the pocket of his tuxedo slacks, waited a moment, and followed Zoie.

———— ◦•◦ ————

Kimberly was immediately surrounded by the mélange that vied for her attention. Zoie stood off to the side and watched the way she moved and smiled, the way her eyes crinkled in the corner, the way her neck arched when she laughed.

She moved seamlessly among the guests, offering a word or two to everyone she met. Zoie noted that she included her husband and daughters in each introduction, and she almost smiled as she watched the twins charm the guests. They looked more like their father, Zoie thought.

"Hey, where did you go? I thought you were going to talk to that anchor woman," Miranda said, sidling up next to her.

"Jackson's here," she said, without taking her eyes off of Kimberly.

"Say what? *Your* Jackson?"

"He's not *my* Jackson."

"If you say so. But what is he doing here?"

"To try to talk me out of confronting Kimberly Graham with what I know about who she really is."

"Hmm, I don't know Jackson, but you know where I stand on this."

Zoie cut her a look. "Thanks."

"So where is he?"

"I left him in the hall—"

Jackson walked up to Kimberly, and they shook hands. She went through her introductions, and Zoie could see, even at this distance, that Jackson was doing that thing he does when he meets anyone—mesmerizing them with his heartbreaking smile and the smooth, southern timber of his voice. He didn't stand out simply because he was one of less than a handful of black men among hundreds of his white counterparts. He was breathtaking to look at. Period.

"Who. Is. That? The hunk talking to her?" Miranda asked, practically salivating.

"Jackson."

"Oh, damn, girl. And you couldn't find a way to work that out? I forgive him for whatever it was you claimed he did to you years ago—'cause we both know how you are. Humph, humph, humph."

Zoie threw her a withering stare. "Would you stop! And for your information, it takes more than good looks and sex appeal."

"It does?"

"Whose side are you on anyway?"

Miranda made a face and took a sip of her drink. "So now what?"

"I'm going to do what I came here to do: introduce myself and interview Kimberly Graham."

Miranda placed a warning hand on Zoie's arm. "Let that be all, Z. This is not the place for a full confession. Please."

"I'll behave. Promise."

Kimberly finally moved away from the group that had corralled her and walked with her family to her table at the front and center of the ballroom. But Zoie's focus was on Jackson. No matter how hard she tried to dismiss what she still felt every time she saw him, she couldn't. He still made her heart race, still made her skin tingle, still made her want him. But she could not let her complicated feelings about Jackson deter her from what she needed to do.

No one seemed to understand why this was so important to her, why she was compelled to get to the seed of every story. There were many nights, sleeping alone, that she had asked herself the same question. It all came back to her, all the holes that she felt in her life. Her insecurities in her own family, that disconnect. She filled all those spaces by finding answers in the lives of others to supplement her own. For a while, it would help; it would salve her wounded spirit. And then the fire in her belly would get lit again, burning off the salve, opening the hole.

She drew in a breath of resolve. "I'll meet you back at the table." Before Miranda could protest, Zoie crossed the room and headed in the direction of Kimberly's table, being sure to steer clear of a last-minute block by Jackson.

Miranda saw Jackson move in Zoie's direction. She had no idea what would happen but didn't think it would be good. She made a beeline toward him and was able to halt his progress midway.

"Hi," she said, placing a hand on his arm.

He turned his head and looked at Miranda. The intensity of his eyes, the up-close smooth chocolate of his skin and his sexy scent made her catch her breath. A slow, curious smile moved across his mouth. His dark eyes crinkled in the corners.

"Do I know you?"

"Not exactly."

He tipped his head to the side in a silent question.

Miranda stuck out her hand. "Miranda. Zoie's best friend."

His thick brows rose a fraction as he shook her hand. "Nice to meet you, Miranda. Did Zoie send you?" he asked with a spark of humor in his voice.

"No, she didn't." She smiled.

"Hmm. Can I get you a refill of your drink?"

"Sure. Thank you."

He placed a light hand at the small of her back and guided her toward the open bar.

⟐

By the time Zoie reached Kimberly's table, the children were seated, her husband had stepped away, and Kimberly was in conversation with a woman whom Zoie concluded was the nanny.

She waited a moment, then walked over.

"Good evening," she stuck out her hand. "I'm Zoie Crawford."

Kimberly turned her fixed sunshine smile on Zoie, and for a

split second her eyes widened and her smile faltered. She shook Zoie's hand. "I feel like I know you already, Ms. Crawford. I'm happy you could make it. How was your flight from New Orleans?"

"Fine. I got in last night. I know this isn't the best time to talk, but I wanted to introduce myself."

"I can make some time tonight, and then we can pick things up at my office on Monday," she graciously offered.

Zoie felt the volcano rumbling in her gut, and she felt the hot lava rise against her will. It spewed out before she could stop it.

"Do you remember Claudia Bennett?"

Kimberly's smile faltered for a moment. A slight line drew her brows together. "Claudia Bennett?"

"Yes. Do you remember her?"

"If it's the same person, she was our housekeeper when I was a little girl. Why?"

"She was my grandmother."

"Oh my, what a coincidence." She pressed her hand to her chest and laughed lightly.

"You have her eyes."

"I beg your pardon."

"You have her eyes, my grandmother's eyes . . . my mother's eyes."

Kimberly's cheeks flushed crimson. "I don't know what you're getting at—"

"She was your grandmother. Her daughter, Rose, is your real mother—*my* mother."

Rowan appeared at her side and put his arm around her waist, then looked from one to the other. "Something wrong, sweetheart?" He turned his focus on Zoie.

Kimberly's throat worked for a moment before words finally came out. "Um, this is the reporter, Ms. Crawford."

"Oh, pleasure to meet you, Ms. Crawford." He smiled broadly and extended his hand, which Zoie shook.

"You as well," Zoie said.

"My wife has been telling me you will be doing some reporting on her and her campaign."

"Yes, that's the assignment."

He hugged his wife close and kissed her lightly on the temple. "Well, you couldn't have picked anyone more deserving, and I'm not saying that because I'm prejudiced," he said with a smile of pure love and pride.

"I think so too, Mr. Graham." She pushed out a breath. "Well, I'll let you get back to your family, and I'll see you on Monday at your office, Mrs. Graham." She smiled and nodded her good-byes.

As she walked back to her table, her heart beat so fast she thought she might faint. What had she done? Once the words were out, she couldn't stop herself even as she saw the look of horror and disbelief wash over Kimberly's face. *You can't put the genie back in the bottle.*

She made it to her table only to find it filled with everyone except Miranda. She scanned the room and caught a glimpse of Miranda—talking with Jackson near the bar. She needed to get out of there. She drew in a breath to calm her vibrating body and walked over to where Jackson and Miranda stood, chatting like old friends.

———⋗◆⋖———

"I see you two have met," Zoie said, sounding more relaxed than she felt.

"Jackson was telling me about the work he's doing in New Orleans. Pretty impressive stuff."

Her gaze slid over to Jackson, who stared back from above the rim of his tumbler of bourbon. "Yes. Very." She turned back to Miranda. "I'm ready to go," she said softly, avoiding Jackson's pointed gaze.

"But the evening hasn't even started. Don't you want to hear the guest speaker?"

"I already have."

Miranda hesitated a second. "Well . . . okay. I was really looking forward to the stringy chicken that they always serve at these things," she said, the words laced with sarcasm. "Really nice to meet you—finally," she said to Jackson.

"You, too." He looked at Zoie. "Good to see you, Zoie," he said softly.

Zoie swallowed. "You too. Good night, Jackson." She spun away and headed toward the exit, with Miranda a step behind.

"What the hell is wrong with you?" Miranda spat from between her teeth. "What did you say to her, and you really better explain what Jackson did that was so horrible 'cause he sure isn't the man you made him out to be."

Zoie stopped short and whirled around. "You know what, you stay. I can get a cab."

"Now you're just being bitchy. What is wrong with you? Talk to me."

Zoie blinked rapidly to stave off the burn of tears. "Can we just go?" she pleaded. Her voice cracked.

Miranda stared at her friend in alarm, then linked her arm through Zoie's. "Yeah, let's get out of here."

CHAPTER 23

Zoie had an apartment in Lower Manhattan on the East Side, a solid half-hour drive from the venue. She was stoically quiet for the entire ride, spending the time staring out of the window.

"Z," Miranda said as they approached the turn onto Zoie's street, "no matter what, I'm your friend. Whatever it is, you can tell me. So what if I judge you and don't agree with half the shit you do? That's what real friends are for."

Zoie rolled her eyes and twisted her lips to keep from smiling. If nothing else, she could always rely on Randi for a bitter spoonful of truth.

Miranda pulled the car to a stop in front of Zoie's building and turned off the engine.

"It's still early, and I'm starved. I know you were feining for that gala chicken, but we can order pizza or Chinese or something," she said by way of apology.

"Only if I get to choose."

"Fine."

⟫◈⟪

"You feel like talking now?" Miranda asked once the food had arrived.

They sat in Zoie's small kitchen with six white containers in front of them.

Zoie opened the lo mein, then the shrimp fried rice, and piled both on her plate. "She looks like my mother," she said softly. "It was like looking at my mother if she was white."

"What did you say to her?"

"After pleasantries . . ." She swirled lo mein around on her plate. "I asked her if she knew Claudia Bennett?"

"You did what? Z, you promised."

"I promised that I wouldn't cause a scene, and I didn't . . . not exactly."

Miranda shook her head. "So then what?"

"It took her a minute . . . and then I let it slip that Claudia was her grandmother, and that her daughter Rose was my mother *and* hers. I told her she had her grandmother's and her mother's eyes."

"You didn't! So what did she say? How did she look?"

"She looked like she thought I was crazy and that she might faint. Her husband showed up like on cue, and the conversation was cut short."

"Damnit, Z." Miranda shook her head.

"I'm sure she doesn't believe me."

Miranda had no words.

Zoie glanced across the table and registered the look of disappointment in her friend's expression. "No comment?"

"What do you want me to say, Z? You want me to give you a rah-rah, go-girl high five?"

"Say what's on your mind. You always do."

Miranda put down her fork and linked her fingers together. She looked Zoie straight in the eyes. "What you did, Zoie, was wrong on so many levels. Kimberly Graham isn't the root of the problem. She's a much a victim as anyone. She didn't do any of this. It was done to her as well. She has a life and a family, for Christ's sake."

"And what about my family?" she lamely shot back. "Don't they count? What about what was done to them? Huh?"

Miranda snorted a laugh. "Funny how your family is so important to you now. This time last month you couldn't stand them and dreaded the idea of having to spend any time with them."

Zoie pushed back from the table. "You have no idea what my life has been like. Not really," she said, her tone softening. "For the better part of my life, my aunts and my mother made me feel unwelcomed, unnecessary, and it was all because of what the Maitlands did. My aunts blamed my mother for having a better life and resented her, and in turn, they resented me. Whatever love my mother may have had for me dried up when my father walked out. The only one who seemed to give a damn about me was my grandmother."

"And who you're really pissed off at is your grandmother. You can't reconcile the fact that she deceived you. But this is bigger than just you, Zoie. The ones you should be going after are Lou Ellen and Franklin Maitland. They seemed to have orchestrated everything."

"Untouchable. If nothing else, Kimberly deserves to know the truth."

"Does she?"

Zoie glanced away. "Yes."

Miranda shook her head. "You can't go through life acting out on your hurt, Z. Do you know that Jackson is still in love with you?"

She jerked her head toward Miranda. Her nostrils flared, and she bit down on her bottom lip.

Miranda continued: "He is, always has been. He told me what happened—his version—and he admits that he should have been there for you when you were dealing with the nonsense from your family, but you never made it easy. You ran him away. I think that underneath this hardened exterior, you're terrified of being loved 'cause you're scared as hell. You spent the better part of your life behind your make-believe wall and hoped that no one would get to the other side . . . You figure if you hurt them first, they can't hurt you."

Zoie sniffed. "Even if you're right, it's too late now," she said glumly. "The proverbial cat is out of the bag. And I still have a job to do. A job that's still important to me."

Miranda spread her fingers on the table. She exhaled a long breath. "At least don't treat her like the enemy. She doesn't deserve that, and I think you know it."

Zoie sighed heavily and twisted her lips. "What else did Jackson say?" she asked softly.

"We talked about the work he's doing, the stuff I already told you and . . . he admitted his feelings for you, and that he wished he could do some things over, but he is accepting the idea that it's finally over between you two." She paused. "Is it?"

"I don't know," she admitted. "Right now, I don't know much of anything."

CHAPTER 24

Jackson slid the card key into the slot of his hotel room door and stepped into the semi-darkness. He pulled off his tuxedo jacket and tossed it on a chair, tugged off his tie and tossed that as well.

The evening hadn't gone the way he'd hoped. His sole purpose in getting Lou Ellen to arrange for him to be there was to try to talk some sense into Zoie. True, he had his own selfish reasons for trying to talk her out of digging up more dirt—and, more important, printing it, which would have a domino effect that Zoie wasn't even thinking about.

But one look at Kimberly's demeanor after Zoie left, and he knew she'd dropped one of her bombshells.

That relentless, obsessive tunnel vision that drove Zoie was the wedge that had pulled them apart. In her work, those traits were admirable, needed, but in a relationship they were lethal, and Zoie had never been able to separate the two. She *was* her work. The work was her. It was as if what she did validated her as a person.

He walked over to the bar and picked out a hotel-sized bottle of bourbon and filled the tumbler.

He'd planned to stay for the weekend in the silly hope that maybe things could work out with Zoie and they could spend some time together before he had to get back to work. But it was past time for him to move on. Rationally, he understood that; it was his gut that said otherwise. Hopefully, the airline wouldn't want one of his kidneys when he changed his flight.

After he made his flight change without too much of a hassle, he realized that he wasn't in the least bit tired. It was barely ten.

He got up from the side chair and dug in his suitcase for a change of clothes. Maybe a walk in the night air would do him some good.

It had been a few years since he'd been to New York. The last time was maybe three years earlier for a business meeting. He'd hoped to "accidentally" run into Zoie then, but that never happened. He probably could have orchestrated it better if he'd had an idea of where she lived. But he didn't.

He put on his jacket over his cotton pullover and jeans, grabbed his phone and room card key, and walked out.

The Manhattan streets were in transition from winter to spring, a time of year when you could expect snow as easily as see flowers budding and trees beginning to bloom.

There was a slight chill in the air, but the vibrancy that he remembered was still present. Yellow cabs still hurled themselves through the streets, pedestrians walked against the lights, illumination twinkled from windows and late-night cafes. Yet there was a pallor that dulled the colors. The voices were muted and the harried pedestrians walked with a new pace, one tempered with apprehension.

He found himself drawn to the place that forever altered America's view of itself and the world. As he came closer to where the center of commerce once stood, he was overcome by the incomprehensible destruction that spread before him.

Giant craters were filled with debris, and huge cranes, like prehistoric beasts, were silhouetted against the night. Local businesses that had not been destroyed were umbrellaed by rows of scaffolding. Armed military patrolled the grounds, which were roped off with miles of yellow tape juxtaposed against row after row after row of handmade memorials of flowers, letters, cards, balloons, and photos of the lost.

The emotion that flooded him was a visceral pain, an emptiness so profound that it weakened his knees and stung his eyes. There were others like him who'd come out of curiosity or to pay homage.

The reverent silence was palpable, punctuated only by soft sobs and softer voices.

It was in that moment that he fully understood Zoie's need to know, to understand, to tell. As he stood there, his anger, his sadness demanded answers for this atrocity because what lay in waste before him defied explanation.

Even months later, the air here was different. The scent of incineration, dust, ash, flesh, chemical fumes, buried cries, and dying hope hung like a specter above them. It was one thing to watch from hundreds of miles away behind the safety of the television screen or to see the images in the newspaper and magazines and imagine what the people directly impacted felt. But to stand here made it real in ways that the media could not.

He spent a few more minutes, then slowly turned and headed back toward his hotel, even though the last thing he wanted to be was alone at the moment. He passed a bar, stopped, turned back, and went inside.

The bar was dark, noisy, and bustling with business—just what he needed. A basketball game was being shown on two large-screen televisions, and it appeared that the room was evenly split on their favorites. He found an empty seat at the far end of the bar.

It took a while for the bartender to get to him over the din and the waiting customers.

"Sorry about the wait," she shouted over a burst of cheers. She wiped down the space in front of him with a damp white cloth, then placed a bowl of trail mix in front of him. "Short-handed tonight. What can I get you?"

"Bourbon on the rocks. And, uh, do you have a menu?"

"Sure do." She pulled one out from beneath the bar and placed it in front of him. "Burgers are the house specialty, but I prefer the buffalo wings." She smiled, and her dimples deepened.

"I'll take your suggestion. Make it a double order with fries. I just realized how hungry I am."

"I'll put a rush on it." She smiled again and hurried away.

Jackson followed her with his eyes and then got distracted by the roar that shook the room.

"Lively crowd," he said to her when she returned with his drink.

"The regulars. There's always some game or the other on. Guess it helps everybody feel . . . normal. Ya know?"

"Yeah," he murmured.

She angled her head to the side. "Don't think I've seen you in here before."

"You wouldn't have. From out of town."

She rested her elbows on the counter. "Hmm, let me guess, somewhere south of New York," she teased.

Jackson chuckled. "You're very good."

"What part?"

"Nawlins."

"Shoulda known. Next drink is on the house." She winked and walked down the length of the bar.

Jackson took his time with his meal, and in between he got his refill and a stop-and-go conversation with the bartender, whose name was Lindsay. She was a last-year psychology major. She said working at the bar gave her great case-study material.

"I guess you must see all kinds of people come through here." He picked up a steak fry and chewed slowly.

Pretty much. "So what do you do in the Big Easy?"

"Land development. Housing mostly."

"Your business, or you work for a corporation?"

"Mine—well, mine and my business partner, Lennox. Started it about eight years ago with rehab, then selling properties, and eventually we secured a bid to put up a row of town houses." He reached for his drink and finished it off.

"Impressive. Is that what're you working on now?"

He pushed out a breath. "Yeah. Don't know for how much longer."

"Oh, why is that?"

"It's complicated. Financing mostly."

"Sorry. So, um, if you don't mind me asking; if your project is having problems, what are you doing all the way up here?"

"My intention was to meet a friend and work out some . . . things."

She grinned. "Oh, *that* kind of friend. How'd it go?"

"Not the way I planned."

"Sorry." She leaned on the bar. "It's gotta be hard, you living in New Orleans and she's up here."

"It's complicated. She's a reporter. Went to journalism school at Columbia and stayed."

"That's why you guys . . . had your problems?"

"Started before she left," he admitted, finding it easy to talk to Lindsay, a stranger.

"Long distance can be hard under the best of circumstances, and if there are issues." She gave a conciliatory shrug. "You said she was a reporter, right? My brother is a reporter. How crazy is that?"

"Wow. Yeah, she was working on an extensive series on the Twin Towers. Maybe you read it."

"Probably. What paper?"

"Hmm." He frowned, tried to remember. "*Recorder*, I think."

"The *National Recorder*?"

His expression brightened. "Yeah, yeah, that's it."

"Get out! That's where Brian works—my brother." She shook her head. "He told me the other night that he was working on the World Trade Center series, change in direction from his boss. Crazy." She blinked slowly. "A reporter named Zoie Crawford had started the series of articles."

Jackson frowned. "You know Zoie?"

"Not exactly. I know *of* her."

"From her work, coming in the bar?"

"No, she used to date Brian. Small world, huh?"

"Yeah," he dragged out the word, blown away by what she'd said.

"She must be something," Lindsay said with a bit of sarcasm to her voice.

"Meaning."

"Meaning that whatever number she did on Brian, it took months to peel it away."

He wrapped his hands around his empty glass. "Zoie can be intense."

"That's not the word that Brian used, but I get it. From what he told me, their biggest problem was you." She looked him in the eye.

"Me?"

"Yeah, not much of anything Brian ever did could compare to you. But you and my brother seem so different. Brian is intense, and you—you seem so laid back, low maintenance."

He chuckled at the description. "Relationships are complicated. People need different things in their lives at different times. I'm getting to accept that now."

"That should have been my line," Lindsay quipped. "You're sounding like the psychologist."

"Not hardly."

"Want a refill? I'm about to make last call. We close at one."

"That late already?"

"Yep."

"Naw, I'm good."

"Cool." She pushed away and went along the bar collecting glasses, giving last refills, and tallying up receipts.

Jackson thought over the unbelievable revelation about Brian. Of all the places, all the bars in Manhattan, he chose the one where Zoie's ex's sister worked. He didn't believe in coincidence. Tossing things off to coincidence was too easy, a way to disregard why roads crossed.

Lindsay finished what she could for the time being and returned with Jackson's tab.

He pulled out his wallet and gave her his credit card.

"Be right back." She took the card and the bill to the register and returned with his receipt. "Here you go."

"Thanks." He put the card back in his wallet. "Guess I better get going."

"Enjoy the rest of your time in the city."

"Heading out in the morning. But thanks."

Lindsay bobbed her head. "Hope you work out your business troubles."

"Yeah, me too." He stood.

"She didn't get over you, ya know."

"Huh?"

"Zoie, your ex. She never got over you. That was the real problem with her and my brother." The corner of her mouth lifted in a half smile.

"Thanks. And thanks for the conversation."

"Next time you're in the Big Apple, be sure to stop by. I'm usually here Thursday, Friday, and Saturday nights."

He tapped the top of the bar with his palm. "I will. Take care, Lindsay."

"You too, Jackson."

He buttoned up his jacket, stepped out into the late-night chill and continued his walk back to the hotel.

CHAPTER 25

Kimberly sat at her makeup table, removed the diamond studs from her ears and put them in her jewelry box, then took off the matching bracelet.

"You looked beautiful tonight," Rowan said as he came up behind her and placed his hands on her shoulders.

They regarded each other in the mirror.

"You always know what to say."

"It's true." He leaned down and kissed the back of her neck. "But all the beauty in the world can't hide the fact that something is wrong. You want to tell me what it is?"

"Just the stress of the whole evening. It was a little more overwhelming than I thought it would be. The people, the questions, the countless photos." She glanced at him over her shoulder. "That's all, really."

Rowan studied her for a moment. "Well, you are going to have to get used to it. This is only the beginning."

"I know." She clasped his hand. "If . . . I don't get the nomination, you won't be too disappointed, will you?"

He sputtered a laugh. "Of course you're going to get the nomination. You're the best choice. Richardson doesn't stand a chance. People hate him. Thomas has a questionable financial past at best. Stevens, well, he might be the toughest adversary, but you have him on legal experience. The fact that you have a great track record in the city, you've championed powder-keg causes your entire career, and you're the only woman in the race—all that counts in your favor."

She was quiet for a moment. "Ro, what if you found out something about someone you really cared about and what you found out changed the entire picture that you had of them."

He frowned. "I suppose it would depend on what I found out and if it hurt other people in the process." He stared at her reflection. "Why? Kim, what's going on with you?"

She pulled in a breath and turned her stool around. She took Rowan's hands in her own. "Political jitters." She forced herself to smile.

Rowan leaned down and kissed her forehead. "I hope that's all it is. You know you can talk to me about anything."

"Of course."

He studied her a moment more. "I'm going to take a quick shower. Have an early racquetball game with Martin at the club. I'll try not to wake you on my way out."

Kimberly offered a tight-lipped smile as he walked away. She stared at her reflection, leaned closer looking for some sign that what that Crawford woman said was true.

Claudia Bennett. She hadn't thought of her in years, yet she was the woman who had pretty much raised her. There had been times when she'd overheard comments about how the help, Claudia Bennett, had those same strange-colored eyes as Kimberly, and how odd, yet amusing, that was.

Ms. Claudia would sometimes sit on her bedside at night and tease her about how they were "secret kin." It was their private joke.

What if it wasn't? What if it wasn't a joke? Her entire body heated, and her temples began to pound. She couldn't wrap her mind around what it all meant—the ramifications, the fallout for herself, her family.

She covered her face with her hands, then looked up and faced her reflection, looking for any sign that she'd never seen before.

Ridiculous. Too many people depended on her. This was some attempt to tarnish her reputation, her record. It's what the media did. Zoie Crawford was no different. This nonsense about Claudia being her grandmother and Rose being her mother was a lie. Obviously, this woman had some other agenda. And if she continued to toss these false stories at her, she would first have her removed from the press pool and then go after her personally.

She picked up her brush and roughly pulled it through her strawberry-blond hair. They would settle this once and for all on Monday, and if she didn't like what she heard, Zoie Crawford would wish that she'd picked another profession.

Jackson zipped up his suitcase and prepared to head out to the airport, checking the room for anything left behind, when his cell phone rang. He pulled the phone from his back pocket and was surprised to see Zoie's name on the screen.

"Zoie. Didn't expect to hear from you."

"I didn't think I'd be calling."

He crossed the room and sat down. "Okay. Now that you have, what's up? I'm on my way to the airport."

"Oh. So soon?"

"No reason for me to stay."

She cleared her throat. "Listen, Jax, I want to apologize for last night."

"Not necessary, Z. Look, I get it. Really I do. I don't have to agree, but I understand."

"Do you?" She sounded as if she really wanted to know.

"Yeah. For real. So, you do what you think you need to do."

"Thank you. I needed to hear that."

"You've never needed my approval for the choices you've made."

She was quiet.

He cut through the silence. "Good luck, Zoie."

"Maybe we can get together or something when you get back—when I get back."

"We'll see. Gotta run, or I'll miss my flight."

"Oh, okay. Didn't mean to keep you. Travel safe."

"Thanks."

"Bye, Jackson."

Jackson looked at the phone for a moment. There were so many things he wanted to tell her, but now wasn't the time. The conversation they needed to have must be face-to-face. In the meantime, he needed to get with Lennox and work on how they were going to keep the project afloat, because if he knew nothing else, Zoie was going forward with her piece, and when she did, all hell was going to break loose.

—•◦•—

"I've been investigating some financing options while you were trying to put out the fire," Lennox said.

Jackson turned the steaks on the grill. His sit-down with Lennox could have waited until Monday, but Lennox agreed that the sooner they had a plan, the better.

"How strong are our chances?"

"Hmm, seventy/thirty. We got thirty, in case you were wondering."

Jackson grumbled deep in his throat.

"This quest that Zoie is on . . . man, maybe if you would have told her what was at stake." He took a long swallow of his beer.

Jackson flopped down in the chair beside him. "I know. Before my trip to New York, I was totally against what she was doing. I couldn't understand why she couldn't let it go, especially with so much on the line. I won't go to Zoie with hat in hand, begging her to do something to save me."

"Man, this is bigger than you."

"I know that. But I wasn't going to use our relationship as the bargaining chip."

"Sometimes, bro, you gotta use what you got."

Jackson took a swig from his beer bottle. "I saw it, man."

Lennox turned his head to look at him. "What?"

"What happened in New York. I visited the site." He went on to tell his friend about the life-changing experience and how it helped him to finally understand what drove Zoie. He left out the part about his meeting with Lindsay and what she told him about Zoie. Lennox would chalk it up to his thinking with his little head. He'd save that story for later, when they had dug themselves out of this mess.

"I suppose I get it, but I can't get with it," Lennox said. "I still think you should have told her about Lou Ellen's tie to the financing."

"I'm not going to guilt her into changing her mind."

Lennox threw up his hands. "Then let's go over this list."

———◦•◦———

Zoie gathered her notes, one of her grandmother's journals, and her phone, and wrapped herself in determination. She had no idea how Kimberly would react once she laid everything out, but she was going to try make it as easy on her as possible. She hadn't told anyone—not Jackson, not even her mother—what her aunt Sage told her about how and why her grandmother was brought to the states by the Maitlands. Kimberly would be the first.

Before she met with Kimberly, she needed to stop by her office and bring Mark up to speed on where she was with the story.

When she arrived at her office, she realized with a jolt how much she missed everything and everyone. The hum of activity was electric and reinforced her determination.

She graciously accepted the "Welcome homes" and condolences from her co-workers as she made her way around desks and cubicles to reach Mark's office.

She tapped lightly on the frame of the open door and finger-waved when Mark looked up from his phone call. He motioned for her to come in and sit.

Zoie stepped in and sat opposite Mark's desk. He finished his call and focused all his attention on Zoie.

"Well, great to see you. How are you? The family?"

"I'm good, still getting things together at home but making progress."

"Glad to hear it." He folded his hands atop his desk. "So where are you with the story?"

Zoie brought him up to speed on what she had done so far, from meeting with Lou Ellen Maitland to her upcoming meeting with Kimberly, including the long-hidden connection between the two families.

For several moments, Mark was silent. Finally, he spoke. "This is major. I mean if all of this is true, which I take it that it is, there will be major fallout. Are you prepared for that? Your article could take down one of the most powerful families in New Orleans, not to mention what it will do to Kimberly Graham and her family."

"Are you saying I shouldn't move forward?" she asked, a part of her looking for a way out.

"Absolutely not. I only want *you* to be sure you are prepared."

She swallowed. "I'm more than prepared. What they did to my family . . ." She shook her head.

He leaned back in his chair. "So Kimberly Maitland-Graham is your half sister." He shook his head in amazement.

"For what it's worth," she murmured.

Mark blew out a breath. "Go for it. Keep me posted."

"I will." She stood and draped the strap of her tote over her shoulder. "My meeting with Kimberly is in an hour."

"How long are you going to be in New York?"

"Until tomorrow. I need to get back. Still a lot to take care of with my grandmother's business."

Mark nodded. He leaned forward and pointed a warning finger at her. "I want you to check and double-check your facts every step of the way. The last thing we need is a lawsuit. I'll have our attorneys look everything over when you're done, just to be sure."

"Of course."

"Good luck, Zoie. I mean that."

"Thanks."

She walked out and headed for the elevator. The doors slid open, and Brian stepped out.

"Zoie! I didn't know you were back."

"I'm not, not really. Just stopped in to talk with Mark."

He bobbed his head. "Everything good?"

"Yeah."

"My sister met a friend of yours."

She frowned in confusion. "Lindsay met a friend of mine? Who?"

"Jackson."

Her stomach jumped. "Jackson?"

"Yeah. And you know Lindsay; she can get anyone to talk."

Zoie tried to keep her expression neutral but was itching to know what they talked about. "I remember that about her. How is she?"

"Good. Almost finished with her degree."

"Tell her I said hello."

He slid his hands into his pockets. "Says he's a really nice guy and has a strong thing for you. Still."

She swallowed.

"We didn't work for a lot of reasons, Z, but I think you're an amazing woman. Maybe when you stop pushing people away, you can see how amazing you really are." He leaned forward and gave her a quick peck on the cheek. "Take care." He walked away before she had a chance to react.

The elevator doors opened again. She stepped on, and the doors slid shut, closing her in with her swirling thoughts for fifteen floors.

CHAPTER 26

Kimberly hurried into her office. She desperately wanted to wash her face to get rid of the heavy makeup that had been applied for her public service announcement. The taping went well, and the girls were thrilled to be a part of it and couldn't wait to tell their friends that they were going to be on television.

"Hey," she said on a breath to Gail. "Zoie Crawford should be here—"

"She's already here," Gail said, keeping her voice low. "I put her in the small conference room."

Kimberly made a face. "Eager," she groused. "Okay, let me put my things down. Give me five minutes, and show her into my office."

"Will do."

Kimberly went into her office and shut her door. Her heart was pounding. Even though she knew that this woman was meeting with her today, there was a part of her that hoped she'd changed her mind or disappeared off the face of the earth. All the activity of the morning and preparing for the taping kept her mind off of the pending interview and the bomb that woman dropped at the gala.

For the entire weekend, she'd battled bouts of anxiety. Hour after hour, she ran a reel of her life in her head, trying to reconcile anything that Crawford woman told her. To believe it, to accept it, would mean that everything she knew about her life was a total and complete lie.

She paced in front of her desk to gather her thoughts and compose herself. She thought of her daughters, her husband, and what this kind of scandal would do to them. True, this wasn't the fifties in the South, but when it came to salacious details that tore down rising politicians, time made no difference. What she must keep at the forefront of her mind was that she would not allow this woman to destroy her family. She would do whatever it took to ensure they were protected.

Drawing in a deep breath of resolve, she pressed the intercom and instructed Gail to show Zoie into her office.

Kimberly stood behind her desk. When Zoie walked through the doors, Kimberly gripped the edge of her desk; her knees suddenly felt weak. Looking at Zoie, in the broad light of day, with her accusations imprinted on her mind, she saw things she didn't want to see—a familial resemblance that she couldn't deny; the slope of the eyes, the forehead, the bow of the lips, shape of her face, and the dimple in her chin. Kimberly lifted her chin.

"Good afternoon," Zoie said.

Kimberly gave a short nod. "Please, come in." She extended her hand toward a chair.

She watched the way Zoie moved with controlled confidence, and she wondered if that was a family trait or something she'd developed over time. She settled in her seat, took out a notebook and what looked like a journal of some sort. Even from across the desk, she could see that it was old by the visible yellow pages and the faded floral cover. Her heart thumped.

Kimberly sat down. "Before we get started, Ms. Crawford, I want to be very clear. I won't sit by and listen to any more of your outrageous nonsense about my family and myself. If you intend to continue to be part of the embedded press for my campaign, we are going to be clear on this from this point forward." There, she'd established the ground rules. She watched Zoie's eyes flash and her mouth move as if she intended to smile but thought better of it.

Zoie opened the journal to one of the many pages she'd marked off, turned it around to face Kimberly, and set it on her desk without a word.

"What is this?"

"Your grandmother's journal."

Kimberly felt her cheeks flush. She snorted her disbelief but still pulled the book toward her. Immediately she recognized the practiced handwriting—the same writing used on the notes that Ms. Claudia used to leave for her in her lunch bag or that she would find on her dresser in the morning to remind her how important she was and that she was loved.

She blinked rapidly to stem the well of tears that suddenly sprang up in her eyes as the memory washed over her, and the space in her heart that she thought she'd filled opened like a sinkhole.

I want to go back home. I know the Maitlands paid good money for me. My mama said so. Said the money would help the family and I would have a good life with the Maitlands in the States in return. They treat me good. I got my own room and the food is good. Not like home. I look after their boy, Master Kyle. He a good boy, not much trouble.

Kimberly felt her chest tighten. She flipped to another marked section further along in the journal.

Ms. Lou Ellen tole me today how lucky I am to be here and what a good thing I am doing for my family. I guess. Most days I don't feel lucky. But Duncan makes it all fine. We spend time when I have a day off and he on leave. I think he gon ask me to marry him. Then maybe I can leave. Maybe I can go back home.

She turned the pages and read the periodic and scattered entries that spoke of Claudia's life with the Maitlands, her courtship with Duncan and their tiny church wedding, little details about Kyle and how he excelled at everything and was the most important thing to his parents. Kyle could do no wrong in his parent's eyes. She wrote about the elaborate parties that the Maitlands hosted. And her slow understanding that being married to Duncan Bennett didn't change her life at all. If anything, it only made it more complicated.

With two young children and one more in her belly, and a man who preferred the service to being a husband and father, she didn't see how she would ever get to leave. Housework, caregiving, and cooking were the only skills she had, and after so many years, her dreams of a different kind of life were all but forgotten.

> *Sometimes in my bed at night I think I'm no better than an indentured servant and my debt ain't never gonna get paid.*

Kimberly shut the journal and turned her glare on Zoie. "This doesn't mean anything." She pushed the journal across the desk. "Is this your proof?" She sputtered a laugh.

Zoie leaned over to the tote at her feet and pulled out another journal. "The entries in this one are about you . . . and *our* mother . . . and your real father." She stretched her arm to hand the book to Kimberly.

Kimberly stared at the black-and-white notebook like it might bite her. Finally, she took it and fought to keep her hand from shaking.

Almost defiantly, she flipped the cover open. These entries spoke of Claudia's worry about her daughter, Rose, and the closeness that she was developing with Kyle Maitland.

> *I keep telling Rose to stay away from him. But she stubborn. I worry every time I don't know where she is. I*

*bring her to the house to keep an eye on her, but she
would sneak off to spend time with him whenever he
home. Kyle a grown man. I knows he think he being nice
to her, but Rose making more of it than it is.*

Kimberly turned to one of the pages marked with a Post-it.

*Dear lord, I know what we doing is wrong, but it's best.
My soul is broken. My chile. My baby. She ain't but sixteen. I told her to stay away from that man. I warned her.
Ms. Lou Ellen and Mr. Franklin almost lost their minds.
Said the family would be ruined. Mr. Kyle would be
ruined. They wasn't gonna let that happen. Evah.*
    *Rose cried and begged, but I ain't got no choice. She
gonna go to New York. Pregnant. No husband. White
man's baby. Jesus. Brought shame on both families. Broke
my heart. Ms. Lou Ellen says they will take care of everything as long as Rose stays gone.*

Kimberly's hands shook as she continued to read.

*Rose gonna have a good life. She don't know it yet, but
she will. Her baby girl white as snow, but she got our eyes.
I scared to think what would have happened if she had
been a little brown girl like her mama. She won't know
her mama, but she'll know her grandmama. They named
her Kimberly after Ms. Lou Ellen's mother. I'm gonna
watch over that baby for as long as I can.*

Kimberly shut the notebook, unable to read another word. Her
head pounded. She couldn't think; a million thoughts ran through
her head at once. The most horrific part of this outlandish tale was
to suggest that her brother was actually her father. The very idea
made her ill.

"What do you want?" she finally said, barely moving her lips.

"I don't want to hurt you or your family, but I want your family to admit what they've done. I want you to admit who you really are. I want you to acknowledge your *real* mother. She deserves that much." She paused. "That's what I want."

Kimberly stared at Zoie. Did she have any idea what this would do to her family, her husband and children? Obviously not. The only thing she wanted was some kind of twisted retribution.

She took the two books and shoved them in her desk.

"You can keep them. I made copies of the important pages. Take your time and read them." She reached in her tote and took out a small photograph. She stood and placed the photo on Kimberly's desk. "That's Rose. Our mother." She picked up her bag from the floor. You have my number. After you have a chance to think it over, call me when you're ready to talk." She turned and walked out.

Kimberly lowered her head, covered her face with her hands, and wept.

CHAPTER 27

Zoie held her head high as she strutted out of the office building and onto the busy Manhattan streets. It wasn't until she reached the corner and had to wait for the light that she began to tremble. Her knees weakened, and she grabbed a pole a moment before she felt herself begin to fall.

A well-dressed young man rushed to her side. "Are you okay?" He held her arm.

Zoie slowly lifted her head and focused on the man holding her arm. She drew in long deep breaths and willed her stomach to stop turning over.

"Yes . . . thank you." She tried to smile. "Got a little light-headed." She straightened and noticed several passersby slowing down to see what was going on.

"You sure?"

"Yes. Thank you so much."

He gave her one last look, then hurried across the street.

The curious moved on. She hailed a cab that screeched to a stop in front of her. She slid in, gave the driver her address, and rested her head on the leather seat back. She closed her eyes, and Kimberly's stricken expression bloomed in front of her.

She thought she would feel some sense of ultimate satisfaction, some vindication. What she felt was sick.

"How'd the meeting go?" Gail asked when Kimberly stepped out of her office. "Hey, you okay?" She started to get up from her seat.

Kimberly motioned for her to sit. "I'm fine. Um, I'm going to take the rest of the day off. Forward any important calls."

"What about your three o'clock with the campaign committee?"

"Please reschedule."

"Sure," she said slowly.

"Thanks." She walked out, took the elevator to the underground garage, and got her car.

On the drive home, she took intermittent looks at the damning notebook and journal on the passenger seat. She didn't want to believe it. If she did, then where did that leave her? How could she ever explain it to her husband, her children, and her friends?

Her gaze settled on her hands, which gripped the steering wheel. They looked the same. The same hands, the same face. Yet they weren't.

For her entire life, she had believed herself to be the daughter of Lou Ellen and Franklin Maitland, pillars of southern society. But she wasn't. They were in actuality her grandparents, and the man she believed to be her brother was her father. They'd all deceived her. Her existence was built on a mountain of lies. Her so-called family was no better than modern-day slaveholders, having "purchased" Claudia Bennett from her own family and ultimately her descendants.

Her stomach started to churn. Heat swept through her body and exploded in her head. She quickly pulled over to the side, opened her door, and threw up.

⟶⊷⟶

"Mrs. Graham, you're home early. Everything okay?" Farrah asked when Kimberly walked in. She closed the oven and set it for three hundred.

"Just a headache. I'm going to take a shower and lie down for a bit. Would you still stay until the girls get home from school and get settled?"

"Of course. Do you need anything?"

Kimberly felt the sting of tears burn her eyes. She swallowed and forced herself to smile. "No just a nap. I'm sure I'll be fine." She quickly turned away and hurried to her bedroom.

Once inside, she shut and locked the door. She toed off her shoes, crossed the carpeted floor, and flopped face down on her bed.

The conversation, the revelations, the words, and the picture swirled in her head. What was she going to do? She couldn't even fathom the far-reaching outcome if this story was ever revealed. She didn't care so much about herself, but what about her children and her husband?

She turned over onto her back and draped an arm across her eyes. If Zoie wrote and printed this ugly story, this buried piece of history, her run for office would be over. That much she was certain of. The scandal alone would overshadow whatever she wanted to accomplish. Voters wouldn't give a damn if she was the best candidate or not, only that she was mired in the kind of ugly past that the country still wanted to pretend hadn't happened.

She needed advice, but there was no one she could turn to. No one. She pulled herself upright, swung her feet to the floor, and went to retrieve her bag with the books. She took out the photograph of her mother, Rose.

Kimberly stared at the image. Did she now know that the daughter she believed to be dead all these years was alive and well and living the life of a white woman? God, it sounded like something out of a fifties movie. But it wasn't. It was real, and it was now, and she was the star.

Her mother was beautiful. Kimberly saw a shadow of herself in the face that looked back at her. She even saw pieces of herself in her half sister, as much as she was unwilling to admit it.

Yet none of it mattered. She could not allow her life with her husband and children to be destroyed.

Rowan wasn't an outright racist, but he often had opinions about black people that up until now did not include her. They did have black acquaintances, but none that they could say were actual friends. They didn't, as a couple, travel in mixed circles. And the more she envisioned the people in their immediate circle, the more she realized how sterile it actually was.

She could never tell him. Never. What she had to do now was decide what she was going to do about Zoie and her story. She was a lawyer. She was trained to look at every scenario, every obstacle, and find a way through or around it to get her client clear. This time she was her own client, and she had something that she was pretty certain that Zoie Crawford didn't have—money and power. What she needed to figure out was how to use what she had to neutralize the obstacle in her path.

<hr/>

Zoie shut the door to her apartment and went straight to the bathroom to splash water on her face. She snatched a towel from the rack and patted her face dry. Momentarily, she was stunned by her reflection. There was hollowness in her eyes, a dull tinge to her skin, and a downturn of her lips as if the vitality that fueled her had been drained.

She pushed away from the sink and the telltale reflection.

CHAPTER 28

Jackson walked out of the offices of Henderson and Dupont. They were the last of three possible financiers, and he'd done no better with them than the others. They all applauded what he was attempting to do but weren't in a position to assist.

He knew what they really meant. Lou Ellen and Franklin Maitland had far-reaching arms. No one in New Orleans would go against them. If they believed that the Maitlands had doubts about the progress of the development or were pulling their funding, then no one would be willing to fill that gap.

Plan B was a failure, and if Lou Ellen did as she threatened to do, he and Horizon were finished.

Maybe he should do what Lennox said and tell Zoie the truth, try to talk some sense into her. He opened his car door and got behind the wheel. He pounded his fist into the steering column. There had to be some other way. He wasn't going to beg Zoie to save him.

He pulled off and headed back to his office.

———

"I can tell by the look on your face that this meeting was a bust, too," Lennox said, as he stood in Jackson's open doorway.

Jackson took off his glasses. "Pretty much." He massaged the bridge of his nose.

Lennox came in and sat down. "So now what, bro? If she prints all that mess about the Maitlands, we are royally screwed. End of story. You know that."

Jackson frowned. "How many more units need to be completed?"

"Eighteen. That's not including the grounds and the façade. We still have vendors to pay and the crew."

"Right now, we're still in good shape and on track."

"Yeah. For now."

Jackson slowly nodded his head and pursed his lips. "It won't matter if Zoie prints her articles or not."

"Say what!"

A slow smile moved across his mouth. "If there is something the Maitlands hate more than anything, it's scandal. Right?"

"So? What the hell do you think this will be?"

"Exactly. So we head it off." He leaned forward. "We get proactive."

"You're losing me."

"I'm going to talk to Lou Ellen. Let her know that, more than likely, Zoie will go forward with her article. But we are going to head it off."

"How?"

"By doing a preemptive strike. Set up some photo ops at the site with the Maitlands and some of the families who will be moving in. Get the local papers to do a write-up on the Maitland's humanitarian efforts." He lifted a finger for effect. "To try to make up for the wrongs that have been done to too many of our black citizens, even by their own ancestors. She can say the Maitlands can't change the past, but they can help ensure a better future."

Lennox heaved a heavy sigh. "I don't know, man."

"Look, even if Zoie does publish the articles, we would have already established that they are aware of the ills of the past and are trying to do right. Then Zoie's article will look like an attack as opposed to a balanced article. Besides, she writes for a local paper. The reach is limited."

"Hmm, maybe so, but she's writing about someone who's running for office. Those things have a way of taking on a life of their own."

"True. But at the very least, if we do it my way, she will have to seriously rethink her approach. This way, no one really gets hurt. Stung a little, but not wounded—other than pride."

"Z is going to be pissed," Lennox said with a chuckle.

"For a minute. But one thing I know about Zoie is that she respects guts. In the meantime, in case all of this is no more than a pipe dream, we have enough in the budget for overtime. I want the men working to get those units finished in three weeks instead of six."

Lennox nodded. "Now that's a plan. I'll get with the foreman and work out a new schedule."

"If we need to hire more crew, then do it."

"With what?"

Jackson swallowed. "I'll get a new mortgage on my house to cover the costs. Just get it done."

"You sure about that?"

"Yeah. I'm sure."

Lennox stood. "You got it. I'll let you know how everything worked out."

"Thanks. And Len . . ."

"Yeah?"

"Thanks."

Lennox saluted with a lift of his chin and walked out.

Jackson exhaled and flopped back in his chair. It all sounded good. Now if he could only pull it off.

Zoie walked into the dimly lit restaurant and went to the hostess counter.

"I'm meeting someone. Miranda Howard."

The young woman scanned her list. "Yes. She's here already. She's at the bar. Whenever you're ready, I'll get you seated."

"Thank you." She walked around the tables, headed for the bar, and spotted Miranda chatting it up with a good-looking guy sitting next to her.

It had always been so easy for Miranda since their days in college. She was open and carefree. People were drawn to her, and she had a way with men. Zoie, on the other hand, always had a hard time establishing relationships. She could count the number of her female friends on less than one hand. And men . . . Jackson was her first real relationship, the first person other than Miranda that she'd let beyond the barriers, and she ran him away. Brian was a rebound, a way to prove that someone wanted her. It wasn't fair to him. So, now all she had was her work, her career, to fall back on, to validate her. No one seemed to understand that.

"Hey, girl," she said, sidling up to Miranda. She gave her a quick hug.

"Hey." She turned to her drinking companion. "Z, this is Terrance Vaughn. Terrance, this is my bestie, Zoie Crawford."

He stood to his full six foot three inch height. He extended his hand, and his smile could have launched a commercial. "Nice to meet you."

"You too."

"Well, it was good talking to you, Miranda. Call me." He patted her shoulder and walked off.

"Who. Was. That?" Zoie asked while she watched him walk away.

Miranda giggled. "He's a professor at the New School. Teaches film."

Zoie hopped onto the barstool. "*He* could be in a film," she said.

"I know, right." She giggled.

"You gonna call him?"

Miranda rocked her head to the side. "You damn right I am. Wouldn't you? Anyway, you want a drink first or get seated?"

"Let's get our table. I need to talk."

━━━━◆━━━━

While they waited for their dinner, Zoie sipped on a margarita and told Miranda about her meeting with Kimberly.

"I thought confronting her was going to . . . I don't know— make me feel good. Redeem my family."

"And?"

"None of that." She took another sip of her drink. "All it did was turn another woman's life upside down. You should have seen her face, Randi." She shook her head. "Kimberly is as much a victim in all this as everyone else. Going after her won't change the past."

Miranda looked at her wide-eyed. "Can somebody tell me where my girl Zoie Crawford went?"

"Not funny."

"I'm serious. I—"

The waitress arrived with their dinner. Miranda waited until she was gone.

"I have to be honest with you, Z. The way you were so hellbent on getting at this woman, her family . . . even for you and your relentlessness, it was over the top. I was getting scared for you, Z. You turned into someone that I didn't recognize or particularly like."

"Whoa."

"It's true. You'd gotten so blinded by this quest that nothing else mattered. But I knew that deep inside you were acting out of hurt. Hurt by what you think your grandmother did as if she did it to you." She shook her head slowly. "You have no idea what it must have been like for her back then."

Zoie lowered her head.

"We do all kinds of things to protect the people we love. We don't always make the right decisions, but we do it out of love. Sometimes that backfires."

"I know," Zoie said softly. "Those are all the things that have been running through my head." She pushed her food around on her plate. "For the better part of my life, I've tried to fit in, to be cared for . . ." Her eyes clouded. She sniffed.

Miranda reached over and covered her hand. "It's okay, Z. It's okay to want to be needed. It's okay to be vulnerable. It's cool to want to matter to someone else. And it's okay to be scared. The thing is, sis, you can't let the scared part ruin everything else. When you're scared, you lash out and you run people off, instead of looking for a safe space with those who care about you." She paused. "We're all human. We fuck up. It's what humans do. You gotta find a way to forgive and move on, or you'll always be in that 'you against the world' position."

Zoie reached for a napkin and wiped her eyes. "I know," she sniffed. "I'm a work in progress," she said, trying to make light.

"Got that right." Miranda's smile was filled with warmth. "So . . . what's next?"

Zoie inhaled deeply, then finally took a forkful of her shrimp scampi. She chewed slowly. "I do want to hear what decision Kimberly makes."

"Why? What does it matter?" Miranda's voice rose in alarm with each word. "You're not going through with exposing the family, are you?"

Zoie glanced away. She slowly shook her head no.

Miranda released a relieved breath.

Zoie stared Miranda in the eyes. "I only want her to recognize our mother, Randi. I want her to acknowledge the rest of her family. I know the Maitlands never will, but she should know what our mother gave up—or, better, what was taken from her."

"You have to know that you can't make her accept your family."

"I know."

"Do you?"

"I do . . . I guess I'm hoping that she will . . . for my mother."

Miranda raised her glass. "Here's to hoping."

CHAPTER 29

Kimberly went to her closet and from the top shelf took down the metal box that contained some of her important papers. She took the box to the table by the window in her bedroom.

She flipped through the plastic sleeves until she found her birth certificate. She took it out and gingerly unfolded it. There'd been plenty of times when she needed her birth certificate: her first driver's license, at different times during college, for her passport, her life insurance policy, and her marriage license.

She'd never really paid much attention to the details before now; she'd simply accepted what was printed and stamped with an official seal to be true. There was no reason to believe otherwise.

Now she stared at the details. Name: Kimberly Alyse Maitland. Mother: Lou Ellen Maitland. Father: Franklin Maitland. Place of birth: St. Cyrian Hospital, New York. Gender: Female.

The only pieces of information that were correct were her name, gender and place of birth. How on earth did her parents manage to get her this fake birth certificate? Whose palm did they grease? She stared down at the lie.

After Kyle died and then Claudia left, she was totally alone. Her mother never treated her the way she imagined mothers treated daughters. Lou Ellen didn't share hugs or girl talk. All her mother seemed to be concerned about was Kimberly being the best at what she did: her grades, how she dressed, the friends she chose, the boys she dated, the career she planned, the man she married.

In the household, Lou Ellen ran things. Everything. But she knew her father wielded a different kind of power. Together they were formidable. If they'd engineered this whole twisted scenario, they would make sure that there were no holes. From the time they purchased Claudia from her parents in Barbados right up to the truth of her birth and everything in between—they had planned it all.

What they hadn't counted on was Zoie Crawford.

"Mom."

She looked up from staring at her birth certificate. "Lexi. Hey, baby." She extended her arm and motioned her to come.

Lexi loped across the room, her blond ponytail dancing behind her, and plopped down on her mother's lap. She nuzzled her head in Kimberly's neck. Kimberly stroked her back.

"What is it, sweetheart?"

"Ryan."

"Who is Ryan?"

"This boy in English class."

"Okay? And is this someone that you like?"

She bobbed her head.

"Is he nice?"

"Yes. Really nice."

"So why do you look so upset?"

"He likes Alexandra."

Kimberly shut her eyes. "Ohhhh."

Kimberly spent the next hour soothing the wounded heart of her twelve-year-old. She assured her that Ryan wasn't the only fish in the sea, and even if he did like Sandi, that didn't mean that Sandi liked him back. There would be times in her life when she and her sister would be on opposite sides, but those times should

never impact their relationship because nothing was more important than family.

———⊷•⊰———

"When do you want me to book your flight?" Miranda asked
when she pulled her car to a stop in front of Zoie's apartment
building.

"I want to give Kimberly a couple of days. See if she wants to
meet again. To talk."

"If she doesn't?"

"I'll let it go. Besides, I still have my grandmother's business to
look after, and whatever is left of my career at the *Recorder*."

"What are you going to tell Mark?"

"I haven't figured that part out yet. Worst-case scenario is I'll
continue to follow the campaign. Give it my all."

"What about your mom?"

She tugged at her curls. "I guess I'll have to tell her the truth
and tell her whatever Kimberly decides to do."

"Okay, sis. You know I got your back, whatever you decide to
do." She squeezed Zoie's upper arm.

"I know. Thanks." She opened the car door. "Love you, girl."

"Back at ya. Hey, Z."

Zoie leaned down and peeked in through the window.

"Call Jackson. See him when you get home. Don't let him get
away again." She pressed the button, and the window rolled up.

———⊷•⊰———

Zoie spent the better part of the morning reviewing her notes
and putting together the pieces to begin writing her article, with
the title "The Rise of Kimberly Maitland-Graham."

From her research and even the limited information Lou Ellen
provided, Zoie had enough to begin the introduction of her series. If, and it was a big *if*, she continued to follow the campaign,
she would be able to flesh out her story with interviews and anec-
dotes from Kimberly's staff and contributors. Her main objective

now was to write a strong enough draft to appease Mark so that he would keep her on the story. With Brian now running the 9/11 series, if this one fell through, she would be relegated to cats in trees stories.

She studied her notes and the stacks of clippings and photos. She picked up one photograph of Kimberly with her husband and children. This woman was her sister. Rowan was her brother-in-law, and those were her nieces. She ran her thumb across the image. There had to be a way to make it right.

Rose deserved to know her daughter and her grandchildren. She set the picture down with the others. She was so torn. The journalist in her wanted to go after the Maitlands with every fiber of her being, blast their tainted history across the pages of every newspaper in America. Then there was the part of her that had spent her own life longing for the love and acceptance of family and didn't want to see another family suffer.

She opened the cover of her laptop, clicked onto her Word program, and began her draft.

———⇒•⇐———

Rowan snapped open the newspaper. The main story, which had been in the news for weeks, was the sensationalized account of a young white officer alleged to have shot and killed a black teenager in a Bronx hallway. The jury had failed to indict the officer, and protests were sprouting up all over the city.

"I don't understand what these people want," Rowan complained with a shake of his head. "What do they expect to happen when they live like animals? I'm sure the officer was scared for his life, just like he said. I know I would be."

Kimberly's throat constricted. For the first time in her life, she really heard the words of her husband and their underlying meaning. Was she now "these people"? Over the years, he'd said similar things, and so had their friends, but before it didn't matter. It didn't affect her or relate to her. Her stomach seesawed.

"You tossed and turned all night, babe," Rowan said. They sat at the breakfast nook, sipping coffee. "What's going on? Are you feeling okay?"

"I'm fine." She brushed her fingers across her forehead. "A lot on my mind with the campaign, the office." She forced a smile.

Rowan looked at her over the rim of his mug. "We've been married for eighteen years, Kim. I know you, and I know when you're lying to me. What is it? Something with the girls?" He put down his mug. "Are you sick?"

Kimberly immediately held up her hand. She looked into eyes of sincere concern. Eyes of love for the woman he believed she was. "No. No. I'm not sick." She couldn't tell him. She could never tell him. If she had never understood it before, she understood it now. "I did have a very interesting conversation with Lexi yesterday . . . about boys."

"Boys! Heaven helps us. Not yet." He chuckled. "So tell me."

As she told her husband about Lexi's revelation and the motherly advice she had offered their daughter, she realized, even as her heart was breaking, that this was her life, the life she'd built with this man who worshipped the ground that their daughters walked on. She would do nothing to ever jeopardize that, no matter the cost to her.

⋯⋯

After Rowan left for work and the girls were off to school, Kimberly made her decision and called Zoie. She sat in her bedroom with the journals and the photograph in front of her while she listened to the phone ring on the other end.

When she heard Zoie's voice, for a moment she froze and debated about hanging up. But the next phone call, because there would be one, would be no different.

"Good morning. This is Kimberly Graham."

"Good morning. I don't know if I was expecting to hear from you, to be honest."

"Not much of anything is what we expected, is it?"

"I suppose not."

"I . . . read everything."

"And . . . do you believe me now?"

"Funny, a part of me believed you when we met at the gala. I always felt . . . different," she slowly confessed. "And I was closer to Claudia than my own mother, but I always attributed it to my mother being a cold and distant person and nothing more. Claudia and I used to joke about having eyes of the same color, but as a kid, I didn't make much of it." She sighed heavily. "I don't know why my mother and father did what they did all those years ago, and maybe I never will. It was a different time, and we've all paid a price because of it. I've built a life, a good life with a man I love and children whom I adore beyond reason. I won't lose that. I can't."

"What are you telling me?"

"I'm telling you that if you go ahead with exposing the past of my family and my connection to yours, I will use everything in my power to ruin you, your newspaper, and your family."

Zoie heaved a sigh of disappointment. "For some bizarre reason, I thought way in the back of my mind that you would find a way to rise above the debris your family caused and speak out about who they are and who you really are. I'd stupidly hoped that you might find a corner in your heart to care about your real mother, the woman who gave birth to you, the woman who spent her life believing that you were dead. You talk about family, you glorify family . . . that is your family. I am your family, too."

"You don't understand," Kimberly said softly. "I don't expect you to."

"I understand more than you think. Thank you for calling."

Kimberly listened to the dead silence and slowly put down the phone. She stared out of the window.

CHAPTER 30

When Zoie got off the plane in New Orleans, she was surprised to actually feel happy to be back. As she drove through the familiar streets on her way from the airport, she was overcome by the bittersweetness of it all.

The past couple of months had been life-altering on so many levels—from the loss of her grandmother to the finding of a half sister, the opening of long-closed doors between herself and her mother, and, most important, slowly coming to terms with what family really meant.

Miranda's wise words still resonated in her soul. She'd spent so many years being angry and hurt and lashing out that she never gave anyone a chance to love her or allow herself to fully love anyone in return. That was a huge void that hadn't been filled.

She'd thought a great deal about her grandmother on her flight home. In the beginning, when the will was read, the first thing she worried about was her job—her life and how she was going to be affected. Never once did she really bother to try to understand why her grandmother had written her will the way she did. But now she was slowly beginning to understand. The task was not to keep the business going. That was only a small part. What her grandmother really wanted was for Zoie to do what she'd been unable to do, and the only way that could happen was to force Zoie to stay, force her to do what she did best: search for answers.

When she pulled up to the house and eased along the driveway, she noticed one of the packing company trucks parked along the side of the house. She parked, took her carry-on from the trunk, and went inside.

The kitchen was bustling with activity. Her mother, Aunt Sage, and even Aunt Hyacinth were busy sorting the fruits and vegetables and packing them. What really surprised her was when Jackson walked in from the back door to announce that one more box of corn and a box of green peppers were needed for this shipment.

Jackson stopped short when he saw Zoie. All eyes turned in her direction.

"Welcome back," Sage greeted. "Might as well just put that bag right on down and get to work. We behind schedule."

Rose smiled. "Welcome home."

"I always did like that Jackson fella," Hyacinth said with a wide grin.

"Hey, Zoie," Jackson said softly.

"Hey . . . everybody." She cleared her throat and willed her heart to stop hammering her chest. She tore her gaze away from Jackson. "So what do you need me to do?"

In no time, Zoie found herself fully entwined in the shenanigans of her family. While they worked, they tossed raucous stories back and forth about their uppity neighbors, local marital scandals, and just plain juicy gossip. Zoie could hardly believe the saucy language her upstanding, church-going aunts and mother used, but they were quick to beg baby Jesus' forgiveness for the things that fell out of their mouths.

As she looked around at the joy on the faces of her family while they worked, a new revelation hit her—this was why her grandmother had started her business. It wasn't only to make money and serve the community; it was to build a bond between her daughters and now Zoie. She was a part of this intricate web that her grandmother had spun. In order for it to succeed, they all had to work together instead of against each other. And then there was Jackson. Somehow, Nana had managed to factor him into her plan as well.

"The last of the boxes are stacked in the shed, ready for pickup tomorrow," Jackson said, reentering the kitchen and wiping his forehead with a paper towel. He placed the clipboard on the kitchen counter.

Aunt Sage poured glasses of sweet tea. She handed one to Jackson.

"Thank you, ma'am."

"You always been a big help 'round here," Sage said.

"Sure have. We definitely make use of your muscle," Rose added.

Jackson finished off his sweet tea in three long swallows. He set down the glass. "Anytime. Glad to help." He took a quick look around. "I gotta be going."

"Why don't you stay for dinner?" Rose asked.

"Thank you, but maybe some other time." He snatched a quick look at Zoie. "Y'all have a good evening." He headed for the door.

Aunt Hyacinth kicked Zoie under the table, and she yelped. "Go walk that boy to the door, chile, 'fore he get away."

"What?"

"You heard her," Sage said.

"Go," her mother added.

Zoie huffed, untied her apron, tossed it over the back of a chair, then hurried after Jackson. He was opening the door to his car by the time she got outside.

"Jackson!"

He stopped and slowly straightened as she approached. "Did I forget something?"

"No." She leaned on her right leg and stuck her hands in the back pockets of her jeans. "Um, thanks for all that back there."

"No need for thanks. I helped your grandmother and promised her I would help your aunts." He started to open the door.

"Wait."

"What is it, Zoie?" he said, sounding mildly frustrated. "You were pretty clear last time we spoke. So . . . what's changed?"

She paused a moment and then looked him right in the eyes. "I have."

He nodded. "Good. I'm glad to hear that. Look, I really have to go. Maybe we can talk another time. Not now." This time he opened the door, and Zoie had to take a step back to let him get in.

Zoie watched the car until it reached the corner, signaled, and turned. She had some ridiculous hope that, like in a TV movie, he would come to his senses, stop the car, jump out, and run back to her. She turned and went back inside.

Her aunts were gone from the kitchen, leaving her mother to clean up and get dinner started.

"Can I help with anything?"

"You can get this floor swept and take that bag of garbage out back for me." She washed down the table and returned all the table items—shakers, napkin holder, and knife rack—to their rightful places.

Zoie got the broom from the closet next to the door and began to sweep.

"You gonna tell me what happened in New York?"

Zoie looked up from her sweeping. "I've been trying to think of a way to tell you."

Rose's lids lowered over her eyes. Her lips pinched. She took a breath and looked at her daughter. "Only way to tell me is just to tell me." She pulled out a chair from under the table and sat down. "What's she like? When is she going to come see me?"

Zoie leaned on the broom for a moment. "I met her . . ." Slowly and with as much care as she could, she told her mother everything—from the moment she met Kimberly for the first time at the gala, to the meeting at her office, up to and including their final phone conversation. Her mother's eyes continued to cloud over, but she didn't shed a tear. She was stoic as she listened to this daughter talk about the daughter she never knew and maybe never would.

"You said she has twins," Rose said in a faraway voice.

"Hmm-umm."

"What are they like?"

Zoie smiled. "They're twelve. Beautiful girls. Identical. They look more like their father."

"So she really was passing all these years. Always thought that was some mess that you read about. Never thought it would be something to happen in my own family." She looked off. "I can't blame her, though. It's not a choice that she made. She didn't know the difference."

"But she knows now. She knows the truth *now*."

Rose looked at her daughter with sad but accepting eyes. "We all have to live with the choices we make, Zoie. She will have to live with hers."

"It's just not right."

"One of the millions of things that aren't right with the world. But you can't set yourself up to fix them. What's important now is that you're home. You're here with me, and maybe we have a chance to fix some of the things that are wrong in the world, our world." Her gentle smile lit her eyes with hope. She folded her hands together on top of the table. "When you went away to school in New York, it was like history repeating itself." Her brows drew together. "Families torn apart—for different reasons, but torn apart nonetheless. I know I made it hard for you to stay. I held on so tight because I was terrified of losing another child. I held on so tight that you didn't have any choice but to break free." She leaned forward and implored Zoie with her eyes and the passion in her voice. "It wasn't to control you or run your life, baby. I was scared. But my fear ran you off anyway. Then I resented you for going, leaving me. But you're back now. We got a chance now."

"And Aunt Sage and Aunt Hyacinth resented you."

Rose nodded.

"They thought you got rewarded with the great education and the good life in New York as payment for what you'd done."

"I lived with their scorn for years." She blinked away fresh tears. "But when you came home, when you found the truth, a new world opened between me and my sisters. We haven't talked, really talked to each other about how we feel, in years. We laugh now, tease each other, and reminisce without recrimination."

"I remember," Zoie began slowly, "when I was little and Daddy was still here. There was always laughter in the house."

"Humph." She smiled a sad smile. "You father had charm. I have to give him that. He had a way about him that made even the most mundane activity seem like a major celebratory event. When he left me, he took the laughter with him. He was the buffer between me and Sage and Hy. With him gone, the walls were down, and there was nothing to keep us from going at each other. Not even Mama."

"Why did he leave?"

"Wanted something different than me, I suppose. Just one day said he couldn't do this anymore. Packed a bag and walked out."

Zoie took a moment to let that sink in. In her mind her father's leaving was "the great mystery." When in fact he'd done what many men have done since the beginning of time—he simply walked out. "I think part of me was always looking for him," Zoie said thoughtfully. "And at the same time, I was scared of finding him because he might leave me again." She thought about her and Jackson, and how she worked so hard to push him away before he left on his own.

Rose opened her arms. "Come on and help me get dinner together, girl. Let me see if you learned anything in New York." She stood, and for the first time in longer than Zoie could remember, she stepped into her mother's embrace.

CHAPTER 31

Jackson walked out onto his back deck and stretched out on the lounger. He hadn't expected to see Zoie, and it had unsettled him more than he realized. It took all of his willpower to drive away when what he really wanted to do was pull her into his car, drive away, and keep going.

Maybe he should have stayed to listen to what she had to say. But that would have only complicated things. He knew what he had to do in order to keep the development on track. He couldn't risk allowing Zoie's passion for her cause to outweigh his.

Their Plan C was already in motion. Lennox had set up the accelerated schedule, and the whole crew was on board. He had a meeting in the morning with his banker to discuss refinancing his home if it came to that.

His cell phone chirped. He picked it up to see a text from Lena.

I'M OUT FRONT. CAN WE TALK?

Lena? She was the last person he expected to hear from.

COMING.

He got up from the lounger and strode to the front of the house, while trying to imagine how this impromptu appearance was going to go down. He paused a moment, then pulled the door open.

"Hey," he greeted with an edge of hesitation.

Lena stepped up onto the porch. "Hi."

Jackson stepped aside and held the door. "Come on in."

Lena walked passed him and stopped in the entryway as if this was her first time in his house.

"I was out back." Jackson came around her and led the way outside. "Can I get you anything? Something to drink?"

"Um, water is fine." She sat primly on the edge of a chair.

Jackson's brows flicked in surprise. Lena was always up for a cold brew or a glass of wine. He shrugged opened the cooler and took out a bottle of water and handed it to her.

"Thanks." She shook off the excess water that clung to the bottle, twisted off the top, and took a swallow.

Jackson sat on the side of the lounge chair, facing her, with his arms resting on his thighs. His long fingers wrapped around a bottle of beer.

"There's no other way to put this, Jackson. I'm pregnant."

"Say what?" The bottle clattered to the ground and rolled under the table, spewing a trail of beer and foam in its wake. He held up his hand and angled his head to the side as he spoke. "You and me, we always had safe sex. It was our understanding." He leaned forward and his gaze burned into her. "So . . . explain this to me."

Lena lifted her chin. "I don't know how it happened other than the way all babies are conceived."

Jackson felt like he'd been kicked in the gut. He inhaled deeply, ran a hand across his face, and shut his eyes. "I . . . don't believe this," he muttered and pushed to his feet. He paced. "So how far along?" he asked with more calm than he felt.

"Eight weeks."

He did some quick mental calculations and figured it must have happened the last time they were together before the breakup. He faced Lena, who looked like she would burst into tears if a strong wind blew. His heart softened.

Jackson went to her and sat beside her. He put his arm around her and drew her close, resting his chin on her head. "We'll get through this."

"I'm sorry, Jackson. I didn't mean for this to happen. We had a plan. This wasn't it."

He sputtered a laugh. "True." His thoughts were in total disarray, and he didn't want to say or commit to anything sparked by pure emotion. He needed time to think.

"Look, um, I haven't had dinner. Stay. We'll eat, talk and try to figure some things out. Okay?"

She swiped at her eyes and sniffed. "Okay."

***

Lena moved around in his kitchen the way she'd always done—like she belonged there. Gone was the tentative woman of an hour earlier. She knew where everything was and what he liked.

They worked easily and efficiently together, shelling and seasoning jumbo shrimp and slicing tomatoes and cucumbers for the salad.

While they worked, neither of them talked about the elephant in the room. Instead, they idly chatted about the new restaurant in town, his sister's new job with the museum, movies, and news headlines. It was almost like it used to be—easy and worry free—but it wasn't. They'd crossed a threshold into a new reality.

Lena took the bowl of shrimp out back while Jackson prepared the grill.

"Grill should be hot enough in a few minutes," Jackson said as he closed the lid.

"Jackson." Lena put the bowl on the table. She walked up next to him and placed her hand on his forearm. "I know all this . . . is a shock. It was to me, too." She paused when he faced her. "I want you to know that I don't expect you to . . . marry me. It's not why I told you. I have no problem doing this on my own. I have a great job, and excellent benefits. Family, friends." She offered a tight smile.

"That's all well and good. But this is my child, too. I wasn't raised like that. I don't want to play the weekend father, the holiday visiting daddy." He swallowed. "We get married. We raise our child under the same roof."

"Jackson, I told you about the baby because you deserve to know, not because I was angling for a proposal."

"I didn't think you were. But that doesn't change anything."

She sighed softly and placed her hands on his shoulders. "Yes. It does. I don't want to get married. Not like this. I won't."

Jackson's jaw clenched. "So what I want doesn't matter?"

"That's not what I'm saying."

"Then what *are* you saying, Lena?"

She stepped back. "I'm saying I'm having this baby and I'm not getting married. I would think you'd be relieved."

"Relieved! Why the hell would I be relieved?"

"So you can go back to Zoie without a wife and baby tied to your ankles."

His face morphed into a slab of disbelief. "Are you fucking kidding me? You really worked all that out in your head and had the nerve to say it? When did I turn into *that* guy, Lena? Huh? When?" he shouted, totally losing his cool.

"When you knew you didn't really love me but stayed anyway," she said with a calmness that tossed ice water on his burning outrage.

He stared at her, trying to reconcile this new Lena with the Lena he thought he knew. The pieces would not fit together, no matter how hard he tried to rearrange them. Had he only been going through the motions with Lena? His stiff shoulders slumped. "I always cared about you. Deeply. You know that."

"But it would never be what you felt for her. We both know that." She sighed. "I'd convinced myself that if I gave you enough time, if I loved you enough for both of us, that you'd come around." She paused. "I even tried to play the martyr when I walked out of here that night. But when I saw you in the restaurant with her, the way you looked at her—I knew for certain that you have never and would never look at me like that. And it's okay," she hurried to add. "I want you to be happy. But more important, *I* want to be happy. I deserve it. So," she exhaled and smiled a forgiving smile, "the grill should be ready and I'm starved." She placed a hand on her stomach. "Eating for two."

———◦✦◦———

"What the hell, man. You suddenly got one of those gray storm clouds hanging over your head that follows your ass around or what?" Lennox said.

Jackson almost laughed at the image, but not much was amusing these days. "Feels like it."

"So let me get this straight. Lena is pregnant, and she doesn't want to get married. Now where do you fit into this picture other than be 'da baby daddy'?" He shook his head.

Jackson aimed the remote at the television and changed channels until he found the basketball game.

"She seems to have it all figured out. She'll work for as long as she can, and her sister will stay with her for the first month. Lena plans to take three months off from work. The college has a great on-site child care, she says." He blew out a breath. "As for me, I'm all in. Help when I can, be there for her and the baby. Take care of them financially and make sure I'm a factor in my child's life. I can't make her marry me."

"Welcome to twenty-first century relationships. Guess women don't need us for much of nothing anymore," Lennox groused.

"Hmm." Jackson put his feet up on the coffee table. "She was right, you know."

"Who?"

"Lena. She was right about how I felt about her. I thought I loved her, and maybe I did, but never like Z. I figured if I hung in there long enough, there'd be that fire, ya know? But Lena and I never got passed simmer."

"Hey, man, you know I got you. It'll work out."

"Thanks, man. I hope so."

They both suddenly leapt from their seats and roared as a midair move by Kobe Bryant sent the game into overtime.

"Superman strikes again," the announcer boomed.

Jackson fell back in his seat. Even as he watched the incredible replay, he sure wished that he had some superpower right about now.

CHAPTER 32

The talk with her mother and Rose's revelations about her own past hurts and fears settled gently inside Zoie. They moved and shifted until they nudged and woke up her heart.

For so many years, she'd been utterly committed to her own anger and hurt feelings that she'd never taken a moment to look beyond the surface. In her career, she would move mountains to get at the truth. When it came to searching deep in her own soul and life, she barely scratched the surface.

She realized now that a part of her didn't want to know because if she did she would open herself up to feelings other than anger, and then she would be vulnerable. She could be hurt. Keeping people and emotions at bay protected her. But, as a result, she hadn't been truly living.

She was finally beginning to understand her grandmother's master plan. Forcing her to stay and run the business was the least of Nana's reasons. She knew her granddaughter, and Claudia knew that Zoie would find those journals and wouldn't stop digging until she exposed the truth, a truth that Claudia could never tell, for her own unknown reasons. The uncovering of the past led to a long-overdue healing of the Bennett family. That truth was the real message in Nana's will.

She and her mother still had a long way to go, but they'd begun the process and were determined to keep trying.

Zoie opened the cover of her laptop. She had her story to write. Not the one that Mark was expecting, but her version.

Her cell phone rang. She picked it up from the desk and was surprised to see it was Kimberly. She pressed the talk icon.

"Hello, Mrs. Graham."

"Hello. I've thought about . . . our conversation."

"And?"

"I need you to understand that no matter what threats you make to expose my family, no matter how I feel or what I want or believe, I can't tell my family. It would destroy my marriage, ruin my children. My children!"

Zoie shut her eyes, heard the passionate plea in Kimberly's voice.

"I can't. Please . . . if you have any compassion, you won't do this. They can't find out this way." She paused. "At least let me do it my way in my own time. Do you have children, Zoie?"

"No."

"Then you can never understand that a mother will do any-thing—anything—to protect her children."

Zoie thought about her great-grandmother, her grandmother, her own mother and the sacrifices they'd made, the losses they'd endured, the deals they'd made, and the secrets they'd kept, hop-ing for a better life for their children.

"I think I do," she said softly. "You don't have to worry about me or any story that would hurt you or your family. I promise you that. Good luck with whatever you decide to do, Kimberly. Maybe one day we'll see each other again—as sisters."

Zoie pressed the CALL END icon and slowly set the phone down. She turned to her laptop, opened her Word program to a blank page, and began to write her article on Kimberly Maitland-Graham.

She wrote nonstop for a steady three hours before she was satisfied with the piece. After a last spell-check, she hit SEND, and off it went to Mark. He would be disappointed, to put it mildly. It wasn't the story they'd discussed. It wasn't even close. But it was the story seen through her new eyes. A story about a young woman who built her own life and was determined to help the lives of others. At least she would be able to sleep at night.

She went to look for her mother. They had a lot more talking to do.

———◆◆◆———

The ringing phone stirred her from sleep. With one eye open, she groped for the phone on the nightstand.

"Hello?" she mumbled.

"Turn on the television—not that local mess, a national channel," Mark barked into the phone.

Zoie fumbled, bleary-eyed, located the remote, and turned to MSNBC. There was a BREAKING NEWS banner running across the screen.

"It was just announced at Graham campaign headquarters that Kimberly Graham has withdrawn from the race for state senator, citing family concerns as a reason. Graham was considered a shoo-in for the nomination, and all the polls indicated that she would win by a large margin over her Democratic opponent," the announcer said.

Zoie still held the phone as she watched in stunned silence.

"Are you hearing this?" Mark said, snapping her to attention.

"Yes. I'm watching."

"So much for your series. Not much point now."

"I suppose not," she said absently.

"And what was that crap fluff piece that you sent me on Graham?"

Zoie drew her knees to her chest. "A change of heart. All that other shit isn't as important as I thought it was."

"I see." He pushed out a breath. "When are you coming back to work?"

"That's another thing, Mark. I don't know when I'll be coming back . . ."

Jackson finished speaking with Lou Ellen Maitland. For whatever reason, she'd decided not to pull her funding. He didn't care what her reasons were as long as the project went through as planned. Now he didn't have to mortgage his house, he didn't have to leverage his relationship with Zoie, and he never had to tell her that it was her pursuit of her story that nearly cost him his business and his reputation. Now his crew could go back to their regular schedules and lives.

With that near disaster out of the way, the next thing he had to tackle was talking with Zoie and telling her the whole story about Lena and the baby and, most of all, that he was still crazy in love with her and that with her by his side, they could make it work. He was willing to do whatever it took.

Zoie peered out of the attic window, surrounded by the strong spirit of her grandmother. Below she glimpsed her mother and aunts walking arm in arm down the pathway toward the street.

Her grandmother's method may have been unorthodox, but she achieved what she'd longed for—having her family together again.

Jackson's car eased down the driveway. The trio waved and continued on their way. He'd said that he loved her and he needed to talk about them and their future . . . and about Lena. Whatever it was, she would deal with it because she loved him; from the bottom of her heart, she loved him, and he needed to hear that from her—finally.

She'd spent her life searching, but what she'd been looking for had been right here all along—love and family in all of its forms. There was nothing more important. She looked around the room at all the nooks and crannies, all the places that held the family secrets and its legacy.

"Thank you, Nana," she whispered.

She went downstairs to open the door for Jackson.

A HOUSE DIVIDED

Donna Hill

ABOUT THIS GUIDE

The suggested questions are included to
enhance your group's reading of
Donna Hill's *A House Divided*.

Discussion Questions

1. Zoie Crawford is a complicated character. She comes across as strong and focused, but what would you see as her real weakness and why?

2. There have been dozens of stories about 'passing.' What made this story element different for you?

3. Claudia Bennett was the matriarch of the family. What are your feelings about what she did, holding onto that secret for so long?

4. Truth was the driving force behind everything that Zoie did. How did her search for truth change her in the end?

5. Family is at the center of the novel. What are some of the quirky elements or family secrets that you may have discovered in your own family?

6. What was the biggest surprise for you in the novel and why?

7. If you were in Zoie's shoes, what would you have done if you'd found out about a sister that you didn't know you had?

8. Why was it so hard for Zoie to connect with her mother Rose?

9. What was your favorite and least favorite element of the novel and why? What would you have liked to see but didn't?

10. What are your thoughts on the Maitland family and their dark history?

11. Once the novel ended what do you see happening to the characters? Specifically Zoie and Kim?

12. Would you recommend this novel to a friend? If so, what would you tell them?

DON'T MISS

COLD FLASH

In Carrie H. Johnson's explosive new series, forensic firearms specialist Muriel Mabley takes a one-way plunge that's outside the law . . .

Enjoy the following excerpt from *Cold Flash* . . .

CHAPTER 1

Lord only knows the things we'll do or how far we'll go for the people we love.

Flailing around in the pool at the Salvation Army Kroc Center this Friday morning was my "thing" I was doing for my girl Dulcey. She has breast cancer. I committed to doing a triathlon, as in a quarter-mile swim, twelve-mile bike ride, and three-mile run. Mind you, I am scared to death of the water, have not been on a bike since childhood . . . that would be forty-plus years . . . and have not run with any speed since the police academy more than twenty years ago.

The SheRox Triathlon Series raises funds for breast cancer research. I admit the whole triathlon thing is a smoke screen for coping with the fear of losing Dulcey. Somehow my crossing the finish line will turn the nightmare into a fairy tale, with a happily-ever-after ending.

So here I am, three months into my training. It's not like I never work out. At five foot three and 140 pounds, it is necessary to keep all my parts in check. I work out on a semi-regular basis, three or four times a week for a month or two, then I'm distracted by any good reason. Not this time. At least not for another month until after the July event.

I learned to swim five weeks ago and have since mastered a slow, steady stroke. Grab the water, push it away in an S motion with flat hands. Turn my head, suck in air, put my face in the water, blow out air. Each time I turned my head to gulp air, I saw this guy whipping the lifeguard, Pam, with his pointer finger. White guy, six feet, 250 pounds maybe. He was wearing a green, black, and silver sweat suit and a black Eagles cap pulled low on his brow. At first I thought maybe he was a disgruntled parent of an eel, pollywog, or fish—names that indicated a child's level of swim achievement.

Children's squeals bounced off the pool's dome, signaling the end of adult swim time. The sounds were muffled each time I put my face back in the water. I dug deep to squeak out the last lap, which totaled sixteen, a half mile. I got to the deep end and flipped to retrace my path for the final length.

When I reached the shallow end and walked up the stairs, the guy had Pam's arm pinned behind her back. He pressed against her body, talking into her ear, red-faced like a heavy drinker or druggie. His other hand was stuffed in his pocket, which bulged with what I suspected was a gun.

A quick check had the children on the opposite side of the pool with their instructors, making enough noise to part the waters.

Pam wriggled under his hold. Her wide eyes darted in every direction until they set on me. She watched me walk past them and sit on the bench. I dried my feet, my arms, and my head, the whole time pleading with the good Lord to move this guy along or grow me large enough to pound him.

He yanked Pam's arm backward. Pam yelped like a hurt puppy. Damn. I approached from his blind side, aware of my inadequate clothing and dwarfed size in comparison to him.

"Is everything all right here?" I asked, my voice steady, my nerves shivering.

"Mind your damn business, lady," the guy said, twisting Pam's arm harder.

"You're hurting me, Bunchy," Pam whimpered.

"Shut up. Do what I'm telling you or I really will hurt you."

Pam pulled away from the guy and screamed. I pushed her to the side and stepped in front of her.

"Easy, mister. I'm Philadelphia Police. Take your hand out of your pocket, slow."

He pulled his hand out, holding a Beretta. I rushed in with one shoulder down and grabbed his arm. He got off a shot. Loud screaming. I knocked the gun from his hand, spun around, grabbed his wrist, spun around again and twisted his wrist, bringing him to the floor. I jammed my foot into his neck. He squirmed, trying to get loose.

"I'll break it if you don't keep still," I said.

"You stupid bitch. I'ma kick your ass. I'ma kill you." Spit sprayed from his mouth with each word.

I twisted his wrist a little harder and stepped into his neck a little deeper. "Not today," I said.

Pam came up the stairs from the pool with the gun in hand. She walked over to us and pointed it at Bunchy.

"Put the gun down, Pam. He's not going to hurt you or anyone else. Believe me, you do not want to kill him. He's not worth it, Pam."

"He'll just come back. I tried to get the police to do something. A restraining order doesn't do any good. He'll just come back."

"Not this time. This time he'll go to jail. Put it down, Pam. Think about your little girl."

She kept pointing it.

"Don't shoot me, Pam. I'm sorry. I love you," Bunchy pleaded, relaxing his pull on my hold. I dug my foot deeper into his neck.

She lowered the gun as police stormed into the dome. An officer took the gun from Pam and pulled her arms behind her back for cuffing.

"She's good," I said. He released her.

Three officers gathered to relieve me of my charge. "You sure you need our help with this guy?" one of the officers joked.

I stepped off Bunchy's neck. Bunchy growled as he rose up and lunged forward headfirst, pushing me backwards. I went down.

"Welcome back."

Fran Riley, my partner, put his hand out to stop me from trying to sit up. "You should stay put a few." I brushed his hand away. He sighed a helpless verse and pulled me forward to a sitting position.

I tried to speak, but the words stuck in my throat. I looked around at the uniforms helping the parents and children to calm down. Other uniforms were snapping pictures and asking questions. A little girl lay out on the deck, an EMT bent over her. I stretched my neck to locate Pam. A police officer restrained her, blocking her path to her daughter. I rubbed my eyelids but failed to clear my blurred vision.

"Muriel? You all right? You with me? Muriel?" Fran asked, as he waved his hand in front of my face. I brushed his hand away and nodded. I tried to stand with his help. Halfway up, another EMT interfered and I was back on my butt.

"That might not be a good idea yet." The EMT motioned Fran to move, then knelt and flashed a light in my face.

I could see he was talking to me. The sounds were muffled, as though I was still under water. My ears popped. I covered them with my hands, a buffer against the sudden loudness of the hollow voices. ". . . a bump on your head. You'll be fine. You're lucky he didn't break your neck." The EMT turned to Fran and said, "Keep an eye on her for a few hours. Precautionary."

Detective Mosher, who I knew from the fifth district, stood in front of me. "What happened here, Mabley?"

I took a deep breath. "Is the little girl . . ."

"She's alive. Now, what happened?"

I settled down. "The guy . . . he was having words with the life-guard, with Pam." I closed my eyes and put my head down to ward off a rush of dizziness.

"You good, Mabley?"

I looked up and continued. "I was in the water doing my last lap. He was cursing her out. I noticed a bulge in his jacket pocket that appeared to be a gun. I got out the water, dried off . . ." Dizzi-ness blurred my vision again. I bowed my head and closed my eyes against the desire to puke.

"Big guy," Mosher said.

I took a deep breath. "Yeah, but he went for his gun." I nod-ded toward the little girl. "What happened? Where's the guy?"

"After you went down, he pulled an officer's weapon and tried to shoot the lifeguard but hit the little girl instead. Grazed her head. She'll survive. She's their daughter. Took six officers to bring him down." He shook his head. "You had him on your own. I need to invest in some of that kung fu stuff." Mosher moved his arms in a chopping motion.

My fuzzy thoughts repelled the humor. "Where is he?"

Mosher put his arms down and got serious again. "He had some kind of seizure. Hopped up on drugs, didn't make it. I would bet some junk—heroin, fentanyl, cocaine, a mix. You know. Mother said the guy is her ex-husband. He's an army vet. Suffered from PTSD, spazzing over custody of the daughter. She's seven. She could have been killed." Mosher walked away, barking orders.

Fran helped me up. "Nice suit." He half-ass smiled, trying to rile me. I had on one of those triathlon suits that cover everything, including thighs. I had no room for his humor either. I cut my eyes and sucked my teeth as loud as I could.

Fran wrapped a towel around my shoulders. "C'mon, I'll help you outta here," he mumbled.

I let him lead me out holding my arm, like I was an invalid un-able to do or say anything but what I was told.

"Can you handle dressing yourself? I can come in and help."

I pulled away from him and gave him a sideways F-U glance and leaned on the door to the locker room. "Don't get your brain in a knot about it."

The locker room was quiet. Clothes, towels, flip-flops strewn in the aisles between the lockers. I sat on the bench and closed my eyes. The uneven quiet seeped in and calmed the tension that squeezed my temples.

I was startled when Fran yelled in, "Hey, Muriel, you about done?"

"Yeah. Out in five."

When I finished dressing, I met Fran back in the pool area. Parents were gathering their children and moving toward the locker room, police were leaving. Fran insisted on driving me home and picking up my car later. I conceded.

"Why were you at the Kroc anyway?" he asked, on the way.

"I'd rather not say, you know."

"No, I don't know."

Fran had been my partner for three months; blond-haired, blue-eyed, Mark Wahlberg–faced Fran. Before him I had the same partner for seventeen years. Laughton McNair. Suffice it to say that Fran is at the opposite end of the spectrum of cool, color, and charisma from Laughton. Laughton and I were partners, friends, and for a time, lovers. I shake off the longing I feel every time he invades my thoughts, like now.

We are firearms examiners in the Philadelphia Police Department. We examine, study, test, and catalog firearms confiscated from criminals and crime scenes, and testify in court about the findings.

"My best friend, Dulcey, I think you know her; she has breast cancer. I'm doing a triathlon in her honor."

The few moments of uncomfortable silence made my insides boil. Really, it wasn't the silence that had sweat dripping off the tip of my nose. While the silence was indeed uncomfortable, the heat was a part of the aging process that came on now and again and made me want to jump out of my clothes; that or punch something or someone. I glanced over at Fran with balled fists.

"Yeah, I met her at your house. We'd just finished our first job together, remember? Damn. I'm sorry to hear that." He hesitated. "You got a call from a Detective Burgan after you left last night. Said she had some information for you."

"She could have called my cell. Thanks. I'll call her when I get home."

"What's it about, Miss M?"

"It's a personal matter."

That is, unless Hamp got his butt thrown in jail, I thought. Hampton Dangervil—Dulcey's husband, aka Hamp or Danger. You think you know a person and then you are slapped upside the head for thinking. I got slapped when Hampton confessed his transgressions to me like I was his priest and could offer him divine mercy. He said he lost some money gambling. He said he was trying to make enough money to keep Dulcey living in style. Silly man. Dulcey loves his dirty drawers no matter rich or poor, right or wrong. I asked Burgan, who runs the Mobile Street Crimes Unit, to do some checking on two characters Hamp said he owed money to. He only knew their street names—Bandit and Muddy— laughable if it weren't for the gurgling in my gut pushing out sharp pangs, which always meant something messed up was ahead.

"I'm not going to push, but if you need me you know I'm right here."

I shifted in my seat and rolled the window down.

"I can turn on the air if it will help."

"Damn it, Fran. Stop trying so hard. We're partners and that doesn't mean you need to be patronizing about everything or try to be inside my head. I'm over everything that happened. I'm over it, despite what you heard before you decided being my partner was right for you."

I cringed at my outburst. I guess you could label me still in recovery. It had not been quite a year since I shot Jesse Boone.

Boone was a psychopath responsible for twenty-plus murders dating back twenty years. He almost took my life and my sister's. His death still sparked much discussion among police officers, with a positive vibe. For me it sparked emotional torment.

Fran kept face forward and did not respond. When we pulled up to the house, Fran opened his car door to get out.

I said, "I can make it on my own."

"Yes, boss," he said in a playful subservient tone.

"Sorry, didn't mean to sound so righteous." I moved to get out and he pressed my arm, stopping me. I turned to match his stare.

"I took this job because it is exactly where I wanted to be. I wanted to learn from the best, which I understood to be Laughton McNair, if he was still around, and you. If there's an issue with me, either embrace it or request another partner."

I wanted to exit the car and slam the door. I wanted to tell him to go to hell, not because I was angry but because a rookie had put me in my place. I felt like I was moving fast down a slope that meant I had no good nerves for police work anymore. Instead all I could muster was "I'm good" as I pushed the door open.

"I'll pick you up in an hour. We can pick up your car on the way to the lab. You have court at one o'clock."

"Yeah, yeah," I said before I closed the door. I turned back and bent down to peer at him through the window. "Thank you."

"No problem," he said, flashing me a cheeky grin.

I waited until he pulled away from the curb before I limped up the walkway to the door. It opened before I got to it. My nine-year-old twin nieces, Rose and Helen, jumped out. The twins are my sister Nareece's children.

Only nine months earlier, the twins lived in a million-dollar home in Milton, Massachusetts, with their mother and father. Now their father was dead, murdered, and their mother was in a semi-unresponsive state at Penn Center, a long-term care facility, the result of being raped and tortured by Jesse Boone, before I killed him.

"Hi, Auntie," they said in unison. The twins are best described as striking. Their father was Vietnamese. Their dark skin, almond-shaped gray eyes and jet-black, crinkly hair, turns heads.

Rose took over. "Travis left us here with Bethany cuz he said he had to go do an errand and he'd be right back, but he didn't come back."

Fifteen-year-old Bethany is our neighbor and the backup sitter. The twins begin attending camp next week. Until then, Travis, my twenty-year-old son, is the designated babysitter. Travis is a sopho-more at Lincoln University, home for the summer.

"What do you mean he didn't come back? How long has he been gone?"

"He left at seven. He didn't even fix us breakfast. He should have taken us with him. He left you a note on the kitchen counter," Rose said.

"Calm down. Nothing happened, right?"

In unison they chimed, "Yeah. We're big enough to care for our-selves. We are on the case to find out where he went and why."

My nieces took on more of me than I sometimes could handle. They started the Twofer Detective Agency in my honor. As in-vestigators, they question, research, and detect everything, and I do mean everything. I liked that they wanted to be "like me" in that way.

Rose said, "We know he got a phone call from Uncle Hamp. After he talked on the phone to Uncle Hamp, he left. From what we heard, we speculate that Uncle Hamp has troubles."

"You speculate, huh. Enough of the speculation."

"Yes, ma'am," they said in unison, standing at attention and saluting.

"Hi, Miss Mabley," Bethany said, emerging from the den. "It wasn't nothing for me to come over," she said, sashaying her way to the front door. Bethany's round baby face—big wide eyes and dab of a nose—made her appear younger than fifteen. She was another version of striking, having a German father and Haitian mother, both musicians. "I'm usually available anytime, so just call when you need me."

Bethany agreed to come back in an hour if Travis had not returned. After she left, the twins sang, "Bethany likes Travis, Bethany likes Travis, and Kenyetta's going to be pissed."

Kenyetta is Travis's girlfriend since freshman year in high school. She ran away from her foster home and was living on the street when Travis brought her home and asked for my help. We found her a better living situation. Their friendship blossomed, not surprising since Kenyetta is a beauty—dark skin, long, thick coiled hair, and curvaceous frame. They have been bound together since.

"Enough. Besides, how do you know Bethany likes Travis?"

"We've been watching them talk to each other and interrogatin' her and Travis, separately of course, about their associations."

I was sorry I asked as soon as the words escaped my lips. "C'mon. I'll fix you breakfast," I said, moving toward the kitchen while checking my phone. There were four missed calls from Travis. I tapped his name in my phone and waited. No answer.

"We already ate. Bethany made us pancakes. We're watchin' *Transformers*," they said, running back to the den. Their voices and footsteps echoed through the large newly remodeled five-bedroom Colonial that we had just moved into a week ago, which was still mostly decorated with unpacked boxes. Nareece and I had grown up in the house. I rented it out after my parents died, until the last tenants moved out a year ago. After everything that happened with Jesse Boone, I decided to remodel it so we could all live here together.

I went to the kitchen and found Travis's note on the floor. Bending to pick it up made me dizzy. I grabbed ahold of the counter and inched my way to an upright position.

```
    Moms, I'm sorry I had to leave the
  kids with Bethany. Uncle Hamp called
```

and said he couldn't reach you and he
needed help. I had no choice. Travis.

Considering Hampton's earlier call to me, for help with his
gambling debt, my feelings of relief at having arrived home cur-
dled into worry.

Connect with Us

Visit us online at
KensingtonBooks.com
to read more from your favorite authors, see books
by series, view reading group guides, and more.

Join us on social media

for sneak peeks, chances to win books and prize packs,
and to share your thoughts with other readers.

facebook.com/kensingtonpublishing
twitter.com/kensingtonbooks

Tell us what you think!

To share your thoughts, submit a review,
or sign up for our eNewsletters, please visit:
KensingtonBooks.com/TellUs.